ÑO CRUZ

MARIKIT
and the Ocean of Stars

FARRAR STRAUS GIROUX

NEW YORK

Farrar Straus Giroux Books for Young Readers
An imprint of Macmillan Publishing Group, LLC
120 Broadway, New York, NY 10271 • mackids.com

Our books may be purchased in bulk for promotional, educational, or
business use. Please contact your local bookseller or the Macmillan Corporate
and Premium Sales Department at (800) 221-7945 ext. 5442 or by email
at MacmillanSpecialMarkets@macmillan.com.

Library of Congress Cataloging-in-Publication Data is available.

First edition, 2022
Book design by Veronica Mang
Printed in the United States of America by Lakeside Book Company,
Harrisonburg, Virginia

ISBN 978-0-374-38909-3
1 3 5 7 9 10 8 6 4 2

To Tasyang and Neneng,
who both shared the same birthday

AUTHOR'S NOTE

As a Filipina, it's my joy to tell the stories I grew up with—
tales of the Aswangs' older relatives spun for naughty, restless
children to behave; ghost encounters told by a friend of a
third cousin of the neighbor who saw it; suspected haunted
houses and then finding out that someone truly lived there;
and almost-forgotten myths written in the soggy, old pages
of our Panitikan.

The Philippines brims with so many stories, being made
up of thousands of islands that throb with tales of their own.
Like the Greeks and the Romans, we, too, had our gods long
before colonizers stepped onto our soil. Our ancestors paid
their respects to several variations of nature deities whom
they believed to provide abundance, protection, and health.

Most of the deities mentioned here are helmed from the
Tagalogs, the region where I am from. I took the liberty
of dressing them in new hats and coats, and in many ways
they will not meet their original cultural depiction. I am

not an authority in this subject. More about these legends, I still—as many characters in this book will say—have to "learn along the way." But please use this book as a springboard for your discoveries. Take these names as a map to find your way back to the legends of the old.

Like many storytellers, I desire nothing but to give you giggles and magic and fun adventures. But books, as life itself, also come with things that terrify us. In *Marikit and the Ocean of Stars*, there is grief, the pain of losing a loved one, the emptiness of being alone. There are encounters with monsters, dives into deep waters, the hot blaze of fire, the sight of sharp teeth, the sting of needles. Please read with caution. Your safety and peace come first, and you are allowed to protect your hearts in the kindest ways you can.

I encourage you to reach out to your nearest Filipino community to learn more about our stories. And our delicious food. *And* the surprising similarities we share. May the magical paths lead us to each other, in a space where wisdom and kindness are infinite, and may we all thrive there.

MARIKIT
and the Ocean of Stars

CHAPTER 1

YELLOW

Marikit. Filipino. adj. *Pretty.* Usually attributed
to stars, fine ladies, and a small girl with thick, wavy hair,
constantly running under the sun in old, remodeled clothes.

Marikit Lakandula was nearly ten and very much certain that shadows didn't blink. Shadows didn't have eyes to do so. Shadows only trailed beneath her soles whenever she ran around the dusty, unpaved roads of Barrio Magiting. Yet when she stooped down to survey the sand caught in her rubber slippers, she had to scrub her eyes and pinch her cheeks two times over. It was there. A shadow, swelling with its dim shade, gaping at her with its big, sun-washed yellow eyes before it closed one of its peepers.

She looked around and wondered if the other kids had seen it. Sixteen heads with the scent of the sun and sticky air bobbed in front of her, and twenty-four more behind her occasionally rose on their tiptoes and mumbled, "Is it open yet?" All of them had been standing in front of a yellow gate that reflected the scorching heat of the cloudless April afternoon. The sun had smothered itself on the tall coconut trees and made shadows of the many leaves, filling the dusty path with many shades of black, under which they took refuge.

"It must be the leaves." Marikit slouched down to look closely at the shadows, blacks upon blacks, swaying at the movement of the wind. The only other reason she could think of was that she was Na-engkanto. Enchanted. Spellcasted. Made an unknown spirit angry, and for that she was cursed.

The crowd of yellow-wearing kids let out a scream, and she jolted back—*did they see it?* But Marikit, upon looking up, only saw two people coming through the yellow gate, carrying a many-tiered yellow cake, passing under a large, yellow banner, on which was written, "Welcome to Jana's Superfabulously Splendid 10th Birthday Party."

"Come inside, children, one by one, and don't push," ordered a lady with shoulder-length permed hair and a yellow gingham dress, waving her manicured hands as she bid the young guests in. One by one, the busy, buzzy crowd followed, stepping over the threshold as the woman examined them before giving them a yellow party hat. Not all came through. Many times, she stopped a child, pushed them back, and turned them away.

"Not enough yellow," Mrs. Solomon told a girl with tiny yellow rings on her bright pink dress. "Not yellow enough," Mrs. Solomon told a boy who wore a shirt with thin beige stripes. The celebrant's mother was very particular about the yellow on the garment, and the closer Marikit got to the gate, the more she forgot about the shadow.

What she feared now was to be found out that her dress wasn't yellow.

If one observed closely, Marikit's party dress used to be white. The A-line frock was a hand-me-down from her mother, with a Peter Pan collar, droopy lace sleeves, and a fake pearl button. It used to be pretty.

That was what Marikit's name meant. *Pretty.*

But like people, things grew old. They shriveled and sulked and cracked their bones and lost their glow. Marikit's dress did. Rust and moth-dusts had clung to its skirt; spatters of yellow stains sloshed all across its corners. How unfortunate that Marikit had no other yellow clothes!

And so, when it was her turn, Marikit closed her eyes and stepped forward, nervously awaiting her judgment.

"Come in," Mrs. Solomon said sharply.

Marikit couldn't believe her ears. "Ma'am?"

She opened her eyes. Mrs. Solomon, instead of surveying Marikit from head to toe, was more preoccupied with her own bright-yellow manicure with French tips, whining about one of her nails chipping. The lady took a quick glance at Marikit, turned her head away, and by the grace of Bathala, only beckoned, "Next!"

Without a second thought, Marikit skipped happily through the gate.

Jana Solomon's Superfabulously Splendid Tenth Birthday Party was almost entirely yellow. The Solomons' sprawling garage was decorated with big, yellow balloons that hovered behind yellow-ribboned chairs set around yellow gingham—covered tables, each of them hiding yellow bags that served as party favors. The center table featured a three-tiered birthday cake enveloped in buttercream and drizzled with golden confetti. Beside it was a mouth-watering lechon that had a golden apple underneath its snout. There was a glass barrel of mango juice with real mango bits, a large platter of pancit, different kinds of yellow puto topped with cheese, overflowing spaghetti, two tubs of mango ice cream, and hot dogs on sticks embellished with yellow marshmallows.

Marikit sat at the end of the celebrant's table, where a wobbly little stool was left empty. Her seatmates, unfortunately, were sharp-eyed, gossipy little guests who took pride in their Actually Yellow outfits: yellow blouses with gold buttons and sequined pockets, tulle skirts with glitters, and yellow corduroy pinafores paired with preppy yellow shirts. Sharp little eyes made it obvious that Marikit didn't deserve her spot.

Ah, poor Marikit! She felt more out of place when the girls pushed their chairs together, far away from her, leaving her outstanding in her pale, discolored dress.

They're laughing at me, Marikit thought.

And she was right.

The shadows were always there, blooming in places where there was no light. These shadows didn't linger under human feet. No, they were remarkably riotous and reckless, going off on their own to make trouble in the dark. They loved feasting on sorrow and dismay, and they found the very girl.

Alone in her corner, Marikit kept her head down as she clutched her rust-tainted skirt. She did not laugh when the yellow-haired clowns bungled their magic onstage. She did not sing when Mrs. Solomon finally instigated the birthday song. She only looked up when Jana Solomon finally appeared, for she heard everyone gasp and say, "She looks like a Diwata!"

Diwata. A fairy.

Jana walked onto the stage with a shimmering crown on her head. She tiptoed on her two-inch-heel sandals with jewels on the straps. Her sunshine-yellow gown dropped to her ankles, with flowy fairy sleeves and a sweetheart neckline and a flower embroidery that dripped down the layers of the chiffon skirt that billowed from the waist. "Now that's a dress!" a girl with a yellow polka-dot shirt said.

"Where do you think she bought it?" asked one girl with a big, fluffy, yellow headband.

"At the mall, of course," answered a girl with a yellow plaid shirt. "Every nice thing can be bought at the mall."

"Looks beautiful," swooned the girl with the sunflower-patterned dress.

"Looks expensive," remarked the girl with the shimmering yellow blouse.

"Not like someone else's dress," hooted the girl with the bright-yellow pants.

All of them passed a hot look at Marikit.

"I'm sure hers is old," noted the girl with the gold ruffle skirt.

"I'm sure hers smells funny," commented the girl with the yellow cat's ears.

"I'm sure she does, too," mused a girl with lemon prints on her pinafore.

Oh, our dear Marikit! She heard it. She heard it all! She burned with so much rage as she hung her head, letting her dark, wavy hair cover the tears that started to fall down her cheeks. "You'll see," she mumbled quietly behind her teeth. "My birthday is coming, and I'm going to look like a Diwata, too."

And so, when the party was over, when the crowd of yellow-wearing children waved goodbye to the celebrant as they carried their yellow packets under their arms, Marikit ran home, her heart thumping with a wild, new thought. She ran on the dusty ground with her equally dusty slippers, past the concrete bungalow homes at Acacia Street, past the swaying bamboo groves at Kawayan Street, and past the boatmakers' homes at Bangkero Street to reach home: Sampaguita Street.

There, a timeworn brown house, outstandingly cramped in between two similarly shabby properties, gaped into the world with its large, broken capiz windows. While the rest of the neighborhood gurgled with all kinds of noise—mothers gossiping by the doorways; fathers clumped at a table outside their houses, grumbling at a game of cards; children playing wildly in the middle of the street—the house of the Lakandulas was quiet. There was no shouting in it. No laughing. No gossiping. The only sound inside was the prevalent *rat-tat-tat-tat* that came from the machine set beside the window, manned by a pair of productive hands that wound the wheels and a pair of eyes that occasionally peeped from the frame.

Marikit slowed down as she passed by their window, having a glimpse of those gaunt eyes. They were very much like Marikit's eyes, except older, more solemn, and they bore less sleep in them. She entered through the door, toed off her rubber slippers, and rose in the steps. "Nanay!" she shouted with all of her lungs. "Nanay!"

Aling Anita sat by the old sewing machine, patiently hemming the edges of a flower-printed fabric. She stopped as soon as Marikit entered the door. "Nanay!" Marikit ran across the wood-slat floor, almost toppling the boat-in-a-glass-bottle perched precariously on the wall. She slid into her mother's lap and looked up with full eyes. "You have not forgotten that my birthday is in June, right?"

Aling Anita softly nodded with wonder. How could she forget? She and her daughter had the same birthday, right on the date of the summer solstice.

"And it's been years and years that have passed, and we never celebrate anything. Not a single thing," Marikit reminded her. "Remember? Last year, we only had warmed-over pancit. Last-last year, you promised we'd eat at Jollibee, and then we didn't. Don't you remember what Tatay always told us? Promises we break will break us."

Aling Anita smoothed Marikit's sweaty forehead with her callused hands. *What is it that you want, anak?* Her fingers flickered into a beautiful dance of unspoken words.

Marikit pressed her nanay's palms with her small, hot fists. "A dress. A new dress. A dress unlike any other. A dress so beautiful, I'll look like a Diwata, on my tenth birthday."

She jumped around so much that the wood-slat floors began to creak. "It should have fluttery sleeves." Marikit twirled. "A balloon skirt with many, many ruffles. A nice little sash, and a large bow to tie at the back. And it must be blue, Nanay," Marikit added last. "Blue! The color of the sky. The color of the sea. The color of Tatay's bangka. Blue, blue, blue!"

All right, dear, Aling Anita gestured. *Now let me get back to work.*

"Promise, Nanay?" Marikit pressed on, not taking her eyes off her mother.

Aling Anita gazed at Marikit with a long, lingering stare.

Marikit knew this look. It was a look as if Aling Anita was trapped in the prison of her own hands. She'd move her fingers, but they would only quake and would not make gestures. Marikit would always think it was one of those joint pains, and that her nanay was having a bad spell.

After all, if one only sewed too much, their hands would get tired, too.

"Nanay?" Marikit asked again, shaking her nanay's thigh. "My dress?"

Marikit, perhaps, would never understand the way Aling Anita's lips quivered. Her teeth blocked a tide of words, words she tried to set free from the tips of her fingers, words that refrained from falling, for it was just like her husband said—*Promises we break will break us.* Yet, at that moment, as she sat in her chair, Aling Anita gave it all until a worn-out smile appeared on her sad mouth. She lifted her quaking palm, the silver thimble gleaming on her finger as she gestured: *Promise.*

CHAPTER 2

THE SEAMSTRESS

Nanay. Filipino. n. *Mother.* Queen of the house who bore
no crown, with hands that only knew how to work, hands
that only of love spoke.

As far as she could remember, Marikit had only worn
clothes her nanay made. Or, more specifically, *remade.*
Like magic, Aling Anita could turn an old paisley night-
gown into a twirly sundress, a retired nun's habit into
Marikit's skirt, a pair of old jeans into a nice denim skirt,
and a secondhand silk scarf into a lovely little blouse. Used
shirts, no matter how many holes they had, could be turned
into sleepwear and blouses and soft tunics that could be
tied with tiny belts. Old things still had value in them if one
knew how to mend.

The clothes Aling Anita made weren't so bad. They just
weren't so plain. They always had too many straps or too

many pockets or too-thick cuffs hemmed at the folds. (In Aling Anita's defense, it was because children tended to grow tall at an unexpected rate, and it was too impractical to buy new bottoms every time their legs grew long.) Marikit always got laughed at for her clothes. But those clothes, in some fantastic ways, saved her life.

When she was three, she would have fallen from a tree, had she not dangled by the strap of her suspender, which had been tightly sewn on her bright-green paper-bag shorts. When she was five, she would have drowned in the sea, had she not learned to float with the help of her giant, ruffled, winged sleeves. When she was seven, she almost got hit by a motorcycle swerving down the road, but her extra-long belt got tangled by the sampaguita hedges and kept her safe by the sidewalk.

Her clothes were looking after her when her nanay couldn't, for she was always running about, always tumbling and skidding and rolling on the ground, coming home with burns and bruises that scarred her young, brown skin. Her family called her Marikit Malikot—restless Marikit—and their neighbors always joked that Marikit must have drained all of Aling Anita's radiance and energy after she was born.

Aling Anita, they said, was fresh like spring, sprightly like a maya. But Marikit couldn't see that. All Marikit could see was a tired, middle-aged woman with a pair of thin hands who attended to her needlework all day long.

Whenever someone needed a seamstress, the people in Barrio Magiting always recommended "the seamstress of Sampaguita Street." Aling Anita could do anything with threads. She could knit, knot, loom, embroider, and make tidy stitches all by hand. Each year, the teachers at Marikit's elementary school made a pilgrimage to the Lakandulas' home to get their uniforms made. Every quarter, the pastor from the next barrio asked for new embroidery for his polo barongs. Most of the neighbors in need of patching a hole or stretching a sleeve made a cordial visit, bringing with them a bundle of eggs or vegetables as a token, relying on Marikit to translate whenever Aling Anita spoke by hands.

Aling Anita's most favorite thing was her Makinang de Padyak, a vintage sewing machine. She bought it from a secondhand merchant at a low, low price and took it home in the back of an old, rusty tricycle. What a wonder that sewing machine was! The wheels spun like a shotgun and put the small needle to work, mechanically hemming perfect seams on each of Aling Anita's clothes. All she needed was to move the flywheel and press the metal pedal with her feet. *Rat-tat-tat-tat-tat*, it resounded. *Rat-tat-tat-tat-tat*.

Marikit loved watching her nanay work. The sewing machine had small wooden drawers where Aling Anita kept all the colorful threads and bobbins and needles and the cute buttons that looked like gems. Marikit wasn't allowed to play with them, of course. Once, Aling Anita caught Marikit using her medida as a jump rope. Twice, Aling Anita saw Marikit inserting a thread on several buttons and using them as jewelry. All those times, Marikit got pulled by her ear, and it hurt for quite a while.

Beside Aling Anita's sewing machine was a large rattan basket where all the scrap fabrics went. There were many of them, heaps and heaps of various colors and prints cut into squares and circles and other shapes Marikit had to learn the names of. Marikit's job was to help gather the scraps. The scraps went to their clothes, covering the tear on Marikit's shirts or adding new sleeves on old, reformed blouses. Sometimes, Marikit used those scraps to practice her needlework. And sometimes, which were her favorite times, her nanay taught her more things about sewing.

In those moments, hands were the loudest in the Lakandulas' house.

There used to be many sounds in their home. Once, it was filled with a boy's laughter. With the sound of a man's whistling, calling for the wind to blow gently in their direction. With the rolling and swirling of shells on the sungka board—and then, the sound of victory, usually the boy's, yelling, "I won again!" (and then Marikit, sobbing, "I always lose to you, Kuya."). There was the running of bare feet across the wooden floors, the sound of loud teasing, and some minutes later, the sound of making up. Breakfasts and lunches came with arguments concerning portions ("Kuya Emman took all the bangus belly!"), from which there rose the calm voice of a man who gave each equal halves. There was, at times, chiding and crying. But, above all, laughter.

Much and much laughter.

But when tragedy hit them, their little home became painfully quiet.

One dreadful September morning, after the sky poured trundles of rain more than the earth could carry, Marikit and Aling Anita waited by the sea, along with the other mothers and daughters and sons of the fishermen who went missing after an early dawn's catch. Marikit joined the crowd who lifted their voices, "Bathala, save them! Bathala, save them, please!" Rescuers searched far and wide. Some fishermen were found, but Mang Fidel and Emman were not.

The sea ate them, body and boat.

Marikit had always thought Bathala did not hear them. That her voice was too small. And even if Aling Anita cried and opened her mouth, no sound came out.

For a good time, there was no sound in the Lakandulas' house other than the sound of dripping tears. And the sound of Aling Anita's Makinang de Padyak, muffling all the sadness and loneliness inside the wooden walls. Three years had passed since their first loss. Three years dulled the gladness and radiance inside the little brown house.

Since then, Aling Anita glued herself behind her sewing machine, forgetting Sundays and birthdays and Mother's Days and all the other days to work. Money had to be made. Stomachs had to be filled. Holes had to be mended. There was only so much a pair of hands could do.

And so, the house of the Lakandulas had only one sound.

Rat-tat-tat-tat-tat spun the sewing machine each morning. *Rat-tat-tat-tat-tat* spun the sewing machine by night.

But sometimes, there was another sound, like the clatter of cowrie shells on the wooden sungka board. Marikit still took it out and played by herself. How she loved that game! In all those times, she looked across her, wistfully imagining her happy-faced brother whom she used to play with.

She had tried so much to imagine.

She still imagined her tatay would come home. After all, he left his fishing hat behind the door, waiting to be picked up by its former owner, who was dearly missed. Marikit took that hat out and wore it herself. Then, she hung it back, thinking her tatay would come looking for it.

Oh, if all could only be imagined!

There were days, however, when Marikit thought she imagined too much. In some afternoons, whenever she walked home from school, she saw the shadows of the sampaguita hedges smiling at her. Hissing at her. Mumbling things at the sound of the wind, singing:

Child of ten, let's make the odds even. Child of ten, come to Shadow-haven.

And for the past nights, Marikit woke up late into the dawn, finding her nanay working quietly beside a candle, pulling rosy, bright threads from the flickering light as if it was a spool. But Marikit only thought she was dreaming and went back to sleep.

CHAPTER 3

MARIKIT'S DRESS

Kaarawan. Filipino. n. *Birthday.* The day of the year when a person honors their first breath. Usually involves gifts and parties and, maybe, new clothes.

Every morning before she left for school, Marikit asked Aling Anita, "Nanay, you have not forgotten our birthday, have you?" She said the same thing when she came back from school, the same thing while they ate dinner, and the same thing as they laid down their banig to sleep.

In all those times, Aling Anita only nodded and forced a smile as if hiding a secret.

There must *be a secret,* Marikit thought, for she knew—she just simply knew—that her Diwata dress was being made. She had seen yards of blue fabric lying on her nanay's sewing machine, folds of chiffon tucked within the cabinet, and a strip of blue satin shimmering under the sun, cut like a wide sash. Surely, this must be her dress!

The excited Marikit told her friends about it, and her friends told their friends about it, until every child in Sampaguita Street and all the other streets knew that Maria Kristina Lakandula, who would be celebrating her birthday on the summer solstice, would have a dress like a Diwata, just like Jana Solomon. And for the first time, she wouldn't be wearing something old.

But not all the children believed it. The children at school scoffed, "You? Impossible!" The children at Kawayan Street told her, "You're always wearing recycled clothes!" The children at Sampaguita Street laughed, "You'll never look like a Diwata!"

"I *will*," Marikit insisted. "Just wait. When I put on my beautiful blue dress, I'll be as pretty as Jana."

"Really now, Marikit Malikot?"

"Really." And Marikit pursed her lips before saying, "Maybe even prettier!"

Marikit endured and waited, avoiding her playmates who teased her, "Diwata? Maybe a *disaster!*" They laughed whenever she passed by. She didn't mind. She knew her nanay was making her dress. Her nanay made a promise.

And promises should be kept.

So she went home to look wistfully at her nanay, hoping that she'd catch a glimpse of her beautiful blue gown. But alas! The yards of blue fabric were not for her dress but for Lola Tacing's curtains, and the yards of blue tulle were for Tiyang Sorsiya's Sunday skirt. Marikit was disappointed, but still, she would not lose hope.

"Maybe it's a secret," Marikit said, in order to comfort herself. "Maybe I'm not supposed to see it yet."

On the twentieth of June, when the sun was fully ablaze on a high noon, as Marikit counted the cowrie shells on her brother's sungka board and played alone, a hand gently tapped her shoulder. She turned around to see Aling Anita's tired and gaunt face all bright under the light, gazing at her with love as she motioned: *It's time, anak.*

Marikit's eyes were already big, black, and luminous, but they sprang larger as her whole face stretched into one big smile. *Ah!* Her broken teeth showed. She was going to see her dress!

Aling Anita wrapped a blindfold around Marikit's eyes and led her quietly to the sunlit desk. The floorboards kept creaking underneath the weight of their feet, but at that moment, Marikit heard nothing else but the sound of her own heartbeat. She walked, humming the birthday song to herself. And then, her nanay stilled her and began removing her blindfold.

Marikit held her breath. She didn't open her eyes at once. In the dark of her lids, she imagined the silvery blue folds of the gown she wanted. A big skirt. A satin sash. A nice bow. And dainty ruffles on her sleeves.

Her lashes fluttered as she slowly lifted her eyes.

Marikit stared at the bright glow of sunlight coming from the open windows. She saw it, a dress different from all others, floating on a hanger, its skirt swaying under the light breath of the wind. Marikit took it all in—the striped green-and-black collar, a pendant of wound pink threads, a pair of different-colored pockets, and a medley of scrap fabrics. The fabrics were not sewn as symmetrically square quilts; each was in various shapes and sizes. Some were squares and long rectangles, rhomboids, and triangles shaped like an upside-down pizza. Then there were shapes like curvy beans or strange oblongs, all set beside each other as if the dress was a giant hole that had to be covered with dozens of patches. The backside had only darker fabrics on it, and there was a conspicuous X embroidered on the bottom part of the skirt, as if her leg was a perfect target.

"W-what's this, Nanay?" Marikit was in shock.

It's your birthday dress, Marikit, came the answer.

"M-my dress?" Marikit closed her eyes, shut her lashes hard, then opened them again. She wasn't seeing things. *This*—not a blue gown, not a flowy ball skirt, not a pair of fluttering sleeves, only a strange assortment of prints and patches—was her dress.

It must be a joke. It had to be a joke.

"Maybe you're hiding my real dress, aren't you, Nanay?" Marikit began swiping the rest of the gowns. But no blue ball skirt appeared, no blue sash nor fluttery blue sleeves. "Or maybe it's somewhere else. It *must* be somewhere else." She stomped with a panic. "Where's my real dress, Nanay? You promised!"

My child. Aling Anita looked forlorn. *There is nothing else.*

Marikit read it all and felt as if her heart stopped.

"No." She quivered. "I told them—they were expecting—I wanted to be—" Marikit hung her head. "I wanted to look like a Diwata."

Aling Anita knelt down to look straight into Marikit's eyes.

Your dress is special. No one else in the world has anything like it. It will wrap you with warmth and keep you company when you feel lost and alone. This dress is what you need. This dress will keep you safe.

"Special?" Marikit's voice was shrill and sharp. "That's not special! That's just your old dress covered with left-over patches. I'm tired of wearing recycled clothes over and over again. It's my tenth birthday! I want a proper dress! I never asked for anything else!"

All at once, Marikit's birthday hopes turned sour. Their small house shook as she stomped her legs, screaming, "You broke your promise! I hate this dress, and I hate you!" Without a hint of apology, Marikit kicked the cowrie shells, flung her brother's sungka board away, and let herself out in an angry dash, slamming the door behind her.

Underneath the sampaguita hedges that lined Sampaguita Street was an inconspicuous congregation, watching, waiting, peering their shadowy ears into human business like tiny ministers of gossip. Nobody noticed they were there; things were rarely recognized in the dark. After all, what could Shadows do?

Nothing, perhaps, but to make the odds even. And make the even odd.

Marikit did not see them, of course. All Marikit could see, as she tearfully flitted across the street, was the ugly birthday dress her nanay had made. A wretched, reformed, flimsy little scrap-dress, spun together from old leftovers of fabric. And as sorrow burrowed in her chest, it breathed to life many woes.

Woes that whispered things to her innocent heart.

What an unfortunate child you are! A birthday dress made out of scraps! How your friends will laugh at you!

Your nanay always makes you wear spare things. Maybe you're not that important. She'd rather sew, sew, sew.

Have you forgotten? Your nanay got very ill when you were born. Maybe this is revenge. Maybe she secretly hates you and keeps you around to make you suffer. How could a mother let her child wear old clothes?

She promised, didn't she? And she broke it so easily. She never meant it when she agreed with you. Poor unloved child. Poor Marikit!

Marikit plucked the sampaguita flowers and crushed them with her little hands, not knowing that underneath the leafy canopies, she was being watched. They exulted at the sight of her, jeering with their pale, yellow eyes, "Ah, the sweet scent of disappointment!"

"She is ripe this time, right?" one asked, in a voice that sounded more like leaves rustling.

"She is ripe *tomorrow*," came a bigger Shadow, one that spread across the curtain of shade, encompassing the silhouettes of the houses stretching as the round ball of light blasted on it with an intense summer heat. "When the clock strikes her tenth sun, she will know, and she will choose. And we shall make her an offer she cannot refuse."

The Shadow slowly rubbed its long beard, examining its young prey, its stomach gurgling with menace.

It was sundown when Aling Anita found Marikit by the hedges, curled and crying while the children around her looked on. Aling Anita stretched her hand and tapped her daughter's shoulder. *Let's come home, Marikit.*

But Marikit looked up with a flash of anger in her eyes. "I will not wear that dress," she declared. "You always make me wear old, used clothes. I never get anything new! Why can't you be like other mothers? Like Mrs. Solomon? I deserve a nice birthday, too!"

And then, it happened again. Aling Anita's fingers stiffened as if they were stitched close. She tried moving them, and she could not, and her small, dry mouth hung with a wordless rebuke.

"What are you going to say now?" Marikit yelled at her mother. "Make me wear that dress? I won't!" Marikit rose and stomped her foot. "Never!"

Marikit darted away, unaware that a Shadow had latched onto the sole of her slipper, extended itself like a thin, long thread, and followed her all the way home.

CHAPTER 4
BIRTHDAY DAWN

Engkanto. Filipino. n. A creature that enchants in the many ways humans prefer to be enchanted—a crystal-clear voice warbling a serenade, the fragrance of a newly cooked adobo, or the spicy thrill of evil mischief set to break the rules of Bathala.

The first thing Marikit did when she got home was stare at the ugly dress by the hanger. Her nanay's pair of scissors was left on the wooden board of the Makinang de Padyak. She could take it. She could cut those patches away until there was nothing left. Nothing of the ugly, yellow-stained, reformed dress.

But it must have been the light coming from the lamp outside—or something else—for the threads somewhat gleamed, as if they spoke to her: *Don't.* And so, Marikit walked away, rolling herself in the banig and covering her face with the blanket. She pretended to sleep when Aling

Anita came inside. She closed her eyes when her nanay checked in on her and wiped her sticky tears with a pair of rough, callused fingers. Marikit stayed so still for a long time that she did, eventually, fell asleep.

And then, she dreamed.

From the black of her mind, she saw something. Some *things*. Something sparkled, something gushed, and something laughed—a laugh that sounded like the wind brushing against a thick cloud of leaves. Something blossomed, sprouting so fast, as if time was in quick motion, and something swirled across the air. Threads. Threads the color of rose and fire, all of them woven on a tapis that sparkled like the gold-speckled waters at sunset. There was a face. The blurry, brown face of a woman with black hair. Marikit tried to recognize them all, but they zipped through her mind so fast, she couldn't get a proper look.

And then, she felt a warm grasp on her shoulder.

Marikit stirred. She opened her eyes to have a glimpse of the clock—it was five minutes before midnight. Her nanay gazed down at her with a troubled face lit by the candle-light. In her arms, the patchwork dress.

Anak, it's time, said Aling Anita, gesturing.

"Time for what?"

Quickly. Get up. We need to get ready.

"What's going on?"

Your dress. You must wear your dress.

"No!" Marikit barked back, sweeping up both of her slippers and running into a corner. She wrapped herself in a blanket and stared at her nanay with defiance. "Don't make me wear that dress, I don't like it!"

Marikit! You have to!

"Why are you so insistent?" yelled Marikit. "I don't want it! I don't! I don't!"

They have found you, my child. And they are coming!

"Who is coming, Nanay?" Marikit asked frantically. "Why are you trembling?"

There was no bell, no chiming, no grand gonging sound, but Marikit heard it. It shook all over her body and rippled in her skin, like a big slosh of wave surging from her toes up to her head. She felt it by the ends of her fingers. She felt it to the tips of her toes.

"Happy birthday to you," came a singing voice. "Happy birthday to you."

Marikit unfurled herself from the blanket and looked around. Was she dreaming? Was someone else in their house? Someone with a voice so strange and menacing and whispery?

"Happy birthday, Halfling." The voice blew in the house like a drafty wind that chilled Marikit's spine. She glanced outside the window and saw nothing but the kamias tree swaying with its ripe, green fruit. She looked behind her and saw nothing but the cobwebs that blanketed many of the wooden decorations that hung from the wooden walls.

Then, she looked down.

A pair of yellow eyes gazed at her from the gaps of their floor.

"AAAHHHH!" Marikit shrieked, throwing her blanket and running into Aling Anita's arms. They watched the creature move. Its body gurgled, oozing up into the slats like a thick, velvety liquid, slowly forming into the shape of a human wrapped in a big black cloak.

Hi-hi-hi, the Shadow laughed, showing off his crooked, muddy teeth.

Hi-hi-hi.

Marikit tremblingly clutched her mother's arm. "Nanay," she whimpered with teary eyes, only to notice the cold, stoic expression on Aling Anita's face, as if this spectacle was not new to her.

"Don't look at me like that, Diwata. Or should I say, *Diwanlaon*," the Shadow murmured from the corner where it was dark. "I am not here to fight."

"Diwata?" Marikit glanced at her mother. "Diwanlaon?"

"I have only come to place our bid, to take our share, to make the odds even." The Shadow stretched out his ink-black cane. "I have only come for the Halfling."

Aling Anita hid Marikit behind her and grabbed a hot

candlestick. The fire atop the wick exploded in a warm, pinkish light. Long, blazing strands rippled from the fire-tip. Aling Anita pulled them all with her fingers, like threads unspooled from their roll. The pink strands danced in the air and glowed in the dark, swirling with a spark like a thick live wire.

"How could Nanay do that?" Marikit gasped.

"I told you, I wasn't going to fight," sighed the Shadow in despair. "I don't wish to fight. I'm not the kind of Shadow to. If we had known you still had your powers, Sitan would have sent a proper mambabarang to curse you to your fingernails."

In the air, the candle-thread formed the words, *Leave, then.*

"Ah, but I can't leave," the Shadow reasoned. "Look, both our sides are bound with the laws of consent. That's why Sitan wants to tell the Halfling, your daughter, this." And he sank into the floor, kneeling so that his eyes fell directly on Marikit's. "Sitan will give you everything you like if you come with us. All the power, all the wonder, all the beauty mortal man cannot afford. He will feed you until you are sated. You will wear all the nice clothes you want, whenever you wish."

Marikit glanced at her birthday dress.

"Not like that, of course," laughed the Shadow. "Diwatas lie. They tell you one thing and give you another. Poor Fidel thought the woman he married was just a young, innocent seamstress. Wouldn't it be much better if you had given him all the gold he needed so that he didn't have to set out into the sea that morning? With your son, of all people?"

"Nanay, what is he saying?" Marikit saw Aling Anita purse her lips.

"It was all because of an Oath, wasn't it?" The Shadow grinned. "Promises you make, promises you break. However, this one bound you like a well-stitched thread."

Leave! Aling Anita narrowed her eyes.

"I told you, I just need to take the girl." The Shadow's cloak started rippling, stretching, creeping toward Marikit's toes. "Most parents gave their Halflings to us. They're easy to convince, those petty-minded humans. Of course, I have never met a Diwata after the Laon before. This is a first."

As the Shadow spoke, the tip of his cloak quietly wrapped around Marikit's ankles. "But I tell you, there's no better choice. You broke the law. A criminal in Bathala's eyes. You can't return to your own land. Might as well be on the other side."

The Shadow made a strong tug, and Marikit fell down. "Nanay!" Marikit yelped.

Hi-hi-hi. The Shadow grinned, showing his dirty death-dust teeth as he dragged Marikit toward him. *Hi-hi-hi,* his body gooped and rumpled.

Aling Anita latched her flashing threads around

Marikit's wrist. She made a good pull, too. *Heave!* went the threads. *Heave!* went the Shadow's cloak. Marikit cried at the pushing and pulling, feeling as if her body would break.

One gentle breath from Aling Anita, and the strands—thin and wispy—grew into thick, flat ribbons. They drizzled inside the room like rosy-pink snakes, and Aling Anita, with a loop and a knot, pulled Marikit back into her arms, burning a bright light on the Shadow's black cloak.

"Fire! Fire!" the Shadow screamed, attempting to put it out.

Aling Anita wasted no time. She immediately perched Marikit on the top of the sewing machine. *Wear the dress,* she commanded.

"Opo." Marikit obeyed. She slipped the dress over her sando and shorts, and it fell flimsily above her knees. It was warm, like an embrace.

This is not just a dress, Marikit. Aling Anita gestured with her hands. *It's a map. A map that will guide you through the land of the Engkantos. My once-home. And, if you will it, yours.* All at once, the lengthy fire-ribbons followed the tips of Aling Anita's fingers, swirling, darting, whistling in the air, forming into curves and curls.

"No, I won't allow this!" threatened the Shadow. "Your child will not step foot in that place!"

Aling Anita pulled a needle from her pincushion and

stuck it on the pink embroidery of threads underneath Marikit's collar. *In the place where you will go, you will not lack anything. The needle will be your compass. The stitches will tell your way. X will be your destination, so, my child, do not stray. And remember*—Aling Anita gave Marikit a tight squeeze—*never take this dress off. No matter what.*

"But I don't want to go, Nanay!" Marikit began to cry. "I don't want to leave! Don't make me leave, please!"

Aling Anita held Marikit's face for the last time and kissed her forehead. All of a sudden, Marikit could read it—her nanay's thoughts, running through *her* head.

I was afraid of this, but I was ready. Oh, all that I have given to be with you! Ten years was splendid. I wish there could be more. But there were ten years. I will always think of you. Always, always, always.

The fire-ribbons had taken form by then, into a pair of wings in layers of light. Aling Anita looped and knotted them behind Marikit's back. They began to flutter.

"No! Stop! This Halfling is for us!" the Shadow squawked, gurgling down the wooden slats like melted black lava.

But Aling Anita was quick. *I love you*, she motioned, before giving Marikit a final push.

Marikit fell from the window, her fire-wings lifting her body into the cloudy black sky, beyond the Shadow's reach, beyond her wooden home, beyond her mother's gaze, and into the star-speckled night.

CHAPTER 5
MANGHAHABI MAGIC

Sinulid. Filipino. n. *Thread.* A long strand of fiber used to weave, stitch, knot, or knit. Occasionally employed to make magical wings.

N anay is a Diwata?"

Marikit could not believe it, not even as fire-wings flapped behind her and carried her across the rusty roofed neighborhood of Barrio Magiting. Why, her nanay never showed any hints of magic! Never twiddled her callused fingers to cast a spell at the irritating clients who made fun of her disability. Her nanay had only been sordidly quiet, a gaunt, pale figure that stationed herself behind a sewing machine for as long as Marikit could remember. The only time someone alluded to Aling Anita's powers was whenever she held a small needle, as if that tiny object possessed all her fiery magic.

"I thought Diwatas and Engkantos were just stories!" Marikit spoke loudly as she glided across the evening sky. "And if they were true, Nanay hardly looked like a Diwata! Aren't they supposed to be well-dressed and pretty?"

Some of the ribbons unfurled from her back and tapped her shoulders as if they were two hands, their edges stripping into smaller lines that bent into cursive letters:

Yes, she was a Diwata. And yes, they are real, child.

"AHHHHHHHH!" Marikit squirmed in the air. "What are you? Don't hurt me! Just put me down, please!"

We're just threads. Threads of luminous light. Threads your mother made.

Marikit's eyes widened with wonder. "So it's true! All those nights of seeing her weave threads from candlelight. But . . ." She pursed her lips. "I don't understand. What's going on? Why did this happen? Where are you taking me?"

One by one, please. We can't answer it all.

"Take your time, then."

The ribbons did take their time. They swirled and bent and curved and folded as they answered. *Firstly, you are officially a Halfling. Second, it's precisely because you're a Halfling. And third, where all the Halflings must go. To the land of the Engkantos.*

"Engkantos?" Marikit shuddered. "But aren't there more monsters there?"

Not monsters, the ribbons told her. *Magickind.*

"Does that mean I am a Diwata, too?"

Not yet. You are only a Halfling. Half that's about to be whole.

"Is it because I have a Diwata mother and a human father?"

No. Being a Halfling means you only have half of your power. The land of the Engkantos has your other half. That, which you must find.

"Nanay should have told me." Marikit scowled as she flew over the tall coconut trees that lined the beach. "She has power! Magic! Why did we have to live in an old house and eat stale food? We could have been rich! I could have had my blue dress if she wished it!"

There are rules, even for the Engkantos, child.

"Well, if I was a Diwata, I would definitely use my powers differently," Marikit declared. "I wouldn't let anyone laugh at me or look down on me. I'd wear pretty, new dresses all the time, not like the old clothes Nanay makes me wear!"

Are you mad at your mother?

"Mad? Of course I'm mad! I'm also sad and lonely and I want to scream!" Marikit did, shocking the two bats hovering nearby. "She never told me about herself or myself or those monsters. And now she's just going to make me leave?"

She was bound to keep a secret, the ribbons said. *It was in a contract. There were rules.*

"I don't care!" Marikit stomped her feet in the air. "Nobody told me a thing! Now I don't know what happened to her or what will happen to me. Why do I have to do this alone?"

The ribbons swirled in the black sky like a flash of rosy lightning. *Child, where you are going, your nanay cannot come. But she is with you. In the stitches and patches and every fiber of this dress. Her love is as intact as every hem. Every seam. Her threads will watch over you. Besides, you have other problems.*

Marikit followed the ribbons' hands as they pointed down, and she saw them.

The Shadows.

They were not letting up. In fact, they followed Marikit and called more of their companions—Shadows upon Shadows rippling on top of each other as they surged across Sampaguita Street. They gazed at Marikit with their many yellow eyes, with their white, sharp teeth, hissing, "You can't run away from us, Halfling!"

"Go away!" Marikit shouted at them. "Stop following me!"

The sky and the wind were between them—surely, Marikit was out of reach. But not for long. One must remember that Marikit's wings were just made up of threads. Bright, blazing, ribbon-breadth threads that slowly burned and evaporated into the sky. In a few moments, just as they passed the edge of Barrio Magiting, they began to sag.

They began to tear.

Marikit felt it. The weight of her body, the weight of her questions, the weight of her sadness. Sadness, most of all, was a heavy thing, and gravity made its pull.

Marikit began to droop.

"There's no escaping us now!" laughed the Shadows underneath. "We will catch you, and we shall make you one of us!"

Black, goopy, shadowy hands shot to the sky and aimed for Marikit. The wings successfully evaded them, flying Marikit off the Shadows' path, but they were burning. They were dissolving.

"No!" Marikit tugged the strings and pleaded, "Don't let me fall! Don't leave! Please! I don't know what to do!"

Oh, but we must, child. Our job is done.

"But how can I get there? To the land of the Engkantos? How can I be a Diwata?"

They were on the top of the bamboo groves, where thick, green poles extended themselves to the heavens, ready to pierce any fallen object with their sharp edges. It was then that the fire-wings breathed their last blaze. *Find the X, child.*

The last strands pointed at the bottom of her skirt. *The X.* The wings unlooped themselves behind Marikit's back and scattered in the sky like a sudden burst of fireworks. Marikit fell from the sky, shouting with her lungs, "Nanay!"

But before the sharp tips could touch her, the bamboo stalks at Kawayan Street bent sideways like fingers uncurling on a hand, receiving Marikit into the depths of their palms before snapping to a crisp close.

CHAPTER 6
LUNTIAN FOREST

Alitaptap. Filipino. n. *Firefly.* A small insect gifted with
a glowing ball of light, a constant imagery of magic and
nostalgia at night, said to guide spirits or humans to secrets
gods are not willing to share.

Marikit crashed straight into the ground, into something deep, into something dark.

"OUCH!" She hit the grassy floor, the soft blades grazing against her small hands, wrapping her nose with the
fresh fragrance of the morning dew. Marikit tried to peer
clearly, but all she saw were shadows of stalks that stretched
far beyond recognition and the speckles of stars that glinted
in the still-night sky. As she carefully rose to her feet, something on her dress lit up.

It was her collar. A print of black and green stripes began
moving like tall bamboo poles swaying in the dark, coming
alive through the stitches and threads that rippled through

it. Words began to form from the stitches, in the same script Aling Anita used to write in the air.

Luntian Forest, it read.

"Wow. That's some strong Diwata magic you got there," rang a voice in the dark.

Marikit clenched her fist. "Don't come near me," she warned as she surveyed the darkness. "I'm not scared of you."

"That's good to hear," came the answer. "There's positively no reason to be scared."

"Don't come near, I say!" Marikit swung her hand in the dark.

"I'm not going to hurt you. I can't. I absolutely have no hands, just tiny, wobbly legs. Can't throw a punch against a human."

Marikit paused. She turned around and saw nothing but darkness. "Show yourself."

"I'm just right here," the voice laughed.

"Where?" Marikit gazed to her left, then to her right.

"Nope, not there," she heard it say. "Here. Up heeeeere."

Craning her neck up, Marikit looked at the sky. There were only stars. Stars that glowed in light, bright colors—in white, pale yellow, orange, red, and blue. Strange. One of the stars started growing bigger, almost to the size of the moon, until it became a ball of light that hovered around her. She squinted.

The hovering light illuminated her face before staying put, lending her cheeks a warm, amber glow. "Whoa," Marikit gasped. "You're a star!"

"Not a star. I'm an alitaptap," the amber light corrected her. "A firefly."

In an instant, all the starlike light from the sky drew close as if long strings pulled them down. There were hundreds—no, thousands—floating by the bamboo forest, their tiny glow illuminating the dark bamboo groves. When Marikit looked up, all the glittering speckles vanished, and so did the sky. There were only the tips of bamboo leaves filling up the entire atmosphere.

"Hi," they greeted in chorus.

"H-h-hi," she greeted back, putting one hand over her

eyes as she cowered under the light of the fireflies. "My dress said I am in Luntian Forest." She looked around. "But *where* is Luntian Forest?"

"In the earth's enduring roots," answered one firefly. "Holding the planet's pillars for trillions of years."

"I am under the earth?" Marikit gasped.

"'Center' would be more geographically correct," one answered promptly, "since the roots grow inward. And don't tell us we're wrong; we Infinites have been around for millions and billions of whences, and no other living thing with skin can tell us otherwise."

"I'm sorry. *What* are Infinites?"

The fireflies glowed their brightest. "Us. We exist like the stars, tens of thousands of forevers, and never die until the galaxy finally sleeps into existence."

Marikit tilted her head with wonder. "But doesn't forever mean not having an end?"

"Not really," someone in the luminous crowd chimed. "Forevers are just long, loooong years. For example, when people get married, they make cheesy wedding vows like 'I'll love you forever'—which in some cases is true—until they die and live their next life. Then they can choose another partner if they want to. That's fulfilling a contract. Some break their forevers, though. And when they do, they get massive amounts of bad luck. Maybe not in this life, but in another life they'll live."

"We have other lives?" gasped Marikit.

"Most certainly. You have a life with flesh, and you have a life like a star. A life of promise. A life of many possibilities."

Marikit waited for her skin to glow, but it stayed as it was—brown and fleshy and plump.

"Not like that, child." One firefly swished its tiny head with displeasure. "Ugh. Humans are so dense, they hardly understand anything about the universe."

"You, of course, aren't one," another firefly commented.

"Dense?"

"No. Human." A firefly swirled around Marikit, and the rest followed until she was engulfed in a festoon of tiny radiant fireballs, breathing and burning alive. "You are a Halfling, aren't you?"

"Yes," she answered timidly.

"You are here for your Diwata Journey, then?" A cluster of fireflies inspected her.

"Diwata Journey?" Marikit fidgeted.

"Yes, for becoming a Diwata."

"Can't you just sprinkle some sparkly magic dust on me so I can get home?" fretted Marikit. "A Shadow attacked my nanay, and I don't know what happened to her!"

"Oh, *magic dust*," a firefly in red sarcastically repeated. "What an upside-down notion you've got. That's not how it works, child. Let me explain. Have you ever been to school?"

"Yes . . ."

"And you won't graduate until you finish the number of required years, right?"

"Uh-huh."

"It's precisely like that," said the firefly with amber light. "You go through different stages so you can graduate. And to graduate as a Diwata means that you have acquired skill, experience, common sense, fulfilled Oaths, broken curses, and gods' kisses along the way. You need the land's magic to rub off on you, so Sitan won't ever bother you again."

"But my nanay!" Marikit cried.

"Oh, shush, child. Your nanay is perfectly safe." Another firefly came forward. "Shadows are only after Halflings. At least for now. No Engkanto would wage a war against another unless it's on schedule. Bathala is very particular about dates. We'd know if someone wrote it on the Destruction Scrolls."

"Ugh. I get headaches explaining to Tens," sighed an olive-colored firefly.

"It used to be so easy when the adults took the Journey," a blue-colored firefly grumbled. "Back then, when the rules were not yet tampered with, the grown-up Halflings accepted their fate and soberly went on their way. But ever since the Shadows learned the secret, they've tried to bait the younger ones with just about anything, from candy to a mundane Heart's Desire."

"What secret?" Marikit was confused.

"Magic starts to spurt from a Halfling's fingers around their first decade," answered another firefly. "That's when powers can be trained and bent into things, like singing and dancing and growing plants and drawing pictures—"

"But aren't those *human* skills?"

"Well, where do you think those skills come from?" a firefly bleated. "They all come from us. From the Engkantos. *We* taught you things. *We* slipped into your world to share our wisdom. Sadly, some of us got too entangled with your affairs and preferred to stay. That's how this mess started."

All the fireflies blinked their many lights in agreement.

"It is unlawful for a Diwata to stay for more than a complete sun-cycle in the mortal world," one rose-colored firefly explained. "That's when their powers weaken. That's when their hearts forget. That's when the land of the Engkantos ceases to remember their name when they pass by the Door That Wasn't There. Bathala always warns them about this, but many seem to be taken by your world's allure, and I don't see why."

"True," answered one firefly with white light. "So much politicking and patronizing and planet plaguing. I would never want to end up in the mortal world, even if Bathala asked me."

Marikit, who was already confused, only managed to say, "*I* would like to go back, please."

"You can only go back to the mortal world once you

finish your rite of passage as a Diwata," said a deep-blue firefly that sounded like a lady. "It's in the Hirang's Clause."

"Hirang's Clause?"

Out of the black, a scroll as big as Marikit *poof*ed into existence. All the fireflies clumped behind it, rearranging themselves in the shape of a man, complete with arms that extended to the edges of the scroll as if they were holding it. "Ehem," started one, whose voice was unusually deep for someone so small. "As mandated by the High Council of Kaluwalhatian, all Halflings must return to the land of the Engkantos to carry out their individual Diwata Journey, utilize their inherited vocation from the Branches, and regain their Infiniteness by obtaining permanent Engkanto residency, which gives them the right to traverse the Many Worlds in complete freedom and gain apprenticeship under designated god-mentors." The firefly paused, then balked. "Uh, do I still read that part?"

"What part?" one firefly asked, glowing hot red.

"The part that shouldn't be here but is?"

"Oh." A sea-blue firefly shone. "*That* part. It's badly written, too. Shadows have the ugliest handwriting."

A few fireflies crowded close to the scroll. "The High Council of Kaluwalhatian is still convening over whether to affirm the changes or not," one argued. "After all, this is still tampering."

"But it's written in the Scroll," insisted another.

"Everything that has been written in the Scroll is effective the moment the ink dries. Come now, if you won't read it, I will."

The firefly took the first reader's spot and continued. "Failure to Journey within their first decade implies automatic designation to the Shadows. Consolations and Consequences apply. This law is made true and binding until the end of time."

The scroll vanished with the same *poof*, and all the fireflies scattered.

"I don't want to be with the Shadows," Marikit moaned.

"For sure, you don't!" one firefly told her. "All those unwashed dirty cloaks used over and over again? Who knows what creatures live there?"

Yikes. Marikit began scratching her arms. "Can you tell me how to be a Diwata, then?"

"That's easy," one firefly bragged. "All you gotta do is reach the X."

"Oh, that's what the ribbons told me." Marikit glanced at the patch at the bottom left of her dress. "Can you tell me where X is?"

The fireflies gaped at her before huddling together, buzzing a *wis-a-wis-a-wis-wis* sound. They scattered again, blinking with their own colors. "We don't know."

"Why?"

"Your X appears to you and you only," they explained.

"It's like finding your favorite book in a library or falling in love. *We* can't find your favorite things or fall in love for you. You have to learn things along the way."

"Does that mean I have to guess it?" Marikit tilted her head.

"No, that means you need to unearth it," came the answer. "It's there, tucked deep somewhere in your fate. The good news is you'll get a reward for finding it."

"Some say you'll get to rule kingdoms, marry royals, live in rooms of pure gold, get served by nymphs, and order all the sweets you want to eat. I'm not really sure, though; all the Halflings who passed this way never came back. You don't return to a place twice in a Diwata Journey."

Marikit's eyes grew wide. "I can get rich?"

"Extremely so, if you stumble upon treasure chests or old magic castles with hidden gold rooms."

"I can get servants?"

"Of course, if you manage to trick a king or concoct a compelling spell to lure a town to appoint you to a high position."

"And power?"

"Yes, power. Diwatas are all about power, don't you know? All the power, all the wonder, all the beauty."

Marikit clasped both of her hands to her mouth. Power. Wonder. Beauty! Why, she could make herself richer than anyone in Barrio Magiting. Even richer than Jana! She could magic cars, a big mansion, servants to follow her around with umbrellas as she walked around the sun, and above all . . .

Her dream blue dress!

The clothes she'd wear all day would be so nice that Jana's gown wouldn't compare. Each time someone in her class displayed their new things, she could magic hers and show off, too. She wouldn't have to shrink in the corner of the room because all she had were old things. She'd be powerful, so powerful every kid would envy her.

Marikit's thin, small lips stretched to a remarkably wide smile.

"Don't get too happy." A blue firefly whooshed across her eyes. "Getting to X comes with a price. You have to face a challenge."

"Like what?" Marikit mused.

"Slay a flying serpent, overthrow a king, start a revolution, outsmart a god, or defeat a princess in a baking contest. It differs per kid."

"But aren't those too much? I just turned ten!"

"Ten, or seven, or fifty-two. Doesn't matter. The gods love sacrifices. It's currency to them. They take nothing without a price, and the price is always steep."

"Ah, this is so hard!" Marikit crumpled to the ground. "Why can't I just answer a quiz?"

"Because the land has to know whether you are worthy

of it," a firefly answered. "And to be worthy of it, you have to argue and wrestle and take it to court until it finally says, 'I give up, you win.' And so, you must win, for losing means forgetting. Losing means being forgotten. If you fail your Diwata Journey, you'll be sent back to the human world with no memory. The gods will wipe your brain clean."

"High stakes, high losses." One rose-colored firefly blinked. "Now that we've told you what a Diwata Journey is all about, here's how you begin."

The fireflies, hundreds of thousands of them, formed into a big, round ball that shone like the sun. "You are here, at Luntian Forest," and the fireflies formed into long stalks of bamboo trees. "It goes for miles and miles, and you'd walk without direction if you were a plain human who accidentally got lost. The only way to get out of here is to see a secret door," and the fireflies formed a rectangular slab creaking open, "found between the three-hundredth-and-second and three-hundredth-and-third bamboo from the Elder Tree. You can't miss it. Halflings will see it if they know how to count."

"Do you know how to count, dear?" someone in the glimmering crowd asked.

"I can!" Marikit answered. "I have already counted past one hundred."

"Good. You just repeat that three times over. Now, this door is tricky; you need to enter it the moment you see it, because if you don't, it disappears in ten seconds and appears somewhere else in the bamboo forest, where you would have to hunt it again."

"Like hide-and-seek?"

"That, exactly. Doors are really playful here," one of the fireflies noted. "Another thing. You don't knock on the door. You sing to it, like a lullaby."

"I'm good at singing!"

"Perfect! She knows how to count, sings, we're all done here, then!" The fireflies clapped their little hands. "All she'll need to do is write her name legibly!"

"Write my name *where?*"

"You'll learn along the way." And the Infinites scattered on their own, dispelling into the night sky like stars rustling back home.

One firefly, however, remained.

CHAPTER 7
A FRIEND'S OATH

Kaibigan. Filipino. n. *Friend.* A life bound to you with an unbreakable loyalty, someone who'll laugh at your jokes even if they're not funny, and who'll make and keep promises no matter how tiny.

A sphere of bright-yellow light dangled in the darkness like a golden pearl. Marikit recognized him. It was the first firefly who had greeted her.

"Hello." She waved her hand. "All of them have gone back now."

"I reckon you need help," the firefly answered, zooming across Marikit's face until she almost got dizzy. "Plus, the Elder Tree is quite moody when Halflings don't talk to it politely. Do you have a pocket?"

"Oh, I do," and Marikit turned her pockets inside out. "My pockets are strange and in different colors. It's not so pretty, but this dress is supposed to be a map, see."

"A map!" he exclaimed. "I have never seen a map! I have never seen much of the world, either. At least, not closely. I have only been hovering around the bamboo groves and gazed into the ages with a sigh. It could be pretty tiring here in Luntian Forest, and I would very much like to get through the door with you."

"But won't they miss you?" Marikit pointed to the other alitaptap.

"Perhaps." The firefly shrugged. "But when you've been with the same folks for a long time, it gets a bit tiring."

"It's not." Marikit wrinkled her small nose before hanging her head down. "I wished we had a long time, because I still miss them."

"Who?"

"My family." Marikit pursed her lips, swallowing a sorrowful lump in the back of her throat. She clutched her skirt and glanced at the firefly before asking, "Do you have a father, Mr. Alitaptap?"

"Ali, please," the firefly told her. "And no, I don't have a father."

"I do," replied Marikit. "I mean, I *used* to. He was tall and thin and loved to whistle to the wind. He always carried a hat. He'd be gone before dawn because he was a fisherman, and a fisherman must always head out before the sky welcomes the morning. I'd always smell the sea on him. I loved the sea."

"Hmm. Interesting man," Ali commented.

"He was!" Marikit leaped. "He'd always carry me on his shoulder and call me Marikit. Tatay gave me that nickname. My full name is Maria Kristina. He'd tickle me, make jokes for me, and cook for me, too. He was very good at cooking! It's just—" Marikit's voice dwindled. "I miss him. It's been three years since he's gone, and I wasn't able to say goodbye properly."

"Three human years is merely a wink for me," Ali said. "Feels like yesterday. But you'd be surprised how time worked differently in the Many Worlds." He then blinked with a blush. "Infinite years will feel like a wink in the mortal world, too."

Marikit thought for a while. Fireflies in *her* world easily lost their glow and lost their life. Maybe that was what he meant. "Do you have a mother?" she asked next.

Ali *pffft*ed. "We're Infinites, Marikit. We're—"

"*I* have a mother," Marikit cut in. "She was a Diwata, but she never told me. She'd always just sew and sew and sew!" Marikit stomped on the grass so many times that it shriveled under her slippers. "She said she was ready. Ready for what? She never told me. *I* wasn't ready. All I wanted was a blue dress for my birthday, but she made me leave home, and I don't know if I can ever go back! I wish she had told me. I wish there was another way."

Tears streamed down Marikit's cheeks, straight onto

Ali's wings. *How heavy a human tear was!* Ali thought. So much sorrow and burden and salt. Ali tried to shake the weight of the tears away, when some of it washed his Infinite body and warmed his cold, immortal heart.

"Do you have a sibling?" Marikit asked after she had calmed down.

Ali gazed at Marikit, his light blinking softly. He knew she wasn't just asking questions now. He knew she was telling a story.

Her story.

"No, Marikit," Ali answered, hovering closely where she could see him.

"*I* had a sibling," Marikit answered keenly. "A brother. He'd always help me with my assignments and play sungka with me, but he'd always win. I told him I was going to practice hard and beat him. But before I ever did, he—" Marikit stopped. "He—"

Ali's heart softened as he gazed at Marikit. What should he say now? He wasn't born the way Halflings were. When he blinked his first light, he was already surrounded by fireflies. Loud, brilliant fireflies. And they were always happy. Always in bright, merry clumps.

He glanced at the firefly-lit sky before clearing his tiny throat. "I think I have siblings, after all. Since we Infinites came from Bathala."

"H-how?" Marikit asked curiously, wiping her wet lashes and gazing at Ali with new interest.

"Well, they say that when Bathala laughs, a light appears in the corner of Luntian Forest. A small, minuscule glow—"

"Smaller than you are?"

Ali scowled as Marikit sized him up with her fingers. "Yes," he growled. "Smaller than I am. I am not the smallest thing in the world, you know. Have you heard about atoms? Atoms are smaller than me." He cleared his throat and began hovering around Marikit's head. "Anyway, light. The light beats with its tiny glow, and the entire forest welcomes it by singing 'Happy Birthday.'"

"Like humans do?"

"Possibly." Ali tried to recall the lyrics in his head (he could not). "And then we linger. We study the law and play games and join pajama parties and learn how to fly backward. I myself was born not too long ago, when Bathala smiled fondly at two siblings who helped an old woman carry her heavy load up the mountain. Infinites must be born out of noble things, see. Nobody wants a forever born out of a heartbreak."

"Is Bathala like your father, then?" Marikit mused.

"Maybe." Ali shrugged. "All things are created by Bathala. I guess I have a father, too."

Marikit eyed Ali with a sidelong glance.

"Why are you looking at me like that?"

"Does Bathala look like you?"

"Me? No!" Ali snapped. "A god is big and mighty and flamboyantly dressed. And terrible, in many sorts of ways. I'm just a firefly that lives forever. Unless . . ."

The last word was spoken so mildly, Marikit didn't hear it. The only audible sound was a loud lungful as she hid her face behind her thick, wavy hair.

Ali knew it was his turn to ask.

He flew toward Marikit, toward her hair-covered face, and pushed away some of the thick strands so he could see her eyes. He perched himself right over the small mark on her nose and asked, "Do you have a friend?"

Marikit nodded lightly. "I do. Out there. In my world," she answered with her now-phlegmy voice. "There's Lena, who I always share pan de coco with, and Julie, who always lends me her color pencils, and Amy, who braids my hair and makes it pretty. There's also Susie and Gemma and Ruby, who always play with me. I have lots of friends. But—" Marikit sniffed. "I might never see them again, too."

Ali blinked with his warm amber glow and said, "I could be your friend." His radiance was reflected in Marikit's black eyes.

"Really?"

"Yes," Ali answered. "I will walk with you and play games with you and sing with you and make sure to see you through. I will never leave you. Not until you get to X." And this time, with a tiny hand Marikit couldn't see, Ali let out a smile—a smile that came from his tiny, firefly heart that spoke softly, *This is an Oath.*

"About that pocket," he asked aloud, "which of the left or right do you think is better? The previous Infinites say pockets are quite comfortable and are the best way to travel."

Marikit began to walk. "Now listen," Ali explained, flying beside her. "The Elder Tree is at the heart of the forest. It's not far from here. We just have to walk five thousand firefly-miles more—"

"FIVE THOUSAND?!"

"Firefly-miles. *Our* miles. You know, itsy-bitsy miles. It's no longer than a stride. Come along. Follow me." And Ali swooped into the tangled stalks of bamboo, lighting up a straight line and leaving a trail of sparkles behind him. Marikit strode after him, taking big steps, huffing and pushing leaves away as she kept him within her vision in the tunnel of long, neck-breaking stalks and fluttering, where her tired legs couldn't stop but had to run fast, faster and faster, until they stopped, and Marikit screeched.

"Here we are. Elder Tree," he spoke, showing her the browning skin of a bamboo stalk whose trunk was a hundred times thicker than the rest of the trees. "This is where Malakas and Maganda emerged seventeen whence-centuries ago."

"Malakas and Maganda—you mean the legend of the first humans . . . *is true*?"

"Why, of course! Who do you think made up those stories? Humans? No," Ali laughed. "All humans think about is what they can put in their mouths and what they can take away from nature. But dream of epic things? Nah. It happened. Unfortunately, Malakas and Maganda cooled off because she found him flirting with another Diwata. That's not a story for kids like you, though. Are you ready to count?"

Marikit looked at her fingers. It was just many tens. Tens and tens of tens. Marikit had counted a lot of things before—like marbles and petals and the cowrie shells she'd use on the sungka board whenever she played it alone. Counting wouldn't be too hard.

Marikit took a deep breath before answering, "I'm ready."

"When we begin, there's no stopping, so make sure you've got your focus on, because once you're confused—"

"I know! I'll forget! No need to remind me!"

Marikit observed the tall stalks of bamboo lining the way. One, she stepped forward. She looked to her left. Two, Ali tapped the next bamboo tree as a mark. Three, she followed the trail of his firefly light. Four. Five, six, seven, eight. Marikit counted in her head—everything felt more like a dance as she traced the beaming zigzagged lines. Finally, Ali stopped.

There, in the middle of the three-hundredth-and-second and three-hundredth-and-third bamboo was a door made of leaves.

Marikit opened her mouth and sang:

"Maligayang bati, sa iyong pagsilang. Maligayang, maligayang, maligayang bati!"

The door swung open, Ali slipped into her pocket, and both of them stepped in.

CHAPTER 8

EVERWHERE

Daan. Filipino. n. *Road.* A stretch of walkable earth that
leads somewhere, or everywhere, depending on which part
of it you are on.

On the other side of Luntian Forest was a sprawling
rotunda, shaped like a sun spilling its many, many
rays. The middle of the road was generously covered with
glistening specks of pink Engkanto dust and stumps of
gems that eroded in glittery, crystalline chunks. Bundles of
clouds amassed in the pinkish sky of daybreak, where little
lights flashed at their soft edges, dispelling rainbow hues at
every puff.

"Ah, the smell of freedom!" Ali twirled dramatically in
the air, his amber light a striking contrast to the blushing
landscape. He inhaled all that his firefly lungs could muster,
then ended up coughing. The smell of freedom, it turned
out, was the smell of dusty powder and dawn.

"Where are we?" Marikit mumbled, recognizing the dozens of pathways that extended from the center, each one different from the other. There were roads veiled with thick clouds that spilled a heavy downpour, roads covered with lush flora, roads flanked with glistening jewels, and roads that wiggled like giant worms. Some roads were not roads at all, but empty deserts and raging rivers, bridges made of gold or a ladder straight to the sky.

"Good question. But aren't you the one wearing the map?" Ali replied.

Oh, right, Marikit thought, remembering.

Marikit could read maps. There was one on the wall of her classroom, often left ignored until her geography teacher asked the class where a certain country was. Marikit loved finding the places marked in tiny letters, like names waiting to be called. But a map-dress was a different thing. Marikit had to twirl and turn around and look under her armpits or on the other side of her skirt to find a clue. Yet no patch shone. No stitch revealed a name. The only possible hint was a suspicious embroidery that ran across her dress, spreading and zigzagging along the edges, tracing every patchwork like a dotted lining. They all merged into a little sun the size of a button embroidered right under her collar, glimmering and beating with warm pink light.

"Hmmm." She walked around. The needle on her compass began moving. In fact, it moved so much that Marikit couldn't tell which direction it was pointing to. With every step, the needle inched to the north, then wobbled to the west, sprung completely to the east, then dipped to the south.

"There's a street sign over there, if that helps." Ali turned Marikit's attention to the center of the rotunda. A singular pole stood, clumped with many arrows stuffed so close to each other that it looked like a spiked mace. Below it was a large, round rock in reddish brown—a hue outstandingly different from the rosy ground.

Marikit walked toward the street sign with deep interest. She stood on her toes and began reading the words, only to find that the directions were written in an Old Alphabet she could not understand.

"No good?" Ali heard Marikit grunt. "How about we ask someone?"

"Who?"

"Him." Ali flew downward, directing Marikit to lower her gaze.

The rock below the sign was not a rock. A man wrapped in a brown tunic had curled himself on the ground and was fast asleep, snoring loudly as gold earrings twinkled in his ears. His face was smushed against the wood as he embraced a rusty, dusty shovel as if it were a pillow.

Ali examined him closer. "It's a Diwata!"

"*This* is a Diwata?" Marikit leaned closer and frowned at the man's dust-laden garment. "Aren't they supposed to have nicer, shinier clothes and big, fluttery wings and a magical wand?"

"Wherever did you see that?" Ali groaned.

"On the TV."

"What's a tee-vee?"

"A big box where all the shows are," Marikit answered pensively. "There's a morning cartoon where Diwatas are the heroes. They guard their mountain and solve problems and make magic. Only, they find it hard to adjust to our world! They always mix the wrong things, like soups and cereals and milk and juices. They can change their clothes with a snap of their fingers. Big ball gowns and giant sleeves and lovely, long wings. Wherever they walk, they always leave a trail of glitters."

"Outrageous!" shouted Ali. "That's not how it is!"

"Outrag—AHHHH!" The sleeping Diwata stirred, sprang up, and dropped the shovel straight on his bare feet. "Aw! Aw!" he yelped, hopping on one foot, then the other, his sarong flitting as he jumped. Large golden bracelets twinkled on his wrists, chiming like bells. He looked at Marikit and winced, forcing a pained "Hello" as he crumpled down.

"Hi," Marikit answered back.

"A Halfling, I presume?" he said, kissing his injured toes before he managed to stand upright. "Welcome to Everwhere. The highway of all highways, the crossroad of all Engkanto roads. I am Sangdaan, the guardian of the roads," he said by way of introduction. "Proceed at your liberty, please. Mind you, if you are heading to Anitun Tabu's cave, please head to your right. It's the road with the light drizzle; the stormy road leads to Habagat. If you are looking to tour Bighari's Garden, I'm sorry, but the rainbow bridge is under construction and won't be done until the twelfth quarter moon. Oh, and if you happen to meet my mentor Idianale along the way, please don't tell her I've been sleeping on the job."

"Who's Idianale?" Marikit asked.

"Goddess of labor, which you can see I am burdened with," murmured Sangdaan, who proceeded to an empty lot, dragging his feet and shovel.

"There are *other* gods?" Marikit asked Ali.

"Of course, there are a lot more," Ali replied in an as-a-matter-of-fact voice. "There's a god for everything. A god for rains and a god for drafts. A god for searching and a god for hunting. A god for daylight and a god for the night. Someone has to manage these things, you know. Bathala doesn't have the time to keep up with them all."

"Right. Also doesn't have patience with those who ditch their work," remarked Sangdaan, who had begun digging. The rose-colored ground crunched against the metal tip of his shovel. Pink debris scattered in the air, twinkling like powder as it fell.

"What are you doing?" Marikit asked Sangdaan, looking over his shoulder.

"Making roads." Sangdaan huffed as he made another thrust. "That's my job."

Marikit looked around. "But there's a lot of them already."

"Well, tell that to the gods," Sangdaan said, scowling. "They always complain about their Right of Way. No one will take Haik's road by way of Aman Sinaya's. And Bathala's ladder requires constant repair, because the clouds of Kaluwalhatian perpetually drift away."

"What's Ka-lulu-wala—" Marikit stopped short.

"Kaluwalhatian," Sangdaan corrected her. "Heaven, but with more clouds. Bathala's residence, the Palace of the All-Perfect. Look above you."

Marikit lifted her head. An island made of thick clouds drifted on the rose-colored backdrop, its walls glistening in pure, immaculate white. From the edges of the clouds, she could see a shining, pearly dome and sparkling crystal turrets shooting up above the atmosphere.

"Is that the place we go when we're all dead?" Marikit walked around while craning her neck upward.

"That's the place you'll go when Bathala throws a party and invites you. Now step aside. I'm about to dig that part."

Marikit watched him jab his shovel into the ground and then toss dust into the air, all in a uniform cadence. "Aren't you a Diwata?" she asked curiously. "Can't you just—sort of—*magic* the roads?" she asked.

"Magic? Of course I'll magic them," Sangdaan blustered. "It would take hundreds of years to grow those giant trees and carve those waterfalls by hand. But I cannot use my magic without my shovel. I'm a Manggagawa. That's my Branch. All Diwata magic requires some effort from its wielder. Its proportions always equate to our skill."

"Do all Diwatas use a shovel?"

"Some." Sangdaan made another thrust at the sand. "Others use clay pots, or their voice, pens and ink, or the swaying of their hips. Magic has to be manifested through something. A medium. A channel. If not, magic will just dissipate in the air and vanish like dust. Fingers are not trustworthy, especially the dirty, sweaty ones."

Marikit stared at hers. Her fingers *were* sweaty and dirty. "Were you a Halfling, too, Sangdaan?" she asked, seeing that crystalline rocks had begun sprouting out of the plain, dusty road.

"No." Sangdaan shook his head. "I've been a Diwata since my Infinite-birth. But I've met many Halflings. Most of you start here. Some get lost along the way, though. Look there."

Sangdaan pointed to their left. In a dismal path of almost-black rocks was a boy, his now-statue body half bent, his hand on his face and his mouth stuck in an eternal gap as he cried with stone tears. "I told that kid not to pick that road. But he did. He just walked right through it, not knowing that it's the road to Albania, home to a particularly fussy songbird who poops over intruders of her castle, and whoever her droppings land on turns to stone." Sangdaan sighed with dismay. "That boy didn't listen, and that boy is now a stone."

Marikit shivered a bit.

"Are there spells on each road?" Ali wondered aloud.

"Uh-huh," Sangdaan said, nodding. "The gods have had enough of Halflings picking pretty roads with so much treasure on them. Rules have changed. Many, many rules. Now the roads choose you. The roads let you know whether they'll let you pass. They'll send you the message. They'll open the door. That is, if you're really *right* for them, if they're a part of your route, or if you were courteous enough to ask."

"All I need to do is ask?" Marikit was surprised.

"The roads don't always answer favorably, mind you. They're quite temperamental and have no sense of staying put. Many Halflings lose their way on these roads. Not all the Diwanlaons have the foresight to leave their children maps, see."

"What's a Diwanlaon?"

"A Diwata-before." Sangdaan narrowed his eyes.

Marikit's eyes grew wide. "Is that what Nanay was?"

"If that's your parent who had Diwata powers, yes. My condolences, little girl." Sangdaan offered his unoccupied hand.

"But my nanay is alive," Marikit corrected. "She made me this map."

"Where?"

"I'm wearing it."

Sangdaan narrowed his eyes. He pushed his shovel aside then knelt down, studying the flimsy patchwork dress Marikit wore. He turned her aside, then around, then back, mumbling things under his nose. "Is this—?" he began. "Is it—?"

Marikit scowled. "You don't need to say that it looks like a rag. I already, absolutely know."

"Rag? Are you out of your mind?" Sangdaan jolted back, his tunic swishing. "This is a work of art! A masterpiece! A dress made of light and fire and hope and love!" He put down his shovel and held Marikit's shoulders. "You're from the Manghahabi Branch, aren't you? The dressmaking Diwatas, weavers of moon-silk and sunrays, forging the armors of kings and gods. It's been a long time since your kind passed this way. Everyone in the Engkanto lands has been looking for one of yours. We all thought you had gone up the Marilag Mountains and disappeared."

A mangahabi? Marikit thought.

"So that's why Nanay could make nice things with

threads. Except for this. She'd always make me wear something odd and old and strange. This was supposed to be a map," Marikit sighed. "But I think it's broken. Look." She pointed at her needle. "My compass keeps turning and turning and not pointing in any direction."

"Have you tried listening to it?" Sangdaan rubbed the tip of his hooked nose.

"Maps *don't* speak!" Marikit insisted.

"Oh, they do," Sangdaan asserted as he picked up his magical shovel. "They speak in silence. So do coins and twigs and little sticks that point to somewhere. Silence is made up of too many sounds screaming and canceling each other at the same time. That's why you need to pay attention. It's all telling."

"What is it saying, then?" Marikit folded her arms and frowned.

"It's saying that there are many roads ahead. That's what the pink stitches across your dress are for. Those are the highways and alleyways and underways. And the compass cannot tell you directions, because every time you move, it points to a road. A road upon a road upon a road."

Marikit peered as far as she could from the blush-colored rotunda. Each road was busy doing its own thing, raining and thundering and wriggling and splashing and growling with strange sounds. "Look." Sandaan pointed with his shovel. "Even the roads and the sky and the wind speak with signs."

"With signs?" Marikit mused aloud.

"Each morning comes with one." Sangdaan jabbed his shovel into the ground and pressed his arm against it. "The dawn would whisper to the night, *Goodbye!* before the sun slowly crept behind the clouds and lit up the sky. A storm would come with a sign. The wind would blow ahead and say, *It's coming.* The clouds would darken. There would be small drops of water before the big downpour."

Oh, Marikit's eyes brightened. "My nanay spoke with signs, too! Look," she began gesturing with her hands. "This means, 'There's food on the table.' This, 'Don't leave your shoes out in the rain.' 'Have you done your assignment?' 'Don't play too late at night.' 'Are you heading off to school?' This one, 'Take care, Marikit.' And this one . . ."

Marikit stopped as she crossed her hands and made wings across her chest. "I love you," she murmured, remembering the moments she saw her nanay last.

"Yes," Sangdaan agreed. "Those signs were telling, like words trying to get out, all at once. Words upon words upon words."

Marikit looked into the rotunda. Surely, the road would speak. Surely, the road would whisper. It was only a matter of time, Marikit thought.

She only had to pay attention.

And so, Marikit moved forward—slowly, patiently—waiting for any hint from any road. She looked at her map, too. With each step, the threads across her patches glimmered. Her compass rolled, wobbling and rolling until it finally stopped, pointing southeast.

A strong gust of wind blew on a very ordinary pathway, with dusts and gusts rolling toward it as if an invisible door opened. Marikit glanced at Ali. "It's this road!" she exclaimed. "This road opened for me!"

"Good job, little one!" Sangdaan clapped. He thrust his shovel on the ground and walk toward Marikit. "Now remember this. Some lands will share with you their magic; some lands will share with you their toil. Some Nightmares aren't terrible. Some Nightmares, you should avoid."

Marikit gaped at him confusingly. "Nightmares?"

"You'll know along the way." Sangdaan waved his hands. "Now off you go!"

Ali perched himself on Marikit's shoulder as she stepped onto the road that let her in. As soon as they were upon it, the windy gust stopped, as if a door had closed behind them, and the sight of Sangdaan and Everwhere disappeared.

CHAPTER 9

HARVEST HOUSE

Tikbalang. Filipino. n. A burly giant with the body of a man and the head and hooves of a horse, usually dwelling in high trees and constantly engrossed in playing cruel tricks to the wondering and wandering.

Traveling by Everwhere, as Marikit would describe, was a TT, as in "totally tiring," "tremendously thrilling," or "terribly terrifying." She walked through a road that drizzled with bright, white pearls coming from clam-shaped clouds (she tried to catch the pearls, but they vanished as soon as they landed on her palms). Then, she walked through pastel-colored loops without falling as she crossed the ceiling. There were roads that didn't let her through. The roads rolled stones ahead to block her and threatened to bite her. Once, a road filled with sunflowers growled at her like a lion. Another time, a path of pineapples opened their eyes and glared at her as she took the first step. She and Ali ran back in fright.

Ali, who had still not decided which of Marikit's dress pockets was better, slipped into one side for fifteen minutes, and then the other for the next fifteen. He talked to Marikit, sang with her (he had a lovely voice *if* he knew the melody), got startled whenever she hopped like a frog and tumbled on the ground, and worried if she was bruised. Then, he decided to fly close to her to remind her not to get herself hurt. The hopping and the tumbling soon eased to three times per road.

Both of them treaded a wide footpath in between sprawling yellow fields overlooked by several rice terraces. Verdant balconies of wheat reflected the warm color of the noonday sun that hung in the stationary sky. The air dripped with honeyed humidity and carried the fresh scent of harvest as soft hay brushed against Marikit's feet and bundles of wheat were stacked against each other.

Marikit glanced down at her dress. A shoe-shaped patch across her chest started glowing, the threads on its subtle print swaying like long stalks of grass bathed in sunlight. Words appeared in a cursive stitch, glowing in light-threads.

"Ikapati's Farm," she read from her map. "Ali? Who's Ikapati?"

"Goddess of agriculture, the overseer of harvest," came Ali's prompt answer.

"But isn't that the work of the farmers?"

"Not really." Ali sailed beside her as she walked. "Farmers till the soil, plant the seeds, spread fertilizer, then cross their fingers so they get a good return. The one who gives that return is Ikapati. She looks over their shoulders, checks if they are following the proper farming guidelines, and grades them. Then she coordinates with the weather god to keep the storms away. Though sometimes she forgets. Sometimes she argues with the weather god and he gets revenge by raining on her harvest. It's a pretty complicated business."

"Farmers," Marikit mumbled.

"I already told you." Ali rolled his eyes. "It's Ikapati."

"No, I mean there *are* farmers!" Marikit pointed at the golden rice fields. "Look!"

Between the gaps of the tall blades of wheat were visions of straw hats and sickles and towels wrapped around several shoulders. They moved around, bending and pulling off the grains with their own hands. Some hauled bundles of hay on their backs. Boots squeaked in the knee-deep mud, marching in the cadence of a song they merrily hummed.

"Hi!" Marikit greeted as loud as she could, waving her hands and jumping from where she stood.

Ali nudged her. "What are you doing?"

"Greeting people."

"You don't just say 'Hi!' to an Engkanto." Ali flew so close to Marikit's eyes that she got dizzy. "We read greetings differently. To some, it might also mean *Eat me!* or *Here I am, trespassing on your land.*"

Marikit could see, in between the gaps of the wheat, that the farmers had raised their hands, their sickles dancing in the air. "I don't think they disliked it," Marikit pointed out. "See? They're waving back!"

Ali peered into the fields. Indeed, the farmers slogged toward their direction, their feet sloshing with mud, their straw-hat-covered heads rising from the field. But there was something different about them. As the sun hit their faces, Marikit could see that they did not have human noses. Theirs stretched outward, with smoke streaming from their nostrils, some with spots and blazes across their foreheads. Marikit could see their beady, unblinking, round eyes, their conical ears flicking atop their long heads, and their mouths opening to a loud chorus of neighs that made Marikit fall to the ground, shrieking,

"T-T-T-TIKBALANGS!"

Marikit shuddered. Tikbalangs! So they were real! They were not merely hearsays or stories made up by her neighbors whenever she'd play by the tall bamboo stalks. "Oh, they're there," she remembered the elderfolk say. "You'd see them. Horse-headed monsters with the bodies of men, watching mortals with their beady eyes in the dark of the night. They will get you. They'll remember you and follow you home, peek through your windows when you sleep at night and give you nightmares! Nightmares!"

Nightmares, the Tikbalangs were. The sound of their hooves, the sound of their neighs, the sight of their horse heads protruding down their human necks. Marikit didn't want to look back and catch a glimpse of them.

Instead, she ran as fast as she could, speeding across the farm paths, mud and grains splashing over her legs. "I told you not to bother them!" Ali darted beside her. "Look at what you've done!"

"I'm sorry!" Marikit cried. "What do we do now?"

"Ask for a god's help," came Ali's scrambling answer. "Look! To your left!"

Far into the path was a sprawling mansion in earthen colors of wood and stone. Stained-glass windows glimmered under the light, each showing sun and grain and rain, the symbols of harvest. Its large, ornate door, surrounded by the lush botany of tropical plants, seemed reassuringly solid. "The Harvest House." Ali gazed in amazement. "The goddess Ikapati's home. If we ask her for protection, she'll save us from the Tikbalangs."

"Let's go, then!"

With one last burst, Marikit dashed toward the Harvest House. She went straight onto the fern-decorated porch, soiling the terra-cotta tiles with her muddy feet. Desperate, Marikit clutched the knocker shaped like the head of a gold tamaraw. *Tok, tok, tok,* the wood echoed from the inside.

The Tikbalangs were getting closer.

She knocked again. *Tok, tok, tok.*

Tikbalang hooves screeched right before they got onto the porch.

The Harvest House began groaning and waggling, like it was made out of jelly. The balcony waved into giant tile tides. The groaning became louder, stronger, until the door swung with a blast and a loud yell burst like thunder: "Who goes there?"

Marikit stepped aside. A cloud of smoke enveloped the entryway. Flecks of ashes fell over Marikit's head. The fear-stricken Ali swooped into her pocket.

Out emerged a mullet of rough brown and gray hairs, tossed and curled to a brown and white forehead. The being rose ten feet high, with earrings glimmering on his two triangular ears, his body dressed in a black satin vest, a striped shirt, and brown pants. Smoke came from his large nostrils, and he breathed out a puff when he asked once more, "Who knocked on my door?"

Marikit fell on the floor, quivering in fright. "AN-OTHER TIKBALANG!"

The Tikbalang squinted his eyes then gazed at the crowd of farmers standing beyond his porch. "A Halfling?" he yelped. "What's going on here?"

"Ay, Sir Dante." One of the farmers came forward and removed his straw hat. "We saw the girl greeting us and waving her hands. We felt it improper to ignore her, so we came up to say hi."

"And then the little bean ran as fast as lightning. See those tiny muddy legs? She's ruined your porch, sir, but we'll clean it up," said another.

"Y-you weren't going to hurt me?" Marikit asked.

"Hurt you? We're farmers. Our hands sow and reap and grind *your* food," Dante the Tikbalang growled as he helped Marikit up. "Anyway, your pocket is glowing. If you carry what the humans call 'bullets,' I will have them confiscated at once. So many of my kind have died at humans' hands."

Ali flew out of Marikit's pocket, meekly saying, "It's only me, sir."

Dante's big, round eyes bulged with surprise. "Why, it's an Infinite! It's been a long time since I've seen one." The Tikbalang stretched out his human hands and said, "Come here, *little* one, and let me get a nice study of you."

Ali, with all his big feelings, scowled at the Tikbalang's words. But Dante did not see his expression. What Dante did see was a tiny, amber light hanging up in the air, right above his palms. "I thought you were a pearl, you *teeny* thing."

All the Tikbalangs laughed.

"We came for the lady of the house." Ali blinked hotly, quickly changing the topic. "Is Ikapati here?"

Dante the Tikbalang brushed the end of his tobacco on a glass ashtray on the table beside him. "Sad to say, *puny* fellow, but she's not here. Her daughter Anagolay ran away two heroes' harvests ago. Ikapati vented all her anger on her workers until they formed a union and left. No rice has grown here ever since, until she sold the fields to me."

"You own this house?" Marikit whirled around in disbelief.

"Yup. Tikbalangs used to live in trees back in the Fringes, but then I thought, why not have a job and build a better home? Trees are bare and leave us cold on February nights and September storms. I was the first to get a daytime job, you know. Just a courier for loan sharks. But I saved enough, and when Ikapati called for a bidder, I put mine down and promised to pay her all my gold. Ikapati did not think twice; she needed money to find her daughter. Such a problem child, that Anagolay, always getting lost while finding things. She rode her carabao and left. Left all her bounty to me, that is." Dante laughed so hard that he began neighing. "All the fruits and all the crops, all the grains that ever were. All mine!"

The mention of food made Marikit's stomach churn a long, groaning sound. Everyone heard it.

"Um, sorry." Marikit blushed, hiding her face behind her hair. "It's just that I haven't eaten since last night."

Dante made a big puff of smoke from the side of his mouth. "You haven't eaten? Why, kid, you're at the Harvest House. No one is allowed to get hungry here. Come!" He pushed the door to his house open. "Our grains are ripe! Our harvest is plenty! Feast with us, little Halfling." And turning to the Tikbalangs outside his balcony, Dante said, "My friends, join us, for this bounty is also yours, but may I remind you to take your footwear off before entering my abode."

The entrance to the Harvest House jiggled and wiggled as Dante went in, along with the other Tikbalangs, who rose on the porch with their hooves and left their boots outside. Marikit, who stared at her muddy feet, set her slippers aside, then walked through the Harvest Door with Ali. It closed behind them.

There was gold aplenty in the lobby of the Harvest House, all shaped like carabaos standing on their hind legs and spreading their arms as if they were dancing. The house itself smelled like freshly cut hay, surrounded by giant pots of herbs whose large leaves dangled over Marikit's head. Each plant grew from a heap of soil and jewels, with amethysts and onyx acting like stones to keep each plant in place. Marikit reached out her hand to touch one.

"Hold it, Marikit. Engkantos—well, the oligarchs—are exceedingly, selfishly rich," explained Ali. "But be careful not to touch anything. Engkanto treasure is shallow and crumbles at human touch."

Marikit put her hands back in her pockets.

The Tikbalangs were not exactly orderly. Dante's cigar ash, for example, was all over the sofa. There were holes in the silk curtains, despite the efforts of the caterpillars that kept weaving them back. Clothes and boots were scattered across the living room. Big metal horseshoes were on every wall. "For luck," Dante said.

Each time the Tikbalangs passed through an arch, the house had to stretch itself to make sure they wouldn't bump their heads. Even the dining table had to extend itself at the coming of the many Tikbalangs, and chairs made clones to accommodate each guest.

"Sit down, please." Dante took his place at the center of the dark-wood table laden with every food Marikit could ever dream of. There were bowls of glistening, chocolate-swirled sticky rice called champorado, trays of colorful rice cakes called puto, made in many varieties that shone with an inviting glaze. There were heaps of arroz caldo, tiny plates of rice covered with fruits, and mountains of rice cakes in a rainbow of colors. Marikit's eyes sparkled as she took her place beside Dante, her chair lengthening its legs for her. Hovering beside her was Ali, who was quite offended that no chair was offered to him as the rest of the Tikbalangs took their places.

"Eat and be merry, my friends," Dante invited. "And please, do not feel ashamed to eat with your hands."

The Tikbalangs stretched their arms and began grabbing food with their fingers, eating with obvious zeal. "It's like a party," Marikit murmured. "Better than a barrio fiesta! Better than Jana's birthday!"

All the wooden bowls replenished themselves back to the brim. "Magic!" Marikit beamed, stacking her golden leaf-shaped plate with all her favorite things—puto drizzled with cheese, puto topped with ube, sapin-sapin in rainbow colors, and rice mashed with fruits. "Magic, magic, magic!"

"What an appetite!" Dante the Tikbalang laughed.

"On my last birthdays," Marikit said in between gulps, "I only had warmed-over pancit—and cheap mamon—from the panaderia. The last time—my family had—a decent party—was when Tatay was alive. He—always cooked—the best meals—and his tomato-stuffed bangus—is my absolute—favorite."

"Go ahead, little girl," the Tikbalang said fondly. "Enjoy our bounty to your heart's content. Except for you, Infinite. *You* can't eat."

Ali folded his little insect hands and scanned the table, listening to the loud oohing and aahing and chomping and smacking of the hands. He watched the gleaming bowls of rice longingly, wishing he, too, could hold a spoon and revel in a large, satisfying bite. "Wait till I get my body," he huffed under his nose. "When I do, I'll eat everything I want!"

"What's a Nightmare doing here, anyway?" Ali then asked loudly. "Aren't you all supposed to be living in the Fringes?"

All the Tikbalangs stopped eating and stared at Ali as if he had uttered a curse.

Dante cleared his throat with a stricken look. He put down his spoon and lit his tobacco, blowing a man-shaped form into the air. "It's been chaotic there, in the Fringes." He twiddled his tobacco between his fingers. "Sitan's army has been growing. They're everywhere, loitering at the malls and playing in the sidewalks, practicing their untamed Shadow Magic on quiet civilians. They're like plagues. One Tikbalang had a broken spine after a young bruha's spell bounced off a mirror and hit him. Another fell a hundred feet down after a child unknowingly turned his ladder into paper ravens. You wouldn't want to meet those Shadowlings during their errands; those anxious little twitterers would spill a poisoned soda on you with their clumsy hands."

Marikit had licked all the rice off her fingers. "I've heard of him before. Who's Sitan?"

"Evilest of evil. Vilest of vile. Worst of the worst beings on earth, and never takes a bath. He gives us Nightmares a bad rep, but sadly, we can't push him out of the Fringes. So, *we* left, because it was the only way we could live peacefully."

"I wish Bathala would put an end to this," one of the Tikbalangs added. "But even he follows the scrolls to the letter."

"Scrolls?" asked Marikit.

"Yes, scrolls." Dante stared at her with his bulbous black eyes. "Our land is made up of many scrolls. Of many rules. You'll learn these along the way. And, from the way I see it, you have a lot more way to go."

When the banquet was over, all the Tikbalangs rose from their chairs to bid Dante goodbye. "The mud locusts always come around at two fifteen in the afternoon, and we must ward those pests off before they eat all the brown rice," the farmers said. As they left their places, the entire table mended itself back to its former size. Dante rose from his seat, and in an instant, all the clay pots and the grass-woven bilao cleaned themselves of their contents, leaving each utensil spotless and gleaming.

"Have you gotten your fill, Halfling?" Dante asked Marikit as they made their way back to the porch, the entire house stretching itself to make way for the tall horse-headed Nightmares.

"Yes, sir!" Marikit nodded enthusiastically, licking the last traces of puto in her mouth before it disappeared.

"Well, I have something more for you." Dante stuck his big, human fingers inside his trousers' pocket. He pulled out a small bayong. "Here," he said, lurching down as he handed Marikit his gift. "That contains several pusô—triangle-shaped rice wrapped in coconut leaves. I've added adobo inside it. Eat it along the way."

Dante propped himself against the railing and gazed at the far horizon, where dusk peeped into the glowing skies of his sunset farm. "Be careful, little one. The end of this road leads to Dapithapon, a river that swirls from the land of the Engkantos to the Fringes. The goddess who lives there has been in a bad mood ever since she and her brother fought over some unknown thing and she lost her eye in the river. If you happen to cross her, do *not* look at her eye or say something bad about it."

Marikit took the bayong and hugged it close to her chest. "Thank you so much, Sir Dante!" She put on her muddy slippers as Ali floated beside her, blinking with his warm light.

"We should be going now," said Ali.

"You are very welcome, Infinite," the Tikbalang told him. "When you are done with your Banyuhay, which I'm sure is your reason for leaving Luntian Forest, come back and visit me. I'll let you eat all the rice you want."

"What's a Banyuhay, sir?" Marikit cut in curiously.

Dante the Tikbalang only craned his big horse head down to whisper, "You'll learn along the way."

CHAPTER 10

THE RIVER OF DAPITHAPON

Dapithapon. Filipino. noun. *Sundown.* Deep-purple clouds sweeping the sky after the afternoon's terrible heat, reminding one that even the sun, the sky's most powerful luminary, will need to rest.

'You'll learn along the way.' It's *always* 'you'll learn along the way'!" Marikit swung her bayong as she trudged on the footpath away from the Harvest House. "Why can't you just tell me all at once?" she grumbled. "I'm going to learn anyway!"

"Excuse me?" Ali swooped down beside her.

"Adults are so vexing!" Marikit continued complaining. "Everyone seems to know everything, but you all say the same thing. *You'll learn things along the way.*" She paused for a breath. "At school, teachers answer our questions. We have books and dictionaries where we can find those weird words. But here, you keep making me guess things!"

"Petulant child!" grumbled Ali. "You cannot force a secret open just like you cannot force a flower to bloom. Some secrets are sorrowful. Some secrets are frightening. Some secrets require further unrolling, like curtains gently drawn. Life slowly discloses itself. That's what childhood is for; you turn older after Bathala whispers his wisdom to you every year. That's how you transform. That's how you become."

"Well, I hate waiting," Marikit huffed, sending her curly bangs to the top of her hair. "I hate guessing and not knowing and getting into trouble for it. Nanay didn't tell me anything about her being a Diwata, or me being a Halfling, or the Shadow coming for me, or this Journey that I have to take. And now here I am, walking and talking with an insect!"

"Well, I'm sorry!" Ali said. "I'm not just an insect. I am an Infinite, an Engkanto-in-transition. You know what? Everyone was right not to tell you anything, because you don't pay attention. You only think of yourself, and what you want, and what you'll get. Now, if you're going to keep complaining, I might as well leave you."

Ali flew up like a rocket and disappeared into the stark afternoon sky. Marikit couldn't see him through the orange clouds, through the orange sky, through the orange fields. She craned her head, hoping to see his glow, but everything was in the same color.

"Ali!" Marikit called out with her hands cupped around her mouth. "Ali, where are you?"

"Nowhere near a brat," came the distant answer.

"I'm sorry," Marikit pleaded. "Please come back. I don't want to travel by myself!"

It took a long time before a small dot of amber light came whooshing down from the clouds. "You promise to be nicer?" Ali asked.

Marikit held out her hand. "I promise."

"And not say selfish things?"

Marikit glanced sideways. "I promise."

"Don't make promises you can't keep." Ali scowled at her. "Promises to Engkantos will get you into trouble. Promises you break can break you."

"I will *try*, then." And Marikit was earnest.

But, unfortunately, not earnest enough.

Fields that were once a vivid yellow slowly turned into a gradient of deep-blue moss. A chorus of black swept over the sky. Everything was almost unrecognizable, if not for the solitary light of the moon, which reflected on a sad, lonely river.

At their side of the river was a dense forest, lined by trees curtained with heavy leaves like the newly permed wigs Marikit saw in hair salons. There were mourning willows and slumped hedges, looking despondent with their large stems drooping down. The long black patch that slithered across her waist began to shine.

Dapithapon, Marikit read the threads. She clutched her bayong close to her chest as she examined the dark-land, trying to see past the silhouettes. It was as if someone covered the sky with a big, black blanket. There weren't even stars in it, just the billowing, round moon, gazing down like one large eye, and the river that reflected it back.

Ali floated across the waters, the only light in the dim, dark riverbank. "Do you know how to swim?" he asked Marikit.

"Of course I do!" came the prompt answer.

"Oh, you know how to swim!" chimed another voice, cold and melancholic, as dismal as the evening sky.

Under the pale beams of the moon appeared a form. It hovered over the watery surface, veiled by a large cloud of mist that soon dissipated in the air. A woman stood over the water, her skin as pale as the moon itself, glowing in

the dark like a lamp. She wore a long tunic the color of midnight, embroidered with braids of silver and little drops of beads that glistened like tiny stars. Her long train, made with beautiful marks of the phases of the moon, glided atop the river but hardly touched the surface. The train was soft and glittery and misty, like a gauzy curtain in the window. The woman went past Marikit, her glow illuminating everything in the watery surface.

Ali immediately bowed his head, blinking with a pale-red light. "Greetings, moon goddess Mayari."

"Greetings to you, Alitaptap," Mayari answered with a voice so dim, anyone who heard it would immediately feel sad. She glanced at Marikit before adding, "And to your company."

"Greetings, goddess." Marikit curtsied.

Mayari was beautiful. Silver and crystal jewelry wrapped around her neck. Her hair was black and danced in the air like threads of silk, with thin braids woven across each other and bound with silver ribbons. Her lips were of shy pink, curling to the edges like a mild smile. She had a big nose, a pair of arched brows.

Only, she had one eye. Just like Dante said.

"I was gliding over my waters when I heard your conversation. Is it true?" Mayari held Marikit's face close to hers. "That you can swim?"

"Y-yes," answered Marikit, unable to avoid gazing into the blank hole.

"Not all children can swim, you see. Some of them just flap their hands on the water and pretend to fly. Some of them drop down like heavy rocks. Are you like that?"

"N-no, ma'am." Marikit strained her eyes, looking somewhere other than Mayari's face.

"I need someone to find something for me." Mayari's cold breath breezed across Marikit's face. "Something important. Something more valuable than anything else in the world." The moon goddess's grip on Marikit's face tightened. Her countenance changed—a colder, cruel expression with a deathly beauty. "I have been looking for it for centuries, but all the children lost by the river couldn't swim for their life and they all sank." Mayari turned her head toward the moonlit stream. "Deep into Dapithapon."

The goddess looked into the river with disgust. "I don't

know how to swim, you see. Water is beyond my auton-
omy." She scanned Marikit's face with her missing eye, her
icy black hair dripping down her pale cheeks. "If I did, I
would have plucked it out of the river by now. I wouldn't
have asked for someone else to swim and get it for me."

She let go of Marikit's face before drifting over the
river, the way the moon reflected itself on the waters. "My
brother and I have been fighting for decades over who will
rule the heavens. I challenged him in diplomacy. He, of
course, used brutal force, being fiery and hot as he is. One
day, he grabbed me by the neck and plucked my eye out,
throwing it across the edge of Kaluwalhatian, down here,
in the River of Dapithapon. My light has dimmed since
then, and I can't see clearly, even as I spend years going
back and forth."

"Siblings shouldn't be like that!" Marikit stomped on the
grass. "When my kuya was alive, we would fight, too. But
we always made up. Tatay used to say it's best to say sorry
and try to do better."

Marikit glanced at Mayari with pity. How bright and
pretty would the moon goddess shine if she had both of her
eyes? "Maybe I could help," she mumbled quietly.

"Wait, Marikit!" Ali flew in front of Marikit's face. "Listen to me. You need to think this over. Making promises is
dangerous. Oaths, much, much more."

"Quiet!" Mayari clasped Ali with her pale-colored hand
and muffled his mouth. "You were saying, child"—the

moon goddess lurched down with a sickening smile—"that you could help me?"

She loomed over Marikit like the night cast on the setting sun. Marikit wasn't sure now. Her mouth quavered as she gazed into where Mayari's missing eye would be. The hollow gap seemed to suck her in, like an endless pit of sorrow and despair.

"Stop staring!" yelled Mayari. "Do you want to help?"

"Yes." Marikit squirmed.

"Is that an Oath?"

Marikit did not answer—not at once, not until she heard Ali scream between the gaps of Mayari's fingers, "No, Marikit! Listen to me! You cannot be a Diwata if you are bound by an Oath!"

"But the fireflies said I had to fulfill one! Besides, isn't an Oath just like a promise?" Marikit reasoned.

"Yes, a Diwata Journey's requirement," agreed Mayari. "Now, will you make one, or should I crush your puny friend with my fingers?" The goddess began squeezing Ali in her hand, his warm, amber light weakly fighting against Mayari's pale glow.

"Stop it, please!" Marikit held out her hands. "Yes! Yes, it's an Oath—whatever it is!"

"You are, then, bound to me," Mayari said, committing her magic with her silky black hair. Soft strands wound around Marikit's neck, turning into metal chains. A hard, cold choker coiled around her throat. Mayari began pulling Marikit into the river. "You and your friend will have to stay with me, little girl, until I get my precious eye. Now quit fighting and start searching!"

Marikit had no choice. She dropped her bayong and removed her slippers, slowly dipping her feet into the water. She could see her reflection on the dark river, glowing under the light of the moon—small, sad, and helpless.

Mayari lured Marikit close. She kissed Marikit's left cheek and whispered, "I give you the gift of breath—that the water will never trouble your lungs. And here"—she kissed her other cheek—"I give you the gift of pushing on, that your legs will never tire, and your arms will always keep you afloat. Now go." Mayari pushed Marikit downward. The water gulped Marikit up like a thick slosh.

Marikit felt the weight of the liquid as she submerged into it. Everything underneath was as clear as crystal. Colorful fishes swam in all directions, some more beautiful and ornate than others. There was a path of flowers lining the sidelines, each of them breathing with their floaty, wispy petals. Her lungs were not filled with water. She didn't sink or drown. Marikit went on, taking in all the magical scenery on the Earth Below the River, only pausing when the chain of her choker had reached its end. Mayari then moved closer to where she was, and Marikit could see the goddess's light overhead, a pale, round glow.

Marikit began her search. She started unearthing heaps of soil, where a yellow crab got mad at her for unveiling his colony. At some point, she saw small houses with glass windows and flickering lights by the river wall. One had a balcony and two floors and some faces that peeked out of the window as if amused at the giant creature before them. *Duwendes*, Marikit mused. The sprawling structure was marked with "Ho-Ho Hotel" and was painted with a lilac facade. Urchins and other marine plants decorated the exterior.

What fun it was to drift under the sea! Marikit remembered the time when she and her kuya Emman dived underwater to gather shells for their sungka. "Here's one, Marikit!" she remembered him laughing. "And another! And another!" His merry voice still echoed inside her ears.

"Here's one," Marikit murmured, using her fingers to pull the things that got stuck in the sandy, muddy ground. There were many shells. And many other things, too. She found many of the objects similar to the human land—newspapers, old clothes, empty sacks, rusty pots, even old furniture. Fish shot out from holes, eels swam around her, groaning, "How dare you displace us?" and then swiveled away.

Marikit had been digging in the deep for a long, long time when she looked up. Mayari's moon floated like a coin—distant and small. She must have gone too far below.

Far beyond reach.

Like her kuya Emman. Like her tatay.

Suddenly, there was a tug in her heart.

Was it like this? Her heart throbbed. *The way Kuya and Tatay ended up?* Her chest began to feel heavy. Heavy like an anchor. Heavy like a boulder rolling straight into the ocean. Her shoulders flopped; her hands flailed. Water began filling her stomach. Her eyes ceased to see anything else except for the bubbles that started escaping her breath.

She tried to swing up, springing her legs in the water, but she couldn't.

She sank.

Marikit closed her eyes and saw nothing but darkness. She heard nothing but the glugging of water around her body.

How scared she was! The salty tears she cried swiftly mixed themselves into the water. Maybe that was what the River of Dapithapon was made of—tears from the children lost into its depths.

"Nanay," Marikit whispered in her heart. "Nanay."

She would be alone now, Marikit thought. Her nanay would never know that she disappeared under the water, too. Such an end for the Lakandulas. Unable to say their last goodbyes.

Her foot had reached the Earth Below the River when her choker tugged. Something strong pulled her up. Up, up, up. The water sloshed against her. Finally, she was drawn out of the river, her body hung by the metal rope as she was pulled onto the surface.

"I thought children were lighthearted, as everyone tells me," Mayari hummed as she fished Marikit out of the river. "Do you know how many have sunk because of the woes they carry in their chest?"

Marikit coughed, spewing river water out of her nose and mouth. *Oh, I have many woes*, Marikit quietly thought as she gasped for air. About her tatay. About her kuya. About the morning they left. About her nanay. About her blue birthday dress and how she always wore old, reformed clothes.

"Oh, I know what to do." Mayari's thin lips snickered. "Maybe I'll just take your heart. Throw it away so you'll have nothing to weigh you down. We gods are good at extracting things, so calm down. It won't hurt."

"No, please!" Marikit scrambled from her string, but Mayari pulled her close and started touching Marikit's ribs with her pale, blue-tipped fingers. Marikit felt something sting inside her, like an open wound she had when she got pierced by the needle or got cut with a knife. Mayari's fingers inched deeper and deeper. Marikit closed her eyes and clenched her teeth, holding her screams at the remarkable pain.

Just then, a burst of light exploded nearby.

"You always bully the little ones, dear sister." A man's voice, warm and bright, surfaced. Mayari faded into the hot, yellow light, the same light that lit up the cords of Marikit's collar until it burned into ashes swept away by the wind. A big, hot hand helped draw her out of the river and sent her back to shore. She gathered her possessions and hugged her bayong close.

"Apolaki," Mayari hummed, rolling her one eye with disgust. "What are you doing here? Aren't you supposed to be *exclusively* on your side of heaven?"

"It's Eclipse Day," Apolaki answered with a smug look on his face. "You know what happens with eclipses. You and I meet in the same orbit, whether we like it or not—trust me, I don't—for a few moments. Moments I can see you're using very cruelly."

Apolaki tapped his sister's other hand to let go of Ali, who immediately took refuge on Apolaki's arm and fed on the blistering light the god possessed. "Oh, hi there, little firefly," Apolaki greeted.

"H-h-hi," said Ali with a stutter. "You don't know this, Apolaki, but you are my dream god—I mean, I dream to become just like you."

"You could do better, firefly," Mayari swiped.

"Or worse, if you want to be like her," Apolaki snapped back, jerking his hand toward his sister. Turning to Mayari, Apolaki put his big, muscled hands on his waist and muttered, "When Father learns of this, he'll happily punish you for threatening Halflings."

"When Father learns you took my eye, he'll happily take out both of yours," Mayari hissed.

"But you can't, because I'm always beside Father, and you disappear behind my light. Your glow is nothing compared to mine," laughed the bigger, burlier Apolaki. "Now, if you'll excuse me, I've got crops to warm up and people to save. Let them pass through the river."

"Only if you give me my eye."

"Let me think about it," said the god. He started rubbing his chin, which looked like it was made of glass and oil, before turning to Ali and whispering, "To be honest, I don't really know where I threw it. It might not even be *here*."

"So, all that—?" Ali did not finish. Apolaki began lifting him and Marikit in his hand and gave both of them a wink. Ali seemed to have gotten the signal, for he slipped inside Marikit's wet pocket in a flurry.

"Are you afraid of heights?" Apolaki whispered.

"No." Marikit couldn't look up, for it was like facing the sun.

"Good, because I have no time, and this is the only way I can help you break from my sister."

Clearing his throat, Apolaki cradled Marikit in his giant, hot fingers before curling them into a fist. The sun god swung his arm backward and made hot, fiery circles before making a pitch. In a blink, he disappeared in front of Mayari, for the eclipse had ended.

CHAPTER 11

BARRIO BATO

Bato. Filipino. n. *Rock, or stone.* Could be hearts, could be
people, could be the enduring stark-gray minerals
constantly used by kids as markers for hopscotch or missiles
for slings.

Like a shooting star, Marikit whirled into Dapithapon's
night sky and into the humid clouds of daybreak. But
a fireball, Marikit reckoned, was not the best way to travel.
Not only was it hot (even Ali felt burning inside the blazing round sphere), many of Dante's pusô got burned when
they rolled away from the bayong. Marikit managed to save
three, picking them up before they burst into the rolling
fire. Just when the blaze ran out, both she and Ali plunged
toward the purple-colored earth with a sky so green and air
so thin.

The wind howled in Marikit's ears as she plummeted.
She hit the ground bottom first as inertia swung her into

a massive gray slab that stood in the middle of the ground. "STOOOOP!" she cried, holding her bayong close to her head like a shield. Her body screeched against the ground. Her hair flew on her face, and just before she plopped right into the rock, some of her hair got into her nostril, her nose itched, her mouth welled—

Ah-choo!

Marikit flew backward. She tumbled across the ground, her slippers escaped her feet, her bayong swirled in the air along with its precious contents. Ali, dizzy, wheezed out of Marikit's palms, his glow dwindling in the sky.

After the screeching stopped, Marikit pushed her hair out of her face, surveyed her near demise, and exclaimed, "Why, I almost smashed into a rock!"

"Like I'd want you to smash into *me*," quipped a small, perky voice.

Marikit spun her head sideways but found no one.

"Me, fool child." The rock opened its big, mossy eyes. "Do you think my kind wants to be smashed into? Look, most of my skin has eroded, and I don't want a sun-and-petrichor-smelling girl running straight into my face. I don't like the smell of your kind. Unpure. Confused. Don't know whether to be good or evil."

Marikit sniffed as she hoisted herself up, her wet dress sagging from her body. "Who are you, sir?"

"Bato. Benny Bato. I don't have hands to shake yours with, but don't touch me; you might wipe away my moss. I'm growing it."

Marikit and Ali turned to each other with stunned gazes.

Benny didn't like their reaction. He pouted his lips and then murmured, "If you're interested, that is, if they're of any value, a pair of slippers flew over me—probably went over the mud puddle—and a bayong landed somewhere by the tree-fork. Please collect your things. I don't want Halfling trash in my barrio."

"Your barrio?" asked Marikit. "*This* is a barrio?"

"Of course," answered Benny. "Can't you see us?"

Marikit only saw tree trunks with no leaves, ground that had cracked under the sun's heat, and columns of purple-gray rocks piled on each other. But the rocks soon opened their eyes, each of them with two—others, one—blinking sets, their mouths opening with pink tongues and gray teeth, yawning at her.

"You're all rocks!" Marikit mused, picking up a small pebble and examining it.

"Please put me back, I'm growing," it pleaded.

"Oh, of course." Marikit began to put it down when—

Ahh-choo!

"Jeez, girl!" yelped Benny. "Couldn't you have walked away before you sneezed? You might kill my moss!"

"Sorry." Marikit wiped the snot off her nose. "I didn't mean to—"

Ah-choo!

Benny glowered at her. "You better take that soggy dress off before it dooms you to a cold. Tell you what; I'd be happy to volunteer my rock as you let it dry. Wet things are good for me. They make my moss-mustache grow."

"But I'm not supposed to—"

Ah-choo!

"What am I going to do with a dress?" growled Benny. "Do you think I can wear it? Play with it? Run away with it? Kid, I don't have hands or feet. And you're sneezing badly. Get that off before you catch the flu."

Ali spun around Marikit. "I think he's right," he agreed. "You still have clothes underneath. Let it dry."

"But—!"

Never take this dress off. Marikit recalled her nanay's face before she flew from their window. *No matter what.* But all the freshwater brine had gotten into her pockets. The seams were dripping with water. Hadn't she worn this dress for too long? She didn't even like it anyway.

"All right." Marikit wriggled out of her dress. It was a relief to be free from it. It slumped down to the purple ground. Strands of black hair slithered along with the wet fabric.

Marikit picked them up, and the black strands turned silver white. "What are these?"

"Moon-hair," answered Benny. "Those have magic in them. You better keep them. One strand sells for fifty gold nuggets at the pawnshop."

"There's a pawnshop here?" Marikit bundled Mayari's hair into a ball and stashed it inside the wet pocket of the dress.

"Of course there is. We're a very progressive land with various means of business. Now go and get drying! I'm just going to grow my moss here, and if you don't bother me for a good hour, I'd be thankful."

Benny closed his eyes comfortably as Marikit strode away, relishing the strange light of the stark green sky with a stark green sun. The smaller stones trailed after her, rolling across the plain, darting as if they had no weight.

Marikit turned around and asked, "Would you like to play a game?"

"A game!" the stones cried. "We'd love to play a game!"

Marikit ran, and the stones rolled after her. She laughed in the middle of the chase, the stones trying to catch her as she leaped barefoot, cartwheeled, and tumbled into the ground. It was like the many times she played with her neighbors in Barrio Magiting. Only this time, her playmates were rocks.

Ali, watching from the sidelines and many times evading the rocks that smashed upon each other, whispered, "How I wish I had a pair of legs! I wish to run and tumble and stomp on the ground, too!" He stared at the little sticks that dangled down his little body and wobbled them in the air. At the same time, Marikit returned from her wild, loud chase, grinning with satisfaction as she pushed her sweaty hair away from her face while carrying her gathered belongings. "I'm hungry!" she declared.

"Hungry after a game?"

"Hungry after a game, and after flying in the air, and after swimming," Marikit corrected him, slumping down and opening one of the pusô, the scent of the steamed rice wafting in the air. "It's got something in it, too!" Marikit placed it close to her nose, inhaling the delicious harmony of meat, soy sauce, and vinegar spread across the rice. "Adobo!"

Ali lingered with curiosity as Marikit made her first chomp. "How does it taste?"

"A little bit salty, a little bit sour, all bits delicious," Marikit answered.

"I wish I could eat," Ali sighed. "Then I could have big muscles and strong legs and ironlike fists. I want to be like Apolaki."

"Why him?" Marikit chewed loudly.

"Because he is fire. And fire is light. And I am light."

"He was very mean, though. Taking Mayari's eye like that." Marikit pressed her neck as if still feeling the cold metal choker that used to be there. "But Mayari was cruel, too," she whispered under her breath. "Making kids do her bidding."

"Well, I told you all gods are terrible in different ways," Ali said. "Good thing the Oath you made to her has no effect when you're apart. If you signed a written Oath, that changes everything. Ink in Engkanto land binds you for a lifetime. I hear I'll sign one when *I* become a Diwata."

Marikit stared at Ali, unable to see how a tiny dot could become a human with bones and skin. "I still don't understand how you can transform, though," she murmured.

"Of course I can." Ali made a shy sideways glance. "That's what a Banyuhay is all about. Metamorphosis. Haven't I told you Infinites are possibilities? We are the First Life. When we finally step out of the forest, when we finally will ourselves to find our bodies, that's when the transformation begins."

"Are you just going to wake up and grow, then?"

Ali drooped. "I . . . still don't know," he answered sorrowfully.

"I guess we'll learn along the way," Marikit said contemplatively as she licked what was left of the savory, soy-sauced rice from her fingers.

The stones were waiting patiently for Marikit to finish eating when a cry pierced through the silence. "My face! My handsome face! How dare you? How dare you ruin my beauty!" The shout rang across the barrio, startling the rocks so much that they began rolling with a panic. "Benny Bato! It's Benny Bato!"

Marikit immediately ran. With her slippers on her feet and her bayong in her arms, she led the legion of rocks that trailed after her. The giant stone slab began sobbing as a large claw mark ran across Benny's face.

"What happened?" Marikit asked.

"Those murderous criminals! Those lawless Engkantos!" Benny was furious. "Trespassing whenever they wish!"

"Who is?"

Marikit looked at the traces of moss and stone-blood on Benny's face when she began to notice what *wasn't* there. Her stomach sank.

"My dress!" she gasped.

"The map!" cried Ali.

"Mayari's hair!" the stones cried in chorus.

"Where is it?" Marikit looked around Benny's ragged, jagged body. "Where's my dress? It was just here! I left it here!"

"They stole it," Benny answered.

"Who?"

No one wanted to speak. An odd stillness fell before them, and the only sound was the rocks that shook like gritting teeth. Finally, Benny let out a deep sigh of dread, murmuring, "The Aswangs."

Marikit's knees weakened. "A-A-Aswangs?"

She wasn't sure if she had heard right. She hoped she had not. But Benny gazed at her and confirmed with a cold, low voice, "Yes. The Aswangs."

Marikit crumpled to the ground. "Not the Aswangs!" She wrapped her head under her arms. "Not the Aswangs!"

Nobody in Barrio Magiting had ever seen them, but tales of Aswangs haunted the children from the moment they understood the concept of danger. Marikit had grown up hearing about them—creatures in the dark in the shape of wolves, slobbering with their sharp-fanged mouths, prowling on roofs, waiting to sink their claws into anyone with blood. "Dark, dirty Aswangs," Benny continued, scowling as he spoke. "Howls in the dead of the night, lurking in the creepiest crevices of our lands. We didn't want to be neighbors with them after they arrived from the Fringes, but the gods placed our barrio next to theirs so they'd have fewer casualties. Yet even us stone-cold rocks suffer from their mistreatment. They crack us open, slice us, scratch us whenever they want, or use us as heat pillows. Those Aswangs are as foul as they are fierce."

"I shouldn't have left my dress!" moaned Marikit. "Nanay warned me, but I didn't listen. If I had gotten the flu, I'd get well and would still know my way. I shouldn't have taken it off. I should have followed Nanay!"

"It's all my fault," consoled the now-grooved rock. "I wanted to grow my moss-beard, and now my face is a whole mess. And I shan't ever get my old looks back. Is it really bad, kid? It hurts between my eyes."

Marikit looked at Benny. "I think your new face will suit you." She kissed the wounded spot.

"Really?" The rock's downturned face stretched into a smile.

"Somewhat," Ali said, not knowing whether to agree. "But we have to get the map, Marikit. You cannot get to X without it."

"But how?" Marikit stuttered. "It's the Aswangs, Ali! Man-eating, bone-crushing Aswangs!"

She heaved a deep sigh against Benny's cheeks that went right through his stony nostrils, and the rock coughed.

"What did you just eat?" asked Benny.

"Rice." Marikit checked her breath. "Dante the Tikbalang cooked it with adobo."

"Adobo?" Benny snorted. "Like, meat sautéed in garlic?"

"Yes."

"Can you breathe on me again?" asked Benny.

"I just lost my dress!" Marikit cried. "And now you're going to make fun of me?"

"No, do it," Benny insisted. He stared at Marikit before mumbling with certainty, "Because I might just know how to defeat the Aswangs."

CHAPTER 12

LAND OF THE ASWANG

Aswang. Filipino. n. A shape-shifting spirit commonly imagined as a canine disguised as an old woman, with sharp fangs and big claws that feeds on humans in the dead of the night.

I f you follow the trail of the clawed rocks, that's where they are. Barrio ng Lagim," Benny Bato told Marikit. "Watch out for thorns and thistles. Rats run about. Spiders, too. But whatever happens, do not make a sound. If you catch the attention of the Aswangs, they will tear you to pieces in a blink."

He then looked at Marikit's bayong. "What will save you is in there. It's not much; too little garlic will not kill an Aswang, but it's enough to make them sick. If you manage to find the thief and trick them into eating it, they will lose their strength. That's how you will get your dress."

Marikit clutched her bayong close to her chest as she

stood in front of a pitch-black cave labeled, in letters carved by sharp claws, "Barrio ng Lagim." The entrance was made of withered tree trunks and rocks covered with gravel, with hundreds of little eyes blinking from every side. "Sh-should we go in?" Marikit asked Ali as both of them froze by the cave.

"Th-that's what w-we should do," Ali's light began to quiver.

"Then you should go first."

Ali flew in cautiously, blinking with a warning as the many eyes from the dark began staring at him. Marikit walked closely behind, wanting to ignore the sharp, metallic stench that simmered from the cave. From the very little available light, she could see bones scattered on the earth, blood spattered on the walls, and large, hairy legs moving around, crawling with a squeak.

"Turn back, Aswang food," came a hiss. "Or suffer a dreadful death."

"We're not Aswang food," Ali corrected. "We're just here to get something."

"*You* don't get from Aswangs," another murmured. "*They* get you. Turn back if you want to live."

"We can't," Marikit retorted. "They need to return something important to me."

"What could be more important than your life?"

"It's my map," whimpered Marikit. "A map my nanay

made. A map that will help me find my X. A map that will make me a Diwata."

"Oh, is that the Manghahabi map? The one Ruma brought?"

"What a pretty dress that was," one exclaimed.

Pretty? Marikit asked herself. *Why does everyone keep calling my dress pretty?*

"You're in luck," someone spoke from below. "The Aswangs are having their grand show-and-tell tonight. They've gathered around the green fire and will most likely dance and drink fermented palm sap after putting their plunder on display."

"Their senses will be weak with too much liquor. If you're careful enough, they won't see you," advised another.

"Thanks, Scary Eyes," Marikit said.

"You're welcome." Thousands of spiders hiding in the dark appeared, staring at her with their many purple eyes.

The Aswangs *were* having a grand show-and-tell. Hundreds of them gathered in the middle of their underground plaza and reveled around the blaze of a green bonfire whose fiery tip sputtered against the stony roofs. A mass of furry canines sat on the table, drank from their pewter cups, and gnashed bones with their sharp teeth. Some more high-spirited groups looped their arms and swayed with a jovial air as they sang a song without a tune. When one howled, another would harmonize, and the entire place rang with a chorus of menacing, monstrous yells.

Frightful, dreadful, terrible Aswangs.

Marikit stayed close to the ground, crawling underneath the tables as Ali flew overhead, trying to catch a glimpse of Marikit's dress. But there were only heaps of skeletons, stones, rusty shields, animal heads, gold-gilded coats, and large treasure boxes. Not a sight of the map.

"The sword of Lam-ang." One Aswang with bright-red fur rose from his seat and raised a blade. "I have unearthed from the Mountains of Nalbuan a powerful weapon that can challenge even the gods."

"Ah, that's nothing," an Aswang with spots of black on his brown fur scoffed. He stood on the table where Marikit was hiding. "I have a painting of Mayari, rare and ever beautiful, drawn by the Manguguhit of the East."

"I have a tail of a Tikbalang," another Aswang with two uneven eyes said, raising it aloft. "Which is said to tame our co-Nightmares in a whiff!"

Marikit watched them from below, trying so hard to keep still as sharp-clawed paws swung and swooped under the table. She had had this feeling before. The feeling of wanting to stay hidden in her corner every time her class-mates showed off their newly bought bag, or their new set of crayons, or their sparkly new headband.

She'd wither in her chair and try to pretend she wasn't there, for she never had anything to share.

She never had anything new.

"I have something better than any of you!" A sharp shout rose in the middle of the crowd. From one of the bigger tables leaped a young Aswang—unlike the rest of the Nightmares, which were bold and bare in their fur, this Aswang wore a dress.

Marikit's dress.

Ali yelped slightly, his amber light blinking brighter than before.

The young Aswang's eyes slid in his direction, and she put her hands to her waist, snickering, "I found this dress in the outskirts of our colony. It was drying by a rock, and I think a Manghahabi owns it."

"A Manghahabi!" came a chorus of gasps. "Ruma, what a find!"

"And it's got some scent to it, see." Ruma twirled in her dress. "It smells like the moon."

The Aswangs around her began sniffing it, too. "It smells like Ikapati's Farm," another added.

"It reeks of a Halfling."

This last voice was louder than anyone else's, and it came from an Aswang covered in glossy black fur sitting on a stone chair set above a mound of skulls at the end of the room. The great Aswang stood up and rose two times bigger than the other Aswangs, his red eyes nastier, his teeth sharper. The rest of the Aswangs made way for him as he walked toward Ruma, his fists clenching, his claws stretching.

Marikit froze under the table as he walked past. "Smells of a Halfling, all right," he snarled with a voice so heavy Marikit could feel it booming through the floor. "Smells like *food*."

"But, Mael," one Aswang said. "We are not to eat a human, remember?"

"If that child is inside a Quarts' barrio, yes," the Aswang called Mael said, grinning. "But if she's not, then she's free game."

He turned toward the young Aswang and chuckled slyly. "The outskirts, you say?"

"Yes, Papa," Ruma answered.

"Find her!" ordered the giant Aswang. "The first one to give me her heart wins tonight's prize—a barrel of aged palm sap, lambanog!"

"I'm not going," Ruma announced. "I don't want my dress to get soiled."

"Then more for me." Mael smiled.

An ear-piercing howl led the ravished congregation toward the exit. The Aswangs stirred a stampede, creating clouds of dust as they ran with a startling ferocity. Marikit nervously curled underneath the table, allowing the fallen plunder to cover her. She kept still, trembling with a silenced cry until the rush ended and the cave had turned stone-cold quiet.

Seeing everything from above, Ali felt dread in his heart. Even an Infinite knew fear. Even Infinites knew the terrors of Aswangs. And as his light blinked faintly in fright, he did not notice that something had crouched behind him and stretched a pair of long, furry arms until it grasped him with a pair of warm, dirty paws.

"I saw you." Ruma grabbed Ali with her fists. "What's an Infinite doing here?"

She peered between the gaps of her fingers and shook him until he was dizzy. "Ha-ha-ha!" Ruma laughed. "I will put you in a cage and use you as my night-light!"

Now Marikit heard it. Ruma's laughs echoed through the cave and deep inside her ribs and made her shiver. She froze under the table, unable to move or even breathe with ease. But Ali. Ali!

With shaking hands, Marikit pulled herself out of her shelter and, her voice shaking, told the young Aswang, "Stop!"

Ruma turned to Marikit. The young Aswang's sharp snout broke into a smile. "Why, the Halfling meat came to me!" Ruma clapped her hands. "Oh, goody! Only ate a thigh of your kind once, and it was de-licious!"

"I'm not here to be eaten." Marikit held her bayong close. "I'm here to trade."

"Trade what?"

"The dress you're wearing. *My* dress," Marikit pointed out. "For this." She held out her precious woven basket.

"A bayong?" Ruma laughed, jumping down from the loft of the wall and freeing Ali from her palms. "What would I want with a bayong?"

Marikit opened the bayong's mouth in front of Ruma. "This." She fished out the two remaining pusô. "A meal. From Ikapati's Farm."

The young Aswang's ears stood up with a thrill. "Ikapati?" Drool appeared in Ruma's mouth. "You mean the Harvest House? Why, I've heard only good things from it! Endless rice, food tastier than anything in the land of the Engkantos!" She wiped her drool and began fisting her paws. "I want it! I want it! I want it!"

"You'll have it," Marikit said decidedly. "But first, give me back my dress."

Ruma's bloodshot eyes swung from the map-dress to Marikit's bayong.

"I want this dress, but . . ." Her tongue rolled out of her mouth. "I have never tasted anything from Ikapati's Farm before."

"And you won't have another chance. Not for a long time." Ali flew beside Marikit.

It took a few moments for Ruma to decide. Her eyes went to the bayong, to her dress, and back. "Oh! This is hard!" she groaned, before leaping on the table and wildly removing the patchwork dress. She approached Marikit and said sorrowfully, "Here."

Marikit immediately grabbed her possession and hugged it close to her heart. The pink light threads flashed before her eyes. The needle began spinning. "I'm sorry. I shouldn't have taken you off," she whispered as she put her dress back on, the flimsy fabric falling on her body like a soft embrace.

"Hey, how about me?" Ruma stomped her foot impatiently.

"Here you go." Marikit handed Ruma the bayong. She remembered what Benny said. *Too little garlic will not kill an Aswang, but it's enough to make them sick. That's how you will get your dress.*

Ruma didn't waste any time; she grabbed an adobo-filled pusô and began devouring it in sharp, big gulps. She didn't even take the wrappers off. With a satisfied burp, she pressed her paw to her stomach, and then she fixed her eyes on Marikit, grinning. "Hmm. Maybe I *do* want that dress after all."

"Why—" Marikit did not finish, for Ruma grabbed her neck and lifted her up in the air.

"I ate the rice." Ruma licked the sides of her mouth. "And I will still get the dress. Win-win."

"No!" Marikit tried to pull free from Ruma's grasp, but Ruma tightened her fists. With her sharp claw, she started tracing Marikit's ribs. "Now, which side is the human heart again?"

Her nails were drawing across Marikit's skin when a strange smell rose between them. Ruma looked around. "Hmmm." She sniffed. "Something is burning. Looks like my idiot friends have left game meat by the fire."

"It's not your friends." Ali swooped down to dazzle her eyes. "It's you!"

With a spark, red fire broke out of the young Aswang's arm. Ruma yelped and leaped back, letting Marikit go. "What was it?" Ruma saw embers sputter at the tip of her fur. "What did you make me eat?"

"Garlic!" shouted Marikit, stepping back, away from Ruma.

"Garlic? You had me eat garlic?" came Ruma's loud snarl. The fire was unstoppable. It raced across the young Aswang's body as quickly as she had devoured the pusô, the harsh kiss of Apolaki stinging through her skin. "You tricked me!"

"So did you!"

Marikit and Ali darted toward the nearest tunnel without looking back. The cave was long and dark and cold, filled with crushed rocks and broken bones. As Ruma gave out her last cry, hundreds of Aswang feet came rumbling back into the cave. Marikit could hear the sound of a low, booming, terrifying voice. "Ruma! My daughter! Who did this to you?"

They could see the end of the tunnel now. But before she and Ali could reach the exit, two large boulders rolled across their path and blocked their way.

CHAPTER 13

THE VOLCANO
OF IBALON

Bagwis. Filipino. n. *Wings.* Mighty feathered joints that
stretch out from both sides of the body, made to conquer
the gusty winds and the lofty skies, given primarily to
birds, bats, prehistoric beasts, and, sometimes, higher-level
demigods.

The road gave a warning. It shut itself up as Marikit
and Ali approached it, covering its entire passage
with rocks. Marikit's map warned her to go back. Her
needle told her they were taking the wrong way.

"Please let me pass!" Marikit asked the road. "Please let
me pass!"

Yet the road was stiff. The road whispered to her: *I am
trouble. I am terror. When you go through me now, you will only
gain pain.*

"I am ready," Marikit said decidedly. "There is no greater
terror than facing the Aswangs. Please," she begged.

So be it, the road replied, relenting. Rocks rolled away and allowed her to pass, leading her to a fiery red sea, bursting with hot, burning bubbles as steam rose from all corners.

"Oh dear!" exclaimed Ali, surveying the boiling ocean. Marikit's only path was the trail of brown rocks afloat in the stream.

She had no choice.

Hop. Marikit took the first step. The stone fizzed with hot gas. *Hop.* She took the second. Thick, goopy pops of lava bubbles flitted at her. *Hop.* She reached the third. The stone wiggled and waggled, and Marikit had to take the next leap when it slightly turned over. She almost missed it.

Hop. Marikit made it, lengthening the reach of her small legs so she could reach the next stone. *Hop.* When she was midway through the path, Marikit could feel something hot and gooey climb her ankles. She looked down.

The stone was slowly sinking down.

"AHHHH!" shouted Marikit, and she darted across the stone path, tucking her skirt between her hands as she leaped for her life. *Hop.* Lava bubbles burst beside her; still she went on. *Hop*, like a rabbit. *Hop*, like a frog, in the middle of a burning sea, trying to stay alive.

"Who goes there?" a squawky voice called out from the island across from her.

Marikit craned her neck as she made her next jump. "I'm a Halfling, sir!"

"Are you lost?"

"No. I'm heading somewhere."

"Where?"

"To that land, I hope!"

Out of the smoky curtains, a man stood by the skirt of the caldera, one whose long black hair danced in the wind, whose red-gold vest and silver-woven bahag draped his muscular body, and whose arms flapped wildly as if making snow angels out of thin air. Marikit wondered if this was a signal, and so she flapped her hands to imitate him. She looked foolish, especially when the man's arms turned into humongous red wings, his body into an eagle's, his face into a golden plumage.

The eagle-man swooped into the middle of the lava path and hovered above Marikit. "Grab my claws," he said.

Marikit reached out, and the eagle lifted her, clamping her hands with his bright-yellow claws. He flew her high across the lava, away from the fizzing red waves, letting Marikit admire the breathtaking tropical scenery by the edge of the caldera.

"Who—I mean, *what* are you, sir?" Marikit asked him, looking above.

"I am Bagwis," he answered, his wings as big as those of a small plane.

"Are you a Diwata, sir?" Ali flew close by the eagle, only to get caught up in the wind.

"Yes, but I got promoted to lower god because of my good behavior and great strength." The eagle-man winked. "Took me seventy whence-years to get here. I used to just dwell on trees. Now I've got my own place."

Marikit looked down and saw red-hot lava gurgling from the steaming mouth of a volcano. "Here?" she asked, panicked.

"Yup. Here. In Ibalon."

The clouds gave way as Bagwis pierced through them, making a fast, reckless swoop. The eagle flew in loops, like a stomach-churning, intestine-tumbling roller coaster, and Marikit wondered if she would be better off walking. Her curly hair flew, her dress covered her face, and when they slowly neared the ground, Marikit felt close to fainting.

Dust greeted Bagwis's flapping wings. As soon as his feet touched the ground, he became human again.

"H-how did you do that?" Ali gasped.

"Deity perk. Got kissed by Amihan and now I got this wind-animal morphing power." Bagwis proudly showed off his biceps.

"A god's kiss!" Ali exclaimed. "How did you get it? How did you win her over?"

"Wasn't easy," Bagwis answered. "I interned for her at Cordillera and did all the paperwork as she went around and visited fiestas under her name. Her office was chaotic—everyone chirping and twitting and warbling at the same time! On my twenty-fifth whence-year, when I got my Best Employee Award ten times in a row, Amihan put me in a nice silk suit, took me along, and finally bestowed on me a kiss."

"Wow." Ali clapped his little hands and imagined how *he'd* look in a suit. "But how did you change? Tell me, please!" Ali's usually soft amber light glowed into a joyful hue of lemon.

"I've been there, too, young squirt," bragged the eagleman. "I was a normal Alitaptap until I ventured into a higher calling. One that gave me purpose. And this beautiful, glorious body."

"I want to have a body, too," Ali put in. "Tell me how to get one."

Bagwis's jaw dropped. He reached out his human hand and let Ali float on his palm. "You spunky kid. Saying reckless things in front of a demigod like me. Well, you don't just transform, pal. There's a process."

"Then tell me." Ali glowed brighter as he gritted his teeth. "Tell me how to get a body!"

Marikit saw Bagwis heave a deep sigh, the kind of sigh that meant this wasn't going to be easy. "Here's the thing," he started.

"Uh-huh." Ali nodded.

"In order for an Infinite to have a body . . ."

Ali hovered forward. "Uh-huh."

"That Infinite has to die."

"What?" Both Marikit's and Ali's jaws dropped.

"It's the rule, the first of many," said Bagwis, lurching down and taking a seat on the dusty terrain. "Inside an Infinite is something big and powerful. You gotta shake it up, loosen it a little, then finally break the tiny little cell and let it all go. When that happens, all of you, your soul, your ashes, your dreams, and your hopes, explode inside a large container and . . ."

"And?" Ali flew onto Bagwis's nose.

"That explosion forms into skin, bones, human parts, heart and all. You grow outward, like a seed, then you need some time to get 'cooked up.' You wait for your ribs to settle, your heart to be in the right place, your mind to be ripe for learning. And when it's done, some god knocks on the wood of your vessel, and it breaks. Voilà! You're alive!"

"Are you serious?" Ali's light dwindled, pulsating slowly like a candle about to go out. "I have to die?"

"Yes. You *have* to. To achieve something great"— Bagwis stretched out his hand once more to pick Ali up from his nose—"you have to give up something precious. Sacrifices make the special."

"Oh." Ali swung around the air. He sighed, then sighed a bit more, plopping himself down on Bagwis's arm before murmuring, "It's not like I'm not *ready* to sacrifice something. It's just that"—he paused for a bit—"I promised to be with Marikit until she reached the X."

Bagwis shot a look at Marikit. "Was that an Oath?"

Marikit knew what an Oath was. An Oath bound her mother and forbade her not to talk of a secret. An Oath was what choked her neck and bound her to dive into a river for hours she could not count. An Oath made her a slave.

She wouldn't do that to Ali.

"No," Marikit answered. "It's not an Oath."

"It's a promise," Ali insisted. "A friend's promise."

Bagwis folded his arms. "That's tricky. If you manage to reach the X and this girl gets her prize, Bathala will most definitely send you back to the forest. Infinites cannot be vagabonds. You'll have to wait for another Halfling to open the door and start their journey. And that might take several whence-years."

Ali knew it. Of course he knew heaven's rules. He floated sadly in the air, secretly grateful that Marikit couldn't see him cry tiny, minuscule tears.

But she could hear him. Clearly. Loudly. As if his heart spoke to her. She heard the yearning in his small ribs. How he wanted a body! How he wanted to break free from this little light and explode into bones and flesh! She heard his aching for food, for legs that could jump and leap and kick, for big hands that could reach out and shake hers.

Above all, she heard heartbeats. A desire to make sure she was safe. And it was the strongest of all.

She listened well. She listened to the way her needle began to rotate, spinning away far from north. She listened to her own heart. It stung. Just like the first morning she had learned two of her family were dead.

But sacrifices made the special. Sacrifices were the gods' currency.

Marikit choked back her tears and widened her eyes. She started with an *ahem* before saying, in a surer-sounding voice, a voice she forced: "I can do it, Ali. I can read my map. I have Mayari's hair. I was supposed to do this alone, and I'm grateful that you came with me this far. You've been a friend to me and never left my side. Now I'm going to be a friend to you."

She held out her hand and touched Ali's faint glow. "You should go. Make that transformation you have always wanted."

Ali did not answer. He just hovered over her hand with his flickering glow like the first time he met her. With his small eyes, he recognized the tears that veiled Marikit's lashes, tears she was trying to stop. But she looked at him bravely. She had decided her fate.

He, as an Infinite, knew when courage had bloomed.

"What's it now, firefly?" Bagwis rose from the ground. "Because if you want to transform, Ibalon is the perfect place."

Ali did not leave Marikit's palm when he responded, "I'll do it."

"There are many ways for an Engkanto to die," Bagwis said, leading Marikit and Ali up the crater, his eagle-feet leaving a deep trail of footprints on the ground. "You can die drowning in Dapithapon, get caught in Amihan's whirlwind, get ravaged by Aman Sinaya's malevolent waters, but this—" He pointed at the tip of Mount Mayon. "This is also like experiencing a god's wrath."

Ali and Marikit watched lava spurt out of Mount Mayon's mouth. For a moment there, Marikit saw Ali's light wane.

"We will go to the top of the mountain, and you will fly into the mouth of the volcano, where the hottest kiss from Apolaki will burn you," Bagwis said. "But first, we must find you a vessel."

"A vessel?" Marikit asked.

"Yes. The thing that will contain your friend's remains until he comes back to life."

Bagwis magically formed an ax out of the liquid lava

and eyed the small hedges of bamboo that sprouted from the ground. "Remember the story about Malakas and Maganda?" he asked.

"Yes," Marikit answered. "They emerged out of the bamboo as the most beautiful species on the planet."

"There's a lot more to the story," said Bagwis, chopping five bamboo poles with one swoop. "Bathala took two Infinites, shoved their ashes in a bamboo, then planted them in the most sacred, most nourishing soil in the entire world. At the right time, the bamboo broke in half, and out came Malakas and Maganda looking all mighty and fine. It's the soil that matters after death," Bagwis said. "The soil the new you grows in."

Bagwis examined one of the spliced bamboo stalks and scowled. "Too straight," he said, throwing it away. He studied the next one. "Too thin." He did the same for the other, then growled, "Too broad." Bagwis proceeded to cut the rest of the bamboo. He split them into halves before throwing them away. "Too leafy." "Too bald." "Too plain." "Too blue." "Too yellow."

Finally, he gaped at the remaining bamboo sprout in the grassy patch, then murmured, "This."

Carefully, he cut it down the middle. He held the precious bamboo halves and spun toward Marikit. "You, Halfling friend. Hold this."

"Are we going to fly again?" Marikit didn't look too excited.

"Nope." Bagwis shook his head. "When it comes to the pilgrimage of Banyuhay, the Engkanto must traverse there on his own, in his shape, without any magic."

Bagwis, Marikit, and Ali trudged the soft ground of Mount Mayon slowly. Lava had claimed most places, marking them with its charred, black stream that spouted uphill. It was tiring to climb on the high, rough terrain. There was no sign of green, only the bare, rocky skin of the volcano that spewed hot smoke from its mouth.

Marikit hiked until her legs strained and her back hurt. She could feel the blazing heat of the bright-red fire that scattered at the tip of the perfectly triangular volcano. She was tired—oh, so tired—but she remembered that Ali, too, may have felt exhausted on their journey, yet he kept going for her. So up she went, with her fatigued legs and hurting back, following his small, amber glow that flickered under the cloudy sky, the bamboo halves clutched in her arms.

She didn't mind it today.

No. Today, she would lose a friend, but she would be there, watching the very last sight of him.

"Here we are." Bagwis stretched out his hand, all of them pausing by the thickets of jagged rocks before them. When she craned her neck, she saw a pool of thick lava gurgling in a hole as big as their barrio, steaming out enough ashes and dark smoke to make her into charcoal. Bagwis pushed Marikit behind him, taking the bamboo halves from her hands. "This is where your journey ends, my dear," he told her. "But not your friendship."

He then trudged forward with his bird-feet and led the flicking firefly into the volcano's mouth. "Fire may be destructive, but fire is where the earth renews itself," Bagwis said. "In its ashes bloom all the wonderful things you see around here," he said, pointing to the lush, verdant forest that blossomed after the trails of lava. "Fire is where you become new."

Marikit watched Ali's light blink. "I trust you, Bagwis. I am ready to transform," he said. And, with his sincerest gratitude, his color turning to gold, he shouted, from the depths of his firefly heart, "Thank you, Marikit!"

Bagwis's wings stretched from his human back and fanned the steam into the mouth of the volcano. There was, in a few moments, a whirlwind, stirring the volcano's throat. It began coughing red, gooey embers. The ground shook, the rocks rolled down, the surface of the earth jiggling into a force that made Marikit's small body tremble. The wind from Bagwis's wings collided with the hot steam from the volcano, unleashing sharp forks of blue lightning that broke across the sky and pierced the ground. And, without warning, the volcano released an ear-shattering growl, spurting flaming geysers straight into the sky.

It was time, Marikit knew, yet she stood her ground, her wavy hair swishing across her face. Ali slowly passed her by, his eyes set on the column of fire. "I must go now," he whispered gently.

Tears fell from Marikit's eyes as Ali flew straight into

the volcano's mouth. His light vanished behind a thick cloud of smoke. "Ali," she mumbled as the volcano shuddered stronger than before. The ground rippled with a forceful convulsion, and a flash of fire struck high into the sky. The sound of thunder beat inside Marikit's ears, and there, she had a final glimpse of his light. Yellow and bright and burning. "Ali!" Marikit screamed. "Thank you! Thank you for being my friend! I'm glad to have met you! I'm glad you came with me out of Luntian Forest! I'm glad—oh, I'm glad there is you!"

Two wings rose in the bursting sputter of lava. There was Bagwis, carefully collecting Ali's ashes in the bamboo halves with his bare, now blackened talons. The eruption wound down, the sky slowly cleared, and Bagwis flew to the ground where Marikit watched him turn back into a man.

"This is your friend," he told her, cutting a linen strip off his vest and wrapping it around the bamboo halves. "Hold it carefully so it won't burn you."

Marikit clutched the bamboo vessel with her small arms.

"Your job is to plant this stalk," Bagwis instructed her. "Who Ali will turn into will depend on the ground you choose. The desert, the swamp, or even down Mount Mayon. Now farewell, little child, and safe travels! Don't stop to talk to anyone, especially if that someone wears something shadowy and has bad breath. They surely have bad intentions!"

"I understand," came Marikit's meek answer.

"I'm off, then." Bagwis spread his wings and flew straight into the heavens. As Marikit made her slow trek down the mountain, with Ali's bamboo vessel tucked safely in her arms, she saw the demigod soar across the gloomy sky and brush the gray clouds into a hopeful shade of blue.

CHAPTER 14

BRUHA IN THE MIDST

Ligalig. Filipino. n. *Fear, trouble, perturbation.* The uneasy
feeling of worry creeping in a human's chest, whispering
doubts, causing further chaos.

Do not stray. Marikit recalled her nanay's warning as
she trod down the caldera. The needle pointed south,
toward a rust-colored valley, where the air was dry and the
ground was arid. Ali's vessel was still hot and steaming. She
hugged it close to her chest.

Do not stray. Marikit turned around and faced the other
direction. There was a sight of green—a dense, sprawling
forest where canopies of thick trees were enough to cover
the sky. It was a spectacle of life. Of dew and sun and abundance of the earth. She glanced at her map.

Do not stray.

Oh, but did she really ever follow instructions? Marikit

mulled over her options. When the oldfolk at her barrio told her not to play around the bamboo groves, she still did. When the auntie next door told her not to climb the mango tree, she still did. When her nanay told her to not run in the rain or else she'd get sick, she still did. *And* got sick.

"I know it's not the way to go," she murmured, "but Ali needs to be planted where the best soil is. I made a promise, and I must keep it."

And so, she walked toward the opposite road. The road her needle had pointed against. The small piece of metal— perhaps arguing with Marikit's decision—kept wobbling, as if urging her to turn back. But her mind was set. Ali came first.

The road she took was long and leafy, one that easily let her pass. It swept away its curtain of giant palm trees as Marikit stepped into the verdant fringe. She was welcomed by the scent of fresh dew, the sound of animals hooting, the specks of sun glinting through the branches. The leafy palm print of her dress glowed with an emerald tide. *Masigla Rainforest*, the scripted stitches read. Tall trees towered like turrets. Every flower shone like a lamp. Gumamelas were drizzled with a bright orange color, roses with deep red; sampaguitas appeared like tiny stars glistening in their hedges.

Marikit found no one in the forest except for a frog

caught in the pastel-colored rocks, croaking as it glared at her with its diamond eyes. *Maybe it's an Engkanto,* Marikit thought. "Mr. Frog." She approached with caution. "Can you tell me where I could plant my friend?"

The frog's throat billowed and burped. It opened its mouth to an ear-sickening croak when a large white snake sneaked behind it and gulped it with one mouthful.

Glug, glug, glug. The pink frog disappeared in the snake's big, round stomach. It hissed at Marikit with its black tongue.

She decided to talk to it. "Um, hi. I need to plant my friend—"

Hiss. The snake put out its tongue before crawling away. Marikit could only watch its rainbow tail vanish in the grass.

"Well, I guess I can't ask it, either," she murmured to herself.

"*I* know where to plant that."

A bundle of mushrooms, who seemed to be very much alive as they climbed on each other with a frenzy, rolled at her feet.

"Hi." Marikit giggled at the sight of the small, fretful things. "I want to—"

"Not the mushrooms, kid. Me."

From the curtains of a banyan tree came an old woman with a giant braided bun, garbed in an orange-and-purple embroidered dress and walking with a limp. She was aided by a wooden cane carved with a tarsier handle that stared at Marikit with its shining yellow eyes. Yellow like bile. Yellow like a sour gumball. Yellow like all the things on Jana's birthday. The old lady looked like a tarsier herself, with a pair of big, bulging eyes, a small, flat nose, and a large mouth that stretched over her small chin.

She walked toward Marikit with her eyes focused on the linen-wrapped bamboo. "It's still hot. Good." The lady stretched out her wrinkled, black-nail-polished hands. Marikit thought she smelled like raisins. "You're lucky I went out for a stroll. Many Halflings tend to get lost here, see. The forest is so dense, and strange animals lurk around. You'd never know when you're walking straight into a Bakunawa's throat, which is slimy and dark and smells like a freshly cut langka."

"I *like* langka," Marikit said.

The woman only gaped at her.

"That's some taste you have. Anyway," the old lady began again, staring at Marikit with her unusually big eyes. "If you're looking for where to plant that, I can help you. I've been around this place a lot, gathering plants, making potions, tra—I mean, *trailing* after Halflings, who might need my help, you know. I'm very helpful. My name is Ligalig, by the way. I'm a Manggagaway."

"What's a Manggagaway?"

"That?" Ligalig laughed like she was short of breath. "I make people sic—I mean, I *heal* people that are sick. Come, come. Let's start the tour, shall we? It's an excessively big jungle, and it will take us several years to cover it if we don't start now."

Marikit followed Ligalig, both of them slowly making their way through the leafy path. Ligalig swept the heart-shaped leaves with her cane, her arms boiling with mushrooms popping out of her skin.

"This is the narra corner." Ligalig pointed at the columns of giant trees to her left. "Big, powerful trees filling the grounds with roots as strong as the hills. Powerful Engkantos rise here, basking in the earth's natural impulse to endure."

Marikit clapped her hands. "Oh, this is perfect!"

"Perfect? Engkantos who grow from here are lazy and sluggish. There are many other delightful places here in Masigla. Follow me."

Ligalig hummed with her raspy throat as she led Marikit onward, only stopping at the verdant, camellia-covered grounds. An enchanting scent filled the air. "This is the ylang-ylang." She pointed with her cane. "Trees curtained with Bathala's musk and a heavy dose of magic. Engkantos who rise from this soil are charming and good at spells; they conjure glorious incantations, but it's their beautiful faces that leave mortals and immortals bewitched . . ."

"This sounds good, too!" Marikit said aloud.

"Not exactly. They may turn out to be handsome creatures, but they're heartbreakers, and nobody wants another of those romantic delinquents." Ligalig shook her head. "I'll show you the best place for your friend."

With her wrinkly hand, Ligalig pulled Marikit away from the ylang-ylang trees, muttering, "There's a secret, sacred place deep in the rainforest. If you want him to be extra powerful and extra beautiful, I'll take you there."

A powerful and beautiful Ali! Marikit thought. Once he woke up, he'd have to thank her for choosing the best soil for him. "All right!" she eagerly agreed.

Deep into the jungle they walked, into the darker, leafier paths surrounded by big rocks that had permanent scowls on their faces. Gone were the bright roses and the lush green trees. There were only the wilting flowers of the blue-haired willows. Thick vines curtained the swampy groves lit by the purple moss on the rocks. Floating, burping lilies hovered on the surface of the waters. The swamp was murky and muddy, and Marikit felt something gooey and sticky in her ankles as she walked forward.

"Here we are!" Ligalig pushed aside a big canvas of palm that acted as a door to a cave. "My secret place!"

Marikit studied the dark, stony walls around her. The ground was lit with an eye-searing blue. Many bamboos, most of them a dark purple color, were lined in straight columns. "It doesn't look . . . alive," Marikit whispered.

Even Ligalig had changed. The old lady's braids dripped into thin, lifeless strands of white below her waist. "There's no better place to grow an Engkanto than here, in this cave full of magic and peace," said Ligalig. "No animals can topple it, no birds will poo on it, no Halfling can use it as markers on their way home. Now, child, give that to me, and I will plant it in the best spot for you."

But Marikit began to doubt. She didn't like the way the old lady stretched out her bluish, fungi-ridden hands with a thirsty expression. "N-no." Marikit hugged Ali's bamboo vessel close to her chest. "I don't like this place. He needs sunlight and water and space."

"Ah, but we've gone past all that, child," hummed Ligalig. "Why not plant him here? It's a long way back, and the smoke from your Engkanto is fading. You can't let that happen. If the fire in that vessel dies, so will he."

Marikit glanced at Ali's vessel. "Then I have to leave," she said decidedly.

"Now, don't you give me that attitude, miss." Ligalig winced, her eyes now turning into the color of bile, then grabbed Marikit's arm. "Do you think I'd bear all this trouble just to let you leave?" Her orange-and-purple garb had melted into a cloak of black. Her skin started boiling.

Mushrooms sprouted from her body and rolled off until only her bare skin—wrinkly, patchy, and gray—was left. "I stomached wearing that fungi drab and pretended to be a forest nymph. I entertained you. I bore smelling your stinky, sunlit scent!" Ligalig stomped. "All so I could bring that here!"

The old bruha pointed to Ali's vessel. "Now, you have two choices: Plant him here, or let him die."

Marikit clutched Ali's vessel close. "You're a Shadow! You lied to me!"

"Of course I lied!" Ligalig chuckled with a *hi–hi–hi*. "We bad beings lie. We make kings sick and brothers fight and princesses die. We spur jealousy and hatred and war and death. It is our duty to cast shadows!" Ligalig laughed an evil laugh before choking on her hair, which she spat out. "We, unfortunately, are also losing volunteers, so we're stealing Engkantos and incubating them in our own evil, black soil. Your friend will turn out fine. Just choose what kind of a monster he will be."

"You'll never take Ali!" Marikit screamed, trying to hide the vessel behind her back.

"Then I'll have to take him from you." Ligalig scowled, tapping the murky ground with her cane. At once, black vines sprang out like giant snakes. Swift, slithering tentacles sped across the blue-lit cavern toward Marikit. They grabbed Marikit by the ankles and hoisted her upside down, wiggling and shaking her so much that Ali's vessel fell from her hands.

Ligalig picked it up. "What a beauty! A fiery beating heart," she hummed, shaking the vessel and placing it close to her ear. The smoke fizzed her skin. Ligalig jolted back and handed the vessel to her vine-monster. "Now, my roots. Plant this for me, will you?"

The slithering black vines received Ali's bamboo vessel from Ligalig's hand. A few vines had already started digging into the soil. "See what we'll make of your friend." Ligalig grinned at Marikit as she sat on a rock. "I'm sure he'll have a bright—no, a *dark* future here. Just like all the other ashes I have stolen along the way."

"You what?" Marikit hissed.

"Stole." Ligalig laughed as the vines drove Ali's vessel into a pit. "You have chosen the wrong side, little girl. There are cracks in this land. Cracks Bathala has not bothered to look at. Soon, all the Oaths will break, and all of Kaluwalhatian will crumble!"

The vines curled themselves around Marikit's legs. "Why don't you change your mind, Halfling? Why not come with us?"

"No!" Marikit squirmed. "I won't!" She tried to loosen the vines' grip, but they kept crawling back.

Ali, she muttered weakly. *Ali*.

But there was no Ali to help her this time. No Ali to

guide her. No Ali to tell her what to do. Ligalig had taken him. His vessel had begun beating with a blue, Nightmare-ish light.

A stream of tears dripped down her cheeks.

I promised, she reminded herself. *I promised Ali.*

Not all promises are meant to be kept, came a sharp tug in her heart. *Your nanay didn't keep her promise. Ali didn't keep his. So why should you?*

"Tatay said promises we break will break us. I promised a friend's promise," Marikit insisted. "And I won't break it!" A warm, comforting strength spread over her ribs. The needle on her collar started turning, winding up like a clock's hand, spinning and spinning until it stopped.

It pointed sideways.

Her pocket!

Marikit pushed her hand into her pocket. She felt it with her fingers: thin, icy strands slithering across her palm. She pulled the strands out.

There they were, Mayari's hair, shining like beams of silver light, beating and glistening. *Use us, Diwata*, they seemed to say. *Child of a Diwanlaon.*

In the back of her mind, it flashed again—the blurry face of the brown-skinned woman, staring at her, opening her lips, uttering in silence, *Manghahabi*. Thick, black hair danced on her face. Her eyes were familiar. Where had she seen those eyes?

"Manghahabi," Marikit repeated. The vines began curling themselves up to her body. "Manghahabi!"

It was as if her hands immediately knew what to do. She spread her fingers apart and began weaving the threads in and out. Oh, she had done this so many times! Her nanay used to do this. Her nanay taught her how. Her nanay spoke in threads, wrapping Marikit's little hands with her callused ones—hands that had known magic. Hands that had known light.

Hands of a Manghahabi.

From loops upon loops upon loops of strings, tied across her fingers, knotted and woven underneath each other, Marikit made a net. She swung herself beneath the vines— how many times had she hung upside down on the branches of trees? With her net tied in a long string, she threw it straight into the air, in her mouth a loud cry: "Bring me back Ali!"

The moon-thread net flew and obeyed her voice, the loop falling right into Ali's newly cast vessel like a cap. Marikit gave it a tug, the cords tightening the opening. Another tug, and Ali's vessel tilted itself, shaking until it was unearthed. One last tug, and it swung back into the atmosphere, shimmying back to her arms.

"Oh, no, you don't!" Ligalig growled.

The Manggagaway tapped the ground with her cane. The swamp growled like a mad dog, the vines angrily curling and recoiling, following a new order. The black roots that held Marikit loosened, and she fell into the swamp. But with Ali's vessel back in her arms, she began to run.

"You pesky little brat!" Ligalig stomped her cane like mad. "You may have taken it, but you won't be able to get out!"

Vines double the size of what once held her rose from the swamp and hurled toward Marikit. Big, slippery vines sloshing muddy water, attacking her in all directions. Like the scattering of thick, messy cords. Like threads. Big, tangled threads.

Marikit tied Ali's vessel around her body. "No! I won't let you take him!"

A vine shot at her, and she jumped, walking over it like she would a tree branch. Another attacked, but she hopped over it and rode its tentacles toward the dry banks. Then came another, and another, but she did the same thing, evading every tip, every stem, until she magnificently created a giant knot out of the wiggling black vines, none of its parts able to slither away from its tight loop.

"Why, you!" Ligalig groaned. She stomped her cane forcefully into the ground until it crashed into several wooden pieces, and all the vines retreated to the river, groaning in their prison. Ligalig let out a loud scream as Marikit ran safely past the palm-covered door, clutching Ali's vessel close to her heart.

It was cold.

CHAPTER 15

PLANTING ALI

Kabuti. Filipino. n. *Mushroom.* A plucky little fungus nestled on decaying bark or untouched soil; usually an ingredient in potions—magical or not.

Please hold on, Ali. Please."

Marikit rubbed her hands on Ali's bamboo vessel to keep it warm. She darted past the gloomy mangroves, past the muddy banks of the weeping trees and the bright lilies. The steam coming from Ali was slowly fading. She knew she had to plant him soon.

"All I need is to find a place with sunlight and water and good soil." Marikit scanned the grassy patch of land until something tickled her toes.

"Mushrooms!" Marikit gasped as she looked down. "Weren't they the ones that rolled out of Ligalig's skin?"

They wobbled and wriggled and squeaked, gathering by Marikit's feet with an excited buzzing.

Marikit leaned over. "Do you know where I could plant my friend?"

There was only the sound of squeaking. *Squeak, squeak, squeak.*

Marikit frowned. "What?"

The mushrooms rolled into a large mass and plucked Ali's vessel from Marikit's arms. "Hey! That's my friend!" Marikit shrieked. "Come back!"

They did not come back. Instead, they dashed as fast as they could, frantically making their way into a sun-soaked part of the forest bereft of thick, towering trees. Marikit followed.

It was a small patch of paradise set beside a glistening creek, where the light of the sun shone generously from the giant hole in the sky. Rows of fire trees stood at the middle, their tall, slender bodies creating an autumn-like atmosphere as their branches dripped with orange leaves. The mushrooms had stopped rolling, only bustling at a certain portion of the land where the water from the creek lapped softly and gentle birds hummed nearby. They were under the shadow of the fire trees, glorious and strong.

And then, Marikit remembered.

I want to be like Apolaki.

Because he is fire. And fire is light. And I am light.

"You found it." Marikit smiled gratefully. "This is the perfect place! Thank you, mushrooms!"

With her own hands, Marikit began digging the soil. When she had dug deep enough, she unraveled Ali's bamboo vessel from her moon-thread net, the buzzy, chatty mushrooms gathering around her.

"I want you to become happy and strong and warm. I want you to be whatever kind of Engkanto you wish to become," she whispered to Ali's vessel before pushing it deep into the soil. It made a crunching sound as if the ground had small hands that welcomed their new guest. Marikit pushed the soil back around Ali's vessel so that it stood securely in the sun. Ali's bamboo vessel gleamed with a bright emerald light, as if muttering:

Thank you, Marikit.

She gazed at the bamboo case fondly, touching it with her bruised fingers. She did not take her eyes off it as she gathered the moon-thread into a roll and pushed it back into her pocket, nor when she noticed a distant scuffle. From the gaps in the hedges came a juddering of tails, the sound of cautious crouching, and a voice so low that the ground shook when he spoke.

"Have you found her?" Marikit heard him say. "The Halfling who trounced my daughter?"

"No, Mael," another answered. "But we saw broken vines lying around, and they've got a Halfling scent to them."

"Follow the trail. Give me her head."

It was only then that Marikit realized the danger she was in, and without another word, she ran, knowing who those strangers were.

They were the Aswangs.

CHAPTER 16

A CRACK IN
THE FRINGES

Bitak. Filipino. n. *Crack.* A long rupture on a solid surface,
usually caused by being hit by something strong, something
tough, or something shadowy.

They're after me. The Aswangs are after me!

Marikit ran like she had never before, scrambling
forward with her heart squirming in her chest, ready to leap
out any minute. She pursed her lips and silenced a cry, knowing that any sound would lead the Aswangs to her. She could
only wail deep in her heart. *Ali,* Marikit sobbed. *Ali!*

How she wished he was here! That she could still hear
his voice! But the only light she could see came from the
sunrays filtering through the leaves. Ali was gone.

She was all alone.

The leafy trail of the rainforest ended in a labyrinth of
rocky walls that blocked the horizon. Gray, stern, sturdy

walls, rising from all sides. A dark patch on the edge of her dress shyly whispered, *The Border.* Another path far from her X.

My child, do not stray, her nanay had warned her. But she already had. Each step forward was a step away from her path. She had wandered off away from X. Away from becoming a Diwata.

Away from all power. All wonder. All beauty.

"I'm so tired!" Marikit cried. "I'm so tired of finding that stupid X! I'm so tired of always getting in danger because of it! I'm so tired of losing the ones I love! I just want to go home! Please take me home!"

From the stony wall, a dirty slab pulsated with a dark marrow. It was a whirling hole, gaping from a long, giant crack. There was something inside it—moving, dripping. Goops of black leaked from all corners. They sloughed off against the wall, resounding like a hush:

Here, Marikit. Here.

Marikit slowed down and walked toward it. The black goop rumbled and soon tore away into the familiar sight of rusty roofs. Green sampaguita hedges paraded the pavement. From the weather-beaten houses, Marikit could easily make out one brown little cottage whose windows were flung wide open.

It was Sampaguita Street.

Home!

Marikit walked closer. A pair of eyes peeped through the window. Eyes like hers. Eyes so heavy and worn out and lacking sleep, still wet with tears.

It was Aling Anita.

"Nanay!" Marikit called out. "Nanay!"

The crack was big—big enough for her to come through. She only needed to sneak into it.

"I don't need to be a Diwata," Marikit told herself. "I just need to be back with Nanay. My life will be back to normal. Back to the sound of the Makinang de Padyak and Kuya Emman's sungka. I'll meet my friends. Maybe they've been looking for me."

She stopped for a moment, feeling a lump in her chest. "They would have wanted to see my blue dress. I would have wanted to show it off. But I only have this." Marikit clutched her patchwork map.

Suddenly, some of the black goop plopped onto the ground, and it turned to blue. Into a dress. A bright-blue dress with winglike sleeves and a bursting ball skirt that shimmered under the shades of light. White pearls made up the collar and the buttons. A fluttering lace ribbon wound around the waist, like a magical sash whose ends drizzled down the seams.

"It's my dress!" Marikit covered her mouth with her hands. "It's my beautiful, dream birthday dress!"

She knelt down and reached out for it. She slipped it

on. How light it felt! How shiny the fabric was! It was blue, the color of the sky, the color of the sea. It glistened like the waters whenever light touched it.

Marikit twirled and twirled, just like Jana had on her birthday. *This* was all she needed. A perfect birthday dress! It might be too late, but if she returned to Barrio Magiting wearing this, nobody would belittle her anymore. Everyone would tell Marikit, "You are like a Diwata!"

A Diwata.

Marikit stepped forward, placing one leg on the crack. She put her hand on the corners. Black goop dripped against her fingers. *That's it,* she heard someone whisper. *Come here. Take what we offer. The land of the Engkantos is a land of pain. Come here, Diwata. Come here.*

Here, Diwata.

Child of a Diwanlaon.

Child.

Child.

It wasn't a whisper, more like a thought. A thought that reverberated in her head like strings of a guitar being plucked. *Child.* She felt it again, like a warm, comforting hug.

In her mind, the image of the threads. Red, rosy, fiery threads. And the face of a woman wrapped in the most beautiful dress she had ever seen.

Child.

Marikit stopped. She stepped back from the crack. Black goop trickled from her hands. A yellow eye opened.

"AHHH!" Marikit shrieked, wiping the goop on the stone. There were more of them, those eyes. They opened and blinked, staring at her with their sharp irises. Marikit saw them on the goops of the crack. She saw it on her dress—her beautiful blue dress—now turned black, now turned into goop.

"Get away! Get away!" Marikit shrieked, removing the dress and trampling on it. The goop faded deep into the ground, the rest of it sliding off from the giant crack before disappearing. It was gone from her hands.

It was gone.

Marikit was breathing a sigh of relief when a shadow loomed behind her and yelled, "Hey, you!"

The shout sounded like a gunshot. A hand fell on her shoulder, and Marikit whirled around, screaming, "AAHHHH!"

But it was not an Aswang. It was a Diwata wrapped in an earth-colored tunic, bracelets of pure gold dangling from his hands. Sangdaan crossed his brows and tilted his head, his earrings twinkling.

"You need to move away, Halfling," he ordered. "That's

a crack to the Fringes! Home to the Nightmares and Shadows. Didn't the road warn you?"

Instead of answering *No, I didn't get any warning,* Marikit's terror-stricken face soon eased into a wide, wild smile. "You're him, right?" she shrieked. "The guy from Everwhere! We've met before!"

Sangdaan put his tattooed fingers under his chin, studied her, and then mumbled, "Ah! It's you! The girl with the map!"

"Yes, it's me!" Marikit jumped in glee. "It's me!"

"What are you doing here, then?" asked Sangdaan, looking around. "Where is your Infinite friend?"

Marikit swallowed a chunk of fear and loneliness down her throat before saying, "I planted him in Masigla Rainforest."

"You mean, he has done the Banyuhay?" Sangdaan was surprised.

"Yes," Marikit said sadly. "And now I'm—"

Sangdaan took a long look at her and said, "Lost, I presume?"

Lost and alone and afraid, Marikit wanted to tell him.

"I've wandered off." She hung her head and fisted her skirt. "I know I should have followed my map. But there were places I needed to go, not because I *wanted* to, but for someone else. And now I'm left by myself. Maybe this is punishment." Marikit heaved a deep sigh. "Maybe it's because I'm too reckless and restless and never follow directions."

Sangdaan caught her look. "You know, a map only tells you where to go," he told her. "You decide when and how. The journey is not the place. It's you."

He thrust his shovel down and knelt so Marikit could see his vivid brown eyes. "People are allowed to get lost, Marikit. That's how you find the right way. See here?" He pointed at the big black scar that pulsated on the stone. "That's a crack. A crack where one could slip and find themselves on the side of the Shadows. It might have called out to you, but you decided to stay. You chose to be here. You chose to finish your Diwata Journey."

Marikit raised her head and wiped a tear that dripped down her cheek. "I almost *did* go," she spoke honestly. "Almost. Because back there, I felt my nanay speak to me. Not by voice. By thought. By heart. I just don't know how, or if it was truly real."

"Of course it was." Sangdaan smiled gently. There was sadness to it, and Marikit couldn't understand why. "You carry parts of her with you. That's how it is being a Halfling. You are never alone."

"Never?"

"Never ever." Sangdaan began to thrust his shovel into the ground and crushed a few rocks. "You are always connected. It's all a cycle. An Infinite life. Moving and breathing all over again. Now, would you please stand aside?" He pushed Marikit away. "I'm here to fix that wall. There have been many cracks and doors to this land, and the gods are losing track of who's coming and going from the Fringes. Just a while ago, I passed by Aswangs who seemed to be very angry with a trespasser. I don't know *why* anyone would trespass in Barrio ng Lagim. Foolish thing."

Marikit fidgeted. "I know why." She glanced at Sangdaan. "I think they're looking for *me*."

CHAPTER 17

MEETING
JUAN TAMAD

Tamad. Filipino. adj. *Lazy.* Doing nothing, wanting nothing, passing time with either unreasonable hours of rest or a lifelong curse.

Sangdaan stopped, stared at her, then let his shovel drop down to the ground with a loud clash, where it tumbled directly over his feet. "Ah! Ah! Ah!" He hopped painfully, crawling and curling to the ground until the pain subsided. He then rose weakly and focused on Marikit. "Okay, here is what you'll do." His bracelets twinkled as he began pointing in different directions. "Tread this labyrinth and exit on the first left bend. Go straight. Then turn another left. When you see a crossing—"

"I'll turn left?"

"No. Turn right," Sangdaan said smugly. "You'll see a vast grassland. Tread that path. Quarts also travel that way, and the Aswangs won't be able to trail your scent. But hurry! Until you're out of this labyrinth, you're not safe."

"Thank you, Sangdaan!"

"No problem." The Manggagawa smiled anxiously. "But remember, glass is a dead end for a Diwata, so avoid it at all costs!"

"What do you mean?" Marikit cried.

"It means you'll learn along the way."

Marikit had no more time to ask questions. She sprinted toward Sangdaan's directions with one wave of goodbye, disappearing around the bend.

The stony labyrinth ended with a carpet of grass, and the new road greeted her with a gust of fresh wind and a blue sky. It was absolutely still. There was no croaking, no birds flitting about, no animals trudging on the ground with their soft, furry paws. The only thing Marikit heard was the grazing of the grass-blades and her slippers walking on them. Above her were white, fluffy clouds that did not drift; they just hung there like cotton candy waiting to be plucked.

Everything looked the same, like a painting on a canvas.

Marikit was traveling peacefully along the grassy path when she heard a growl. "Smells like a Halfling," came the distant rumble. And an answer: "Smells like a Quart." She caught glimpses of Aswang snouts and Aswang tails behind the grass and immediately knelt down, inching cautiously like a snail. The Aswangs sniffed in her direction but she stayed still like stone, and after finding nothing beyond the wall of grass, they ran away as swiftly as they came, but Marikit did not feel at peace again.

She crouched low and walked briskly, seeing nothing but the blue sky and the grass-blades, until she spotted something else. A scraggly silhouette rose over the tall grass, and Marikit gently craned her neck to take a look.

There, in the middle of the sprawling green plains, was a tree.

The tree wasn't as big as anything in the Masigla Rainforest. It was a common guava tree, slightly tilted, with sparse leaves and a lean trunk. But it bore fruit—lots of them—small, green, and shiny. Marikit approached it with caution, squinting as she noticed something underneath it.

Lying below the tree was a long, horizontal figure; not a fallen trunk or a clump of rocks, but a boy.

He wore a white shirt and khaki shorts, with a Boy Scout scarf around his neck, green and yellow and tied like a triangle with a carabao brooch. Marikit could not believe her eyes.

Was it another Engkanto? Were the Aswangs taking another form to trick her? From what she had heard, they could shape-shift, too.

But what if this was a real boy? What if he needed help? *I should warn him*, Marikit thought, trudging forward.

The boy slept like a log underneath the tree, his eyes closed, his mouth opened wide as he snored. "Hi." Marikit loomed over his face.

The boy woke up with a start.

"Haaa-ahhuhhh-aaah."

"Um, sorry?" Marikit leaned over.

"Ha-uhhaaauhooahhhh."

"That's, uh, difficult," Marikit grumbled. "Sorry. I don't do Engkanto Speak. Can you say it in normal-tongue?"

Ahh aaahh   ooohhuuhhh

"Uhh-aaaahhhauhohhhahhh," mouthed the boy, unable to close his mouth. He, instead, curled his brows and widened his eyes.

Maybe he's annoyed at me, Marikit thought. "Sorry for disturbing your sleep. I just want to tell you that Aswangs are lurking around, and you need to be careful. I'll go ahead, then."

"Aaahh-uuhhaaaoohhaa!"

"What?"

The boy rolled his eyes, from upward to below.

"Are you . . . crazy?" Marikit began to feel scared.

The boy shook his head. He rolled his eyes again, lifted a bit of his head, then stared at his feet.

"You want me to look there?"

He nodded.

Marikit craned her neck to see a piece of paper inserted between the boy's two large toes. She walked farther to read:

My name is Juan Tamad. Do not bother me. I am waiting for the fruit to fall.

"You mean the guava?" Marikit looked up. "Can't you just climb the tree and pick it yourself?"

"Ahh-aaahh-ooohhuuhhh." The boy nudged Marikit to read the rest of the letter. She sat down on the grass and dipped her head close to his toes to read the tiny letters tucked inside a parenthesis: *(I am lazy.)*

"Wow." Marikit shook her head. "Too lazy to even say 'I'm lazy'!"

"Arraaahhuuoooohhaaa-aaaahh."

"All right." Marikit stood up and studied the branch. "I'm going to help you. But you need to help me, too. Deal?"

"Uhh-aaaahhh-oooh."

"I guess that's a yes, then," Marikit murmured, and kicking off her dirty slippers, she began her ascent, hoisting herself up the trunk. The guava tree shook as she made her way, bending and wiggling as if it didn't want her there. But Marikit had climbed so many trees, many of them bigger than this one, that she kept her footing. She grabbed a branch and pulled her weight up, slowly crawling to the nearest guava fruit. She leaned forward and stretched her hand, but the guava slipped from her fingers. "One more try," she mumbled, hugging the branch, slowly inching forward, then reached out—her arms were already shaking—she was too heavy—the branch started breaking off—but Marikit stayed in place, reaching out, stretching her hand . . .

Snap! The branch broke into two—Marikit missed the guava by an inch—both she and the fruit started falling toward the open-mouthed boy . . .

"Aaaaack!"

The guava fell straight inside Juan's mouth. He chomped it, crushing the pink flesh into tiny bits until he made his first gulp. His eyes widened, his hand rose, and when the entirety of the fruit was swallowed, he sprang up, laughing and looking at his legs.

"I'm free! You freed me!"

"From what?"

"From a curse," Juan said, rising beside Marikit and towering over her at the same height as her kuya Emman.

"No way!" Marikit laughed. "*That* was a curse?"

Juan bent over and pulled the paper from his toes, crumpling it and throwing it into the ground. "I'm lazy, but I don't lie. Especially when it comes to curses. Curses are scary things for people like me," he said, dusting the back of his pants. "I was playing in the fields one day when I saw this tree. I decided to eat its fruit, but then again it was hot, and I was tired, so I lay down underneath the tree. The fruit *was* going to fall anyway. But the Engkanto of that guava tree cast a spell, that I wouldn't be able to move until the fruit landed in my mouth. And it's been that way for a long, long time. So long that even the Engkanto of the guava tree got tired and left! I thought I was going to stay like this forever, but then you came, and you helped me out, so thank you! Thank you very much. By the way, who are you again?"

"My name is Marikit."

"Hi, Marikit," Juan said brightly. "You said there were Aswangs prowling around?"

Marikit gazed at the wide, seemingly endless plain. "Yes. Dangerously so."

"No need to worry." Juan scratched the back of his head, plucking off the grass that strayed on his neck. "My town is just nearby. Follow me!"

Juan, who had not walked for years, struggled to lift his legs, for his joints would not bend whenever he stepped forward. He strutted like a toy soldier. Marikit could only laugh.

"See how *you* do after no walking for whence-years," Juan said, scowling.

"I don't think I would." Marikit grinned. "Because there's no way I'd be caught in the same curse as you. Don't all Engkantos have powers? Why didn't you fight it off yourself?"

"Ah, you haven't met a Quart, miss," Juan corrected her. "Quarts don't have powers."

"What's a Quart?"

"Quarter Engkantos." Juan cleaned his ear with his pinky finger. "Our kind descended from the people who were spirited away by the Diwatas. You know, the ones they found cute or annoying—either way, they took us here from the mortal world to live with them. We formed communities and even governments. I think Bathala favors us because he's tired of having stubborn gods for company. Look up. That's his home, Kaluwalhatian."

Juan stretched his arms and pointed up to where a thick bundle of cloud slowly hovered across the blue sky, with a shining white palace crowning it. Marikit had seen it before, back at Everwhere, but she had never looked at it from this angle.

There was something quite different about it. Something strangely odd.

On the shining, all-perfect walls of the fortress, under its tufts of cottony clouds and right on its gleaming white walls, were smudges of black and gray, beating like a wound.

"Juan?" Marikit asked. "Aren't those . . . cracks?"

Juan gave it a good stare. He narrowed his eyes, went on his tiptoes, craned his neck. "Nah. Can't be. Kaluwalhatian is All-Perfect. That must be the shade from the clouds. Come on, now. My town is not far from here. I'm sure Nanay will cook sinigang for you, if I ask her."

"Sinigang!" Marikit's heart skipped a beat as she followed Juan.

At the end of the grassy road was a town, bustling and lively and draped with tall coconut trees and dense acacias.

Bungalows made of wood and stone lined the street that greeted them with a bougainvillea-covered arc. One of Marikit's patches suddenly gleamed.

Barrio Ordinaryo.

"This is my town, Barrio Ordinaryo!" Juan said, stretching both of his arms. From inside the arc, they could see the barrio folk walking about, garbed not in gold-gilded Diwata jewelry but normal human garments—sandos and dusters and shorts and some remade ones with obvious patches, like Marikit's.

It looked like Barrio Magiting. Like home.

"Ah, the smell of sun and sweat!" Juan skipped forward, straight to the entrance of the barrio. "I can't wait to see what ulam Nanay cooked for—"

Pang!

"Oof—" Juan fell back with a groan, touching his big, round nose, which was the most injured of all. He looked up and tried to touch the town. His hand pressed against a transparent film covering the entire gate. "W-what is this?" he asked, panicked. "Why is there a shield around my town?"

"You there!" Two guards in green uniforms appeared on the other end of the arc. At once, the thick film melted as they walked right out. "Why are you skipping class?"

"Skipping? No," Juan shouted back. "I just came home from a very long trip!"

"Veeery long," Marikit seconded.

The guards walked grimly toward Marikit and Juan with books in hand. "Article Five dash Eight of the Ordinaryo Constitution, Section Fourteen," one began. "Every child must be in their appointed seat, in their appointed room, in their appointed school at Barrio Ordinaryo from eight in the morning until four in the afternoon." He glanced at his watch. "And it's still three forty-nine."

"You still have ten minutes to stay in your classrooms," said the other.

"Um, I'm not from here, see," Marikit began. "I'm a Halfling. On a Diwata Journey." She pointed out the needle on her collar to them, but the two guards only looked at each other and shrugged.

"Not enough proof. And what about you?" The guards turned to Juan. "You can't deny it. That uniform is marked with the Boy Scout patch of Barrio Ordinaryo. You're from here."

Juan held out his hands. "Relax, sir. I just got back. I've been cursed, see, and I haven't been to school—or home— for a long time."

The guards leaned over and studied Juan. Juan did his best to look sincere, but one guard squinted his eyes and declared, "Nope. Not buying it." Grabbing Juan by the nape of his neck, the guard pulled the boy in, saying, "You two, come along with us. We're taking you to the Sanctuary."

Marikit and Juan did not fight back. The guards cuffed their hands and brought them in.

CHAPTER 18

SALBAHE
SANCTUARYO

Salbahe. Filipino. adj. *Bad.* Not good. Rude and disobedient,
breaking laws and breaking things, including hearts—
including one's own.

In the heart of Barrio Ordinaryo was Salbahe Sanctuaryo,
a dome-shaped, three-floor concrete expanse in deep-red
walls and bright-blue doors and yellow-framed windows.
The windows looked like portraits—sad ones—bearing
the despondent faces of the children trapped inside. "Don't
worry," one of the guards said casually. "You'll get out after
the principal talks to you."

"I don't remember our barrio having a detention area
before." Juan glowered as he was led in first.

"Well, we didn't, until we lost one of our own, and we
suspected it was the Aswangs," the guards explained, pulling Marikit in before closing the door. "Since then, kids are

forbidden to go outside when it's not yet time. We Quarts have no powers, so we have to protect ourselves with discipline and caution."

The pentagon-shaped room had glossy redwood floors and was bare in the middle. There were cages on its walls containing three or more children, each with their own misdeeds. A desk sat in the middle. Behind it was an old lady with blazing-red hair and an equally red blazer, typing behind a glossy, red typewriter. She nudged her red spectacles slightly as the two newcomers entered the room. The officers saluted her.

"Ma'am Olivares, these delinquents skipped class and were found by the entrance of the barrio. Also, they lied, which is a violation of Code Ninety-Eight, Article Forty-Two of the Misbehaving Quarts law."

"So, skipping class." The principal surveyed Marikit and Juan as she started punching letters on her typewriter again.

"Not skipping, ma'am," said Marikit. "I'm a Halfling on a Diwata Journey."

The principal scanned her with gleaming spectacles. "Do you have a pass?"

"A pass?"

"From Berbania. From Barrio Maulap. From the Masigla Rainforest. Any proof that you came from those lands."

Marikit searched her pocket and only felt Mayari's hair,

plus a few twigs. She put the twigs on the table, but as soon as they left her hands, each of them turned to gems. The principal picked them up.

"You came by Masigla, all right." She inspected the jewels before slipping them in her pocket. Looking at Juan, she barked, "And you? That's definitely a Barrio Ordinaryo patch. You can't lie to me. My family makes those."

"Hold your horses, ma'am, I have an alibi," Juan said coolly. "I just got back from a curse. See, I've been under a guava tree the whole time. An Engkanto cast a spell on me, and I wasn't able to move or talk. I would have stayed there for many years more if not for this kid who saved me. I'm no fool to fool you, ma'am; I'm lazy, but I don't lie."

The principal narrowed her eyes behind her red-rimmed spectacles. "What did you say?"

"I said, 'I'm no fool to fool you, ma'am,'" Juan repeated.

"No. The line you said after that."

"You mean, 'I'm lazy but I don't lie'?" Juan asked.

"Yes. Yes!" The principal jumped out of her chair in shock. "I knew a kid who talked like that. He was the only one who'd lay his integrity on the table when his actions ran short. He rarely did anything, by the way. That boy used to be my seatmate, and he'd come to school empty-handed—no pen, no paper, not even the will to listen."

The principal paused with a sigh. "That boy went

missing for decades, and the seat beside me was empty until I graduated. He never returned. All of us thought he got eaten by an Aswang; that's the reason why we have enforced stricter rules in our land."

Marikit glanced at Juan. "What was his name?" she asked.

"Juan Tamad."

Juan's mouth hung open. "He's got the same name as *me*!"

Marikit hit her forehead with her palm. "Juan, how long did you say you were cursed?"

"I don't know." He shrugged. "I've been lying under that guava tree since playing sipa with George Tanglao."

"George Tanglao? My late first husband, George Tanglao?" cried the principal, who already had three late husbands. "That's when he said Juan went missing!"

The principal ran around her desk so fast, her heels tapping against the floor. "Juan! Don't you remember me? Odessa! Odessa Olivares! I used to sit with you during class!"

Juan gazed at Mrs. Olivares's wrinkly face and recognized her brown eyes. "You mean that girl I'd borrow an eraser from? But that can't be!" He shook his head. "Y-you're supposed to be just twelve. Or something. Because I'm just twelve. Or something. Right?"

He spun toward Marikit, who just shrugged at him.

"People get old, Juan," explained the principal. "We got old. All your classmates got old except you. Where have you been? The entire barrio has been looking for you for decades!"

Juan's face paled. "H-how long was I gone?"

Odessa Olivares heaved a sigh before saying, "Thirty-seven whence-years."

"Th-th-thirty-s-s-seven." Juan dropped down to the floor. "I've been gone for so long? Then my parents . . ."

The old lady moved in front of her desk and knelt down to comfort the shaking boy with her wrinkly fingers. "Your parents moved from barrio to barrio to find you and lost hope," she explained. "They came back here when your mother fell ill. Oh, my dear boy, she died five years ago. And your father, I'm afraid we lost him last year."

Juan's mouth quivered without words as tears streamed down his cheek. He slumped on the floor and gave a loud wail, completely heartbroken.

In a cemetery inside Barrio Ordinaryo, where gravestones were covered in dust, vines, and moss, where wilted flowers were left since the last November first, Juan gazed down at the two markers that indicated where his parents were buried. On his mother's grave were the words "To her who waited faithfully," and his father's "To him who loved endlessly." He folded himself on the grassy post, crying hot tears at the presence of the stones and bones, unable to turn back time.

Marikit watched him from a distance, recognizing loneliness and pain in his silence. She knew those feelings. That feeling of loss. She wiped her quiet, little tears with her palms and grieved for Juan. Juan, who lost his parents. Juan, who lost his childhood. Juan, who spent precious years of his life lying on his back and accomplishing nothing.

There was no loss greater than a life unlived.

Juan shut his mouth like a hard-pressed lid, but sadness came leaking through his teeth. "I didn't know it was the last day I'd see them," he told Marikit without looking. "I ran off and thought it was just another day at school. I went on and did the things I liked. Played around, goofed around, lazed around, until I met the Engkanto of the guava tree who cursed me. I never got to say goodbye to my parents." Juan pulled his Boy Scout scarf from his neck and blew his nose into it. "They were waiting for me. Looking for me. And all I did was lay on the grass with my mouth wide open!"

Marikit hung her head. She, too, hadn't been able to say goodbye. She hadn't said goodbye that September morning when her tatay and kuya Emman left. She just stayed still in her banig and listened to her kuya saying, "Goodbye, Marikit!" followed by the sound of the door closing behind them. That was it. She never saw them again. She didn't even say goodbye to her nanay, either. She just flew out of the window crying and struggling and confused at the same time.

There were many words in Marikit's throat, all clumped with equal parts longing and fear. That was exactly what she felt now—alone and homeless. Ali was gone. And from here, she'd have to continue on the journey by herself. But she had learned things along the way, hadn't she? Met friends along the way. Somehow, even changed along the way.

Maybe all she had to do was keep walking. Maybe that was what Juan had to do, too. "You'll learn things along the way," Marikit began.

Juan gaped at her with now-swelling eyes. "What?"

"You'll learn things along the way; that's what the Infinites told me. That's what Dante the Tikbalang told me," Marikit explained. "It means that this is not the end. It means that as long as there are still roads, there's still somewhere to walk to. We'll learn something new. Meet someone new. We just have to *not* stay—in the same sorrow, in the same place."

Juan's countenance changed. It was as if something clicked. He rose and wiped the grass off his khaki shorts. "I guess I should go. But where?"

He looked at Marikit and watched a patch on her dress shine gloriously. The patch had patterns of houses on it and was inscribed with curly letters: *Barrio Ordinaryo*.

"They say people with maps know the way," Juan began. "If you don't mind, I'll follow you, until I find a home to settle myself in."

Marikit's face brightened like a cloudless, sunny sky. "Are you sure? Are you very, very sure?" She clasped her hands.

"Well, I can't stay here." Juan gazed at the hometown he had just arrived in. "No one's waiting for me. Everyone I knew is old. I'd rather see the world and find my place in it. So, would you take me as a companion?"

Marikit did not think twice. She held out her hand, Juan shook it, and from that moment on, she knew she would not be alone.

CHAPTER 19

THE IMPOSSIBLE
BOTTLE

Kapitolyo. Filipino. n. *Capital*. The provincial center, home
to the seat of the government that takes pride in its illus-
trious buildings, which may or may not be governed by a
corrupt politician with a secret agenda.

Marikit and Juan had not gotten far when they began
to argue. In fact, they had not gotten anywhere at all.

"Oh, no, no, no." Juan shook his head after hearing
Marikit's route. "I'm not taking that road. I'd take any road.
But not *that* road."

"Didn't you just say that 'people with maps know the
way'?" Marikit insisted. "Well, that's where my map told
me to go!"

"Look. If we exit by the main gate, Odessa will find me.
Then she'll make me stay home or keep me in a cage like

the other Salbahes. Besides, don't you want a little adventure? A little wandering off-course?" Juan insisted.

"I got here because I was off-course!" Marikit stomped her foot.

"Then let's stay that way a bit more!" Juan marched toward the hillside. "Come on, Marikit. I promise, we'll follow the map after this. I just don't want to go back there again. Please."

Marikit heaved a good, long sigh. "Oh, all right," she huffed, marching after him down the graveyard. "This is the last time, you hear?"

"The last," Juan promised, raising his hand.

They trudged downhill, where there were thorny brambles and large mirrors embedded on verdant meadow. By and by, they found interesting things. White mice as stout as hogs chomping on grass and running away, only peeking at them shyly by the plants. Rainbow-colored butterflies swirling under a large-bulbed rose that blossomed in between two boulders. Dragonflies the size of small airplanes hovering above, their bodies glistening under the sun. Farther on, as they reached the flatlands, Marikit began seeing objects she has never seen before, in that they were bigger than her.

"Strange," she said aloud. "Small things are bigger here!"

"You got it wrong, Marikit," said Juan. "Seems we're the ones getting smaller. Look!"

He turned Marikit to what he was pointing at: a large, long-necked bottle lying on the ground, whose opening hole was as big as a castle's door.

Marikit gasped. She had definitely seen something like it before! On one of their dusty shelves in their home in Barrio Magiting lay a small bottle with a tiny boat inside. She'd always wondered how the boat got into the glass. And she'd never found her answer.

"It's an Impossible Bottle." Juan spoke as if he was used to seeing them. "Heard of them before. Glassmaking giants used to create towns in bottles to keep all the magic and treasures inside. Thieves may break in and steal, but they can never break out. Funny seeing this bottle lying around; they should be placed on Bathala's bookshelf." Juan craned his neck and glimpsed into the old town, which buzzed with chatter and horse-led Kalesas.

Marikit checked her dress. The Impossible Bottle was nowhere on her map. There was no patch that glowed for it. Even more confusing, her needle did not settle in a particular direction; it only kept spinning and spinning and spinning without settling down.

"Something's wrong with my compass!" she cried, her finger slightly pricked by the rotating needle.

"Maybe we should go in and ask for directions," suggested Juan.

Glass, Marikit thought for a while. Sangdaan had told her something about glass.

What had it been again? She already forgot.

"The bottle didn't look dangerous," she mused. The entrance glittered with a rainbow arc, gleaming with small crystal facets like diamonds. "Maybe I should give it a peek. After all, the road allowed me here. But, Juan, you don't think we'll be considered trespassers?"

"Probably not." Juan put both of his hands behind his head. "As far as I can remember, towns allow everyone to go through, unless the creature about to enter is marked H, as in Hostile, as in Heavily Armed with Sharp Teeth, as in Horrible-Looking, as in Having Issues with Society. The gods have put barricades over human and nonhuman territories because the latter are meat-eaters. Nightmares aren't allowed to go into Quart barrios, unless with some diplomatic agreement."

"Diplomatic agreement?"

"Well, trade-offs. Nightmares offer cheap labor. They're strong and have big claws and don't really ask for much, just meat. Tikbalangs, for one, are good for agriculture work. Kapres, too, as long as you give them enough tobaccos to smoke. Humans, on the other hand, grow farms and breed livestock. You wouldn't trust an Aswang to rear a bunch of ducks, would you?" Juan joked. "Nightmares and Quarts sort of benefit from each other in some way, so we try to live as amicably as possible."

The needle compass kept spinning on Marikit's collar as if it was about to fly off. "Let's try asking for help, then," Marikit said, taking the first step inside the round, glassy entrance. Her footsteps echoed like a chime. It made a nice sound in her ears. Juan followed forward, making loud stomps.

They treaded the glass neck before they reached the town center, where a mass of people walked in their most elegant suits, flitting about with parasols in their hands as a sunlit blue sky shone overhead. Horses drawing ornate Kalesas galloped all along the streets lined with mansions made of stones and garden-like balconies. Cafés with colorful awnings served as shades over the hungry townspeople, who were primly sipping hot tsokolate from their ornate cups. Women walked around with their lovely bags swaying underneath their arms, waving their abanikos as they shyly greeted the gentlemen.

Marikit looked around. The people looked like her, but they didn't dress like her. They wore gowns and suits and lace ternos and had their beautiful hair up in braids and buns and hats. As she and Juan slowly made their way, the well-dressed crowd glanced at her and whispered something under their tall, white noses. "What is that?" she heard someone giggle. "A dress made out of rags?"

"We wipe our floors with that," another remarked.

A writhing feeling grew in Marikit's stomach, the same feeling she had had when she sat down at the end of the celebrant's table at Jana Solomon's birthday party. Juan noticed the change in her face. "Don't mind them. Your dress is nice. They just probably haven't seen anything like it."

"I *am* minding them." Marikit bit her lip, angry and humiliated. "I can't not mind them, especially when *they* keep minding me and my dress as if I'm the weirdest thing on earth! Just wait until I'm a Diwata," she huffed angrily. "I'll make pretty dresses and come back here so they can look at me with envy!"

"They're Principalias. Super-rich Quarts," explained Juan. "The gods give them more gold because they pay more tributes—jasmine-scented tobaccos, fine blue wine, lace dresses, and—" Juan stopped. "Pretty wives."

Marikit scowled. "Wives?"

Juan nodded. "When Diwatas fall in love, it's often with a fair-skinned woman. They don't like morenas. Morenas have toiled along with Idianale, have been kissed by Apolaki, washed by the humid waters of Aman Sinaya. They say brown skin represents much sweat and labor, so they turn toward girls who are meek and stuck at home, with nothing to do but get dolled up and learn housewifely things. I like mestizas, but I bet those foolish Diwatas are just afraid, because morena Quarts are strong and bullheaded, and they cannot be manhandled by magical people who never worked a day in their life. Now, speaking of ladies . . ."

He gaped at each lady with a ball skirt and stopped one in a bright-emerald dress. "Excuse me, Lady with the Most Enchanting Eyes," Juan said courteously. "Could you tell us where we are?"

The mestiza gazed at Juan with her fan fluttering under her chin. "Why, what a polite boy," she acquiesced. "You're in the Kapitolyo, dear."

"Ah, the Kapitolyo!" Juan exclaimed. "Forgive me, madam, but is there anyone who can give us directions? We are traveling, and our map is not showing us the way."

"All inquiries are done in the Purple House." The lady pointed at the biggest building at the end of the street, standing palatial in white. "That's where the governor is. I'm sure he can help you get across."

"Thank you, Your Most Exquisite." Juan bowed down. "Your voice is a comfort to my ears, and I can only wish to encounter your beautiful face once more before we go."

The lady stretched out her hand, and Juan took it, kissing her fingers softly while Marikit frowned behind them. "Juan, let's go."

"Farewell, fair lady!" Juan stepped back, and the lady giggled as she went on her way. Juan turned to Marikit, who stared at him with a scowl. "What?" he asked. "We're guests. We have to be sociable."

"That was called *flirting*," Marikit pointed out.

She and Juan walked through a labyrinth of grand colonial houses that towered so tall, they blocked the rays of the sun. Brocades of bougainvillea hung from the walls and craned over the balconies. Groups of finely dressed adults could be seen from their windows, drinking wine, laughing as they watched from the second story of their home. Once, Marikit smelled the enchanting fragrance of tinola from an open window. At one point, Juan spotted a sad, young face gazing down, and he screeched to a stop.

It was a girl, about fourteen, her chin cupped in her hands as she silently watched the two oddly dressed children make their way through the white, cobblestone street. Good-natured Juan smiled at her, but the girl immediately turned away, her straight black hair as beautiful as Mayari's flitting in the wind before she disappeared by the window.

"That's like the most beautiful girl I have ever seen," Juan gasped.

"You just said that two minutes ago to someone else!" Marikit rolled her eyes.

After many pauses at pretty faces and much pulling, Marikit and Juan finally reached the Purple House. The three-story, marble-pillared building, which took up half of Agoncillo

Street, gazed down at them. "It looks like a giant slab of ube," Marikit murmured. Two enormous hands converged by the entrance, folded in prayer, holding within their grasp a purple gem that rotated in midair. Dozens of smaller hands were imprinted in gold on the marble wall. Another hand acted as knob. When Marikit and Juan were a foot away, the door opened.

They stepped into the lobby, which welcomed them with high ceilings blossoming with upside-down purple flowers, swaying magically like curtains. The floor was all marble, speckled with real gold nuggets, and all the doors had hands on them as they opened and closed on their own. The staff was dressed in purple, walking around busily and carrying documents without looking at their way. Hands shot in all directions, assisting them and making sure they didn't bump into each other.

A big chandelier hung from the ceiling, blinking its glassy eyes. Underneath it was a receptionist, who was so short she couldn't be seen behind the desk except for her elaborate pouf.

"May I help you?" she asked monotonously.

Juan leaned on the desk. "Ah, yes. I'm Juan Tamad, and this is Marikit. We both traveled from Barrio Ordinaryo, and we'd like to ask the governor for help regarding traveling directions, for we have a broken map."

The woman peeped over the desk. She smelled like

ylang-ylang and coffee and bagoong. "Shouldn't you have dressed better?"

"Lady, I've been stuck under a guava tree for decades; I don't even have an income to buy myself a drink, much less new clothes!" Juan explained.

The purple-wearing receptionist rolled her eyes. "Lucky you, the governor told us to never deny anyone," she snorted, picking up the phone and moving the dial with her fingers. "Sir, two badly dressed kids are here, asking for directions. Should I let them in?"

She kept glancing at Marikit and Juan, nodded, and then whispered something on the receiver. "Barrio Ordinaryo. Yes, sir. He's with a girl with a strange dress. *Very* strange." It took her a good minute before she put the phone down. Craning over to look at Juan and Marikit, she said, "You can go to the office now."

"Thank you." Juan attempted to charm her but failed, being rewarded with only a scowl as the receptionist drank from her mug.

Marikit and Juan made their way to the inner court, which had a large water fountain with a statue of the governor and giant bougainvillea gardens creeping from the ceiling. The vines led them to a big staircase with a cold marble railing. The second floor was a grand library, with an expansive stretch of shelves that housed dusty, coughing books. One of the books sneezed as Marikit passed by. There were no other rooms, and the only empty spaces were occupied by paintings of past governors in their gorgeously embroidered barongs. The ceiling to the second floor was a mosaic of glass that let the morning light into the corridor.

Daylight washed over Marikit as she rose up the stairs. She glanced at her skin, sun-soaked and brown, very much unlike that of the many pretty ladies sweeping the lobby with their purple dresses. She glanced at her patchwork dress and burned a bit inside. *If only I had my blue dress!* she thought. *Maybe I'd look better. Maybe these people wouldn't sneer at me.*

She glanced at her reflection in the large, glass window as they ascended the stairs. No, she thought. She could not escape the fact that her skin was too brown or her nose too flat or her teeth too crooked. She could never be as pretty as those Principalias. Never as pretty as Jana.

Marikit could only carry those feelings deep in her chest as she walked quietly, her heart and pride shrinking from the inside.

They reached the third floor, a room with no door, only an archway of marble hands that clapped when Marikit and Juan walked in. It was the governor's office, in which the occupant was absorbed in his phone as he sat at his desk, his white hair radiant under the sun, and his barong woven in purple, similar to the staff. "Ah, visitors!" The man's eyes crinkled as he turned his head toward the entrance. On his desk was a nameplate marked with "His Excellency Governor Artemio Panopio," along with a lot of books, a lamp, and a bag.

The two children shyly approached him.

"Welcome. Come in, please." Governor Panopio gave Juan's hand a good shake and Marikit a soft pat on the head.

"I heard you came from Barrio Ordinaryo. How's life there?" The governor's voice was a balance of scratchy and soothing, like Barrio Magiting's taho vendor Mang Jun, who'd call out every morning selling cups of vanilla-laden soybean curd.

"Still ordinary, sir" was Juan's answer, a truly short statement for someone eager to meet the Kapitolyo's top official.

"I see," said Governor Panopio, who put his palms together and made a loud clap. Answering his call were marble hands that brought two couches for Juan and Marikit, as well as a table with glasses of milk and puto-seko, white cookies so delicate they crumbled in the mouth. "And what do two kids from Barrio Ordinaryo want from Kapitolyo?"

"Oh, sir, I'm not from Barrio Ordinaryo," Marikit answered as Juan downed his plate and licked all the crumbs. "I'm from way beyond there."

"How beyond?" Governor Panopio's eyes narrowed. "Do you live in Barrio Dalamhati? Barrio Bukang-liwayway? Barrio Magaspang?"

"Actually, Governor," Juan butted in, traces of the cookies still evident around his mouth, "she's a Halfling. She's on a Diwata Journey, and we're asking if you could let us pass your barrio."

"Ah, a Halfling!" The governor's eyes twinkled. "Why, it's rare for Halflings to visit the Kapitolyo's Impossible Bottle. You see, we're a dead end." Governor Panopio clapped, and hands magically swept the curtains off his windows. "See the horizon? That hazy sky? That's the edge of the bottle. You can't go through glass, can you?" He laughed nervously. "I wonder how you are going to leave from here!"

"I wonder, too," Juan mused loudly. "But, if you ask me, I could stay here for a while."

"Of course you two can stay," the governor said warmly. "We like having guests and showing off our rich land. There are boutiques and restaurants on every street, theaters and sports coliseums for your amusement. We've been made rich by the gods, see. That's why we were shrunk down to a minuscule size, so no Quart or monster can bother us. Except for, uh, some."

Governor Panopio started sweating at this point, so much so that a hand voluntarily wiped the large trickles of perspiration on his face. He grabbed his chest as if he was having a heart attack, until he noticed Marikit's clothes. "Is that"—he gasped a bit—"a map?"

"Yes," said Marikit.

"Curious, curious," he whispered, stroking his beard as he studied the child's face. "Did you, by chance, pass by Barrio ng Lagim?"

"Y-yes." Marikit gripped the handles of her seat.

"Did you, in some way, encounter an Aswang?"

Juan shot a look at Marikit, whose hands now clutched her skirt as tears formed in the corners of her eyes. "Y-y-yes," she mumbled.

Juan's face paled as he turned to the governor. "Why, Governor? What's wrong?"

Governor Artemio Panopio walked around his desk to sit down on his grand, purple couch. "Weeks ago, three Aswangs came here and told me that they were looking for a girl. A girl who had a dress for a map. That girl defeated one of their kind. Now, you know Aswangs; they don't dress up nicely or even brush their teeth—their presence easily terrorized my staff. They didn't hurt us, though; Mael and I have signed a long-standing agreement that while I am governor, we provide for him two-thirds of our livestock. Which is why my hands are suffering under harsh labor." At this, he glanced at the marble hands that slumped beside him.

"Mael is the one who keeps me in my seat of power, you

see. People vote for me because they know Mael won't enter the Kapitolyo due to our agreement. Now, child." Governor Artemio looked solemnly sad. "He told me to turn over the trespasser if she ever set foot in our barrio. I never thought it would happen, so I agreed. I made an Oath, and it was by blood. No hard feelings, please; this is nothing personal. I just had to maintain my—"

Juan rose from his chair and grabbed Marikit, and both of them sped out of the room before Governor Panopio could finish.

"That's not the way to say goodbye to an official," the governor growled. "Hands, after them!"

Immediately, hands of marble shot from all directions, raining behind Marikit and Juan like bullets. Run, run, run, they did. But the hands were quick. The hands were clever. The hands grabbed Marikit's hair and Juan's arm and began pulling them back. "Let. Us. Go!" Marikit cried, shaking them off.

"We're not coming with you!" Juan threw himself on the wall so that the hands would break.

The books in the library were no help; one coughed at them as they passed by, obscuring their vision, letting them fall into the marble staircase, which did not lend its steps. Marikit and Juan slid down in a horrifying spiral, and just when they were about to hit the floor, a crowd of hands gathered to catch them. "The baluster!" cried Juan, swinging his body into the gaps and jumping down. Marikit did the same.

Both children dusted themselves off as they landed on the main floor, the hands still raining after them. They ran past the snotty receptionist, who murmured, "Have a nice day," as marble hands darted over her and loosened her pouf.

CHAPTER 20

SILVER-SPOONED
SATURNINA

Kutsara. Filipino. n. *Spoon*. A common cutlery with a round, shallow tip and an elongated handle, carved in varieties of metals and sizes. Traditionally used for eating, for navigating, and as a weapon.

Marikit bent her small body behind a large potted plant as Governor Panopio's marble hands tracked them across the street. Juan crawled behind the pillar of a white colonial mansion. "So, you defeated an Aswang, huh?" he asked her within a speaking distance. "With what? A silver knife? A god-kissed sword? An incantation?"

"With a pusô," answered Marikit, who untangled her curly hair from the stems of the gumamela plant where she had taken refuge. "She stole my dress, and I traded her with rice from Dante the Tikbalang. It had adobo."

Juan looked disappointed. "I thought that was some

serious action," he murmured. "You know, those who defeat Aswangs are either heroes or dead."

"I'm not dead." Marikit turned to Juan.

"Not *yet*," retorted an unfamiliar, snarky voice.

The two children looked up.

Above them was a girl with a round face, pale skin, and beautifully lashed but sad, spiteful eyes. Her red mouth curled with malice, and her long black hair dripped down the concrete balusters, which were surrounded by white peonies.

Juan looked up and blushed. "It's her! The prettiest—"

"I don't care for compliments," the girl said, shooting Juan down. Her face would have been divine had she not rolled out a fist—smoke fizzed out of her white skin the moment it was lit by the sun. She pulled it back. "Look," the girl threatened, watching Marikit and Juan from the gaps of her balcony. "I can scream right now and tell the governor you're here. Or you can get up here, this instant, in my room."

Marikit was suspicious. "Why should we do that?"

"Should I start screaming?"

"I'm a man of peace, and very much honored to be invited to—" Juan started.

"Not you, *her*." The girl pointed at Marikit. "You. Climb here. To my room."

"How?" Marikit asked.

"See that pot you're hiding behind? If you move it a bit,

you'll find a tunnel. Follow it and you'll find the ladder straight to my room."

Marikit and Juan looked at each other. The governor's marble hands had stopped inspecting the street, but the Kapitolyo staff in purple had begun running about, their heads swerving at every corner. Left with no choice, Marikit gently pushed the pot behind which there appeared a small manhole, just large enough for a child to fit into. She made the jump. Juan followed her, then he carefully put the potted plant back in place.

The tunnel inside the potted plant was rough and jagged, as if it had been dug out by miners with blunt picks. Marikit followed the path and saw a ladder pressed against the stone wall. She climbed into it and reached a wooden trapdoor. She knocked twice.

"Come in!" ordered the girl.

Marikit pushed the door open and popped her head inside the girl's room. Her eyes widened. The rich girl's room, painted in a cloud of pastel pink, was bigger than Marikit's whole house and had all sorts of luxuries, from a plush bed filled with fluffy pillows lined with silver, to a swirling chandelier made of moon-tears and a sofa bursting with all sorts of stuffed toys, from silver bears to pink kittens to porcelain dolls blinking in their boxes, waving at Marikit as if they wanted to play.

"What finery!" Marikit gasped, immediately feeling envious, especially at the sight of the small dollhouse complete with real pots and pans and a stove. She stood by the ladder and took everything in for a minute, unable to believe that such luxury existed.

"Hey, Marikit, could you move so I can see what you're looking at? It's all dark and wormy here," Juan groaned underneath her.

Marikit slowly ambled up onto the velvet carpet floor and sat by the trapdoor, where Juan rose and sat beside her.

"Wow," he mouthed, looking not at the room but at the strange girl who called them in. Juan took in everything, from her long, black hair and pale-pink dress, her eyes as black as the night, her lips as blushing as a camellia, her face as smooth as porcelain. He walked forward and extended his hand, now covered in dirt, and said, "Nice to meet you. I'm Juan."

"Thanks, Juan, now can I *not* have a boy in my room?" She glared at him so fiercely that Juan ambled down the ladder in defeat, only peeping through the trapdoor.

The girl fixed her gaze on Marikit. "What's your name?"

"Maria Kristina," came Marikit's prompt answer, thinking that her longer name would cover all the flaws in the nickname her father gave her. She looked shamefully at her toes before she added, "But my friends call me Marikit."

"Marikit. That's cute." The girl smiled. "I'm Saturnina. My nickname's Nina, but I prefer to go by my longer name. Less cute."

Saturnina rose from where she sat and extended her hand to Marikit. "It's nice to meet you, Aswang vanquisher."

"Wait!" Juan yelped. "You just ignored me and my hand a minute ago, and now you're shaking hands with her?"

"Did I say you could come?" Saturnina glared at him.

Juan whimpered back down the ladder.

"So, what made you call us here?" Marikit looked at her palms and wondered if Saturnina had magic in her, too. "A-are you going to tell on us?"

"Tell on you? No!" Saturnina laughed as if the idea of doing so was absurd. "I just want you to tell me stories. About your adventure. About the world."

"And then you'll let us go?"

"Sure thing. I don't need you. You're not pink *or* silver; you don't match anything in my room. Plus, I only keep dolls, not dirty humans." Saturnina pointed at her showcase of stuffed toys. "Begin, please."

"Can we at least let Juan sit properly or something?" Marikit begged, seeing Juan wiggle on the ladder more than twice.

Saturnina rolled her eyes. "All right," she said sternly.

"Finally!" Juan crawled out of the trapdoor and sat beside Marikit. "You can begin your story now."

Marikit wondered where to start. There were so many places she could, like at her dress, the beautiful, blue dress she had been dreaming of. Or maybe further. Maybe at the nights she saw her nanay making spools out of light. The many afternoons shadows hissed at her. Marikit cleared her throat, and then began, "My nanay was the barrio's seamstress."

And then, words began to roll. Her birthday. The night she flew into the sky with ribbon-wings. She gazed down at her dress and began pointing at her map. The time she met the Infinites and made friends with Ali the Alitaptap. When they traveled along Everwhere. When they met the Tikbalangs at Ikapati's Farm. How she drowned in the River of Dapithapon, and how she, secretly, had strands of Mayari's hair. How Apolaki helped them escape, how they met the Aswangs . . .

Marikit stopped for a moment and inhaled a deep breath when she recognized that Saturnina had inched so close beside her, clasping her hands while holding her breath. Even Juan was stunned, constantly whispering, "Whoa," in his corner, shaking his head with complete disbelief and wondering how a small girl with a map for a dress had gotten so far. Marikit went on, narrating how Ali died in a volcano, how a witch almost stole him, and how she buried him in the best place in the jungle. She told Saturnina how she met Juan Tamad. The girl laughed at his foolishness, and Juan scratched his hair, before being brought to tears at the mention of his parents.

"Oh please, go on." Saturnina shook Marikit's hands. "Tell me more!"

"That's all there is!" Marikit answered. "I'm now in your room, and I'm anxious to know whether you'll let us free or not."

Saturnina sighed with discontent. "But I want to know more! The twin rivers that revive one to their full health, the mountain of Makiling where a legendary lady-warrior lives, the stairway to the clouds, the kingdom under the sea!"

"I haven't been to any of those places. Aren't you rich? You can go there if you want," Marikit answered back.

"Not me," moaned Saturnina. She rose from her bed and paced across the carpeted floor. "See if you live fourteen whence-years of your life stuck in the walls of your house. That's how you'll get weird. No shopping. No rides in the Kalesas. My cousins would visit me and tell me tales about hero Halflings wandering the land of the Engkantos, while I, I'm just trapped inside this pink, fluffy jail. My parents *never* let me out." She stomped her foot with a passion.

"Why not?"

Saturnina didn't answer, but she stood by the window

and tore the sleeves off her dress. "Because of this." She stretched out her hand into the sun. Her skin reddened. Smoke started fizzing out of her sun-exposed skin before it began bursting into small cracks of fire.

"Oh, merciful Bathala!" Juan gasped. "You're a light-leper?"

Saturnina pulled her hand back and gently brushed her swelling arm. "This is what happens when I go out in daylight. I burn. My parents have kept me indoors since I was a child, and Apolaki's fire doesn't know me. The sun won't settle on my skin. That's why I can't go out. My parents wanted me to be pretty, all white, perfect and flawless, so that one day, when a Diwata finally wanders in this town, I'll get to capture his heart. Hear that? That's the only way I can escape this room. If some magical prince whisks me away to his land."

"You're in for a surprise; Engkanto homes are *nowhere near* as comfortable as this," laughed Juan. "You'd be living in trees, anthills, caves, or worse—right on top of the Bakunawa itself!"

"As if I want to marry. I just want to go out," Saturnina declared. "I want to be there, under the sun, feeling the ground under my feet, meeting magical people, and just! Not! Staying! Indoors!" She yelled so loud that there came a knock on the door, and Marikit and Juan scuffled back to the trapdoor.

A maid peeked in. "Is everything all right, Lady Panopio?"

Saturnina ran to her door to obscure the maid's view. "Y-yes. I'll call you when I need you, Leticia," she answered nervously. "For now, leave my room and don't disturb me."

"As you wish."

The door closed. Saturnina pressed her body against it and stared at the trapdoor. "You can come out now," she told Juan and Marikit.

Two heads poked out of the trapdoor, four eyes surveying her from where they stood. "You're a Panopio? Like the governor?" asked Juan.

Saturnina pulled her long hair to her right shoulder. She fidgeted, evading Marikit's stare, then answered nervously, "He's my father."

There was a scuffle by the trapdoor as Juan and Marikit ran down the ladder. "Please wait!" Saturnina ran after them. "I'm not going to tell on you! I made a promise!"

"Why should we trust the governor's daughter?" Juan growled, leading Marikit out of the tunnel.

"Because I'm the only one who can help you escape without being seen," Saturnina slowly ambled down the ladder with her bare, white feet.

"I don't believe you," Marikit said, chiming in.

Saturnina stood by her ladder and tugged a black cloth that covered the wall. With one pull, she unveiled more holes under the trapdoor, each a tunnel marked with different colors.

"What? How? Who?" Juan could not believe what he was seeing. Before he could even finish, Saturnina pulled something from the dark rubble, glistening in pure silver. It was a spade made out of tiny silver spoons. Marikit could only gape in awe.

"*I* made that," Saturnina said proudly. "Forged in the fire of my own skin. I created these tunnels so I could have a peek of the world outside. Papa has a lot of spoons; he wouldn't mind if I took a few from his collection."

"This isn't a few!" Marikit pointed out.

"Uh, yeah. And there's a bit more in my closet." Saturnina smiled sheepishly. She fidgeted and blushed redly before clasping Marikit's wrist and begging with a tearful quiver, "Take me with you. I have always wanted to go out, but I had no one to tell me where to go, no friends to keep me company. I won't complain, and I'm not as high maintenance as I look. Please." Saturnina held Marikit's hand and pleaded earnestly, "Take me with you."

CHAPTER 21

THE UNDERGROUND MAZE

Lagusan. Filipino. n. *Tunnel.* A passageway made from
rocks and stones and, sometimes, enchanted dirt, usually
unearthing hidden insect colonies and gold nuggets, if only
one looks hard enough.

W hat are you doing?" Marikit watched Saturnina dive
into her closet.

"Packing necessities, of course," Saturnina answered
before tugging at her tidy column of shirts, which fell into
a now-growing sea of lace blouses and frilly skirts, ruffle
dresses and silk camisoles, all of which glowed with sequins
and beads under the light of the chandelier.

"But won't you burn?" asked Juan, who was collecting a
mass of silver spoons from Saturnina's closet and tucking
them inside a shoulder bag.

"I don't know." Saturnina pulled out a pink shirt with long sleeves from her heap of clothes. "I've never been outside for long."

"Won't it hurt?" Marikit cupped her chin as she imagined herself in one of Saturnina's dresses. "Won't your skin sting?"

"Well, I've been burning here in envy. Nothing hurts more than that." Saturnina grabbed a pair of casual trousers. "Do we have everything yet? Spoons, check. Clothes, check. I think we'll need water and food, just in case we get hungry."

"Good idea. Let's have lunch in the middle of the chase while marble hands and Aswangs close in on us," murmured Juan.

Saturnina threw a silver spoon at him. "Well, I'm sorry, Mr. Tamad. I don't know what it's like to be in a . . ."

Tap, tap, tap.

Everyone shuddered.

Hide, Saturnina signaled her guests. She rushed to the door and opened it a small gap, answering with a sweet "Yes?"

"Lady Panopio, your father has arrived early and is in a very bad mood," said the maid. "Your mother is out playing mahjong, and I don't know how to calm him down. Would you see to him? He's in the dining hall, drinking wine."

Saturnina glanced at Juan and Marikit as she slipped on a cardigan to cover her burn. "Coming," she answered meekly, smoothing the collar of her dress and brushing the tangles off her hair as she went out her door.

Juan and Marikit followed her quietly and watched her go down the grand stairs from the balustrade. From the gaps, they peered into the purple-curtained dining room, where a white-haired man sat on the most prominent seat with a wineglass in hand.

"Papa." They heard Saturnina greet her father.

"Ah, Nina." Governor Artemio Panopio weakly held out his hand after refilling his glass.

Saturnina took his cold, quivering fingers and placed them on her forehead. "Why did you come home early?" she asked, pushing the wine bottle away from him. "Did something happen?"

"Oh, *things* happened." The governor slumped his body on the chair's backrest with an exhausted look. "Today, the child the Aswangs wanted to find came to our town and paid courtesy to me. She was younger than you, and a lot greasier."

Juan covered his mouth as he snickered. Marikit frowned. "That's not true, is it?" she asked Juan as she tried to smell her dress.

"Just listen," Juan murmured, pushing his head in between the railings.

Governor Panopio brushed his daughter's smooth head with his velvety palms. "She came with a cursed boy who did not age as he should. They escaped me, though—my marble hands couldn't find them all around the Kapitolyo. And then, to top it all off, Mael appeared with his Aswang minions, in my office!"

"Oh, Papa! That's horrible!" Saturnina gasped.

"What's worse is that Mael threatened me." The governor pounded his fist on the table. "He told me he'll side with my rival in the next election. He told me that I'll certainly lose. That I'll be kicked out of the Kapitolyo, and I won't be governor anymore. Do you know how scary that is, Nina?" He grabbed his daughter's arms. "We'll just be normal Quarts!"

Saturnina rolled her eyes. "And what's wrong with normal? We have a nice house and nice neighbors and maids who get worried when we're feeling down. We have it better than other barrios. You can still wear your purple barong whenever you wish."

"But it won't be the same!" Artemio Panopio cried. "I won't sit there, at the top floor of my building, wallowing in the sight of my town. They'd replace my beautiful, purple banners with my rival's color. Orange! How despicable, the color of a mushy squash!"

"Come on, Papa." Saturnina pressed her father's hand to her cheek. "You can't risk a child's life just for the sake of your own career, right?"

Her father turned to her with fire in his eyes.

Fire and fury and no regret.

"I can."

He made a long sip before gripping the glass to the point that it cracked. "And I just did. Tonight, I allowed the Aswangs to enter the Kapitolyo. I told them to find the girl and take her away. Just her, Nina. Not my constituents. So, you, my dear darling"—he held his daughter's chin— "remain safe."

Juan and Marikit glanced at each other warily. Artemio Panopio rose from his chair and kissed Saturnina's forehead before walking away, swerving like a drunk man. Saturnina stayed still, her hands shaking. She turned her head to the kitchen, her eyes stapled on the leis of garlic that hung in the pantry.

"He's giving me to the Aswangs," Marikit hissed under her breath as she and Juan made it back to Saturnina's room. "He's giving me to the Aswangs, Juan!"

"Let's wait for Saturnina." Juan nervously paced the floor after closing the door. "She said she'd help us out."

"What if she doesn't?" Marikit asked nervously. "What if she changed her mind? I don't see why she'd want to leave. Look at all the beautiful things she has!"

Marikit gazed at Saturnina's mountain of pretty dresses

left scattered on the floor. Oh, how lovely it would be to have one! Maybe she should take the one with the big ribbons. Or the one with a real lace frill. Or the one with layers and layers of tulle. Saturnina wouldn't notice. After all, she had plenty of them.

But something stung Marikit by her collar, as if waking her up, as if telling her, *No, child.* The whirring needle got stuck in the middle of a stitch, and Marikit remembered. She clutched the soft cotton skirt her mother made for her, recalling her nanay's words: *Never take this dress off.*

Right, she agreed silently, turning her eyes to something else. *This* was the dress she had been given. This was her dress.

Somehow, the stitches on each patch glowed with a gentle light, as if telling her, *You have done well, child.*

Just then, the door to the room flung open, and Saturnina rushed in, with a garland of garlic around her neck. "We have to go! The Aswangs are—"

"Coming, we heard," Juan answered. "So, are you with us, or not?"

"Can't you see this?" Saturnina pointed at her new accessory. "I'm sorry the garlic isn't making it obvious. Now, let me change my clothes. Marikit, take the lamp and head into the tunnel with Juan. And, Juan, don't peek."

Marikit and Juan obeyed.

It didn't take long for Saturnina to open it again. This

time, she was dressed in pink long sleeves and cream trousers, her hands covered in gloves and her long hair tied in a slinky ponytail. The lei made of garlic hung from her neck.

"Ready?" she asked.

Juan and Marikit nodded, the light from Marikit's lamp illuminating the rocky walls.

The three of them made their cautious way through the tunnel. Saturnina examined the colored markers. "Let's see." She tapped her chin. "I *knew* I dug one for the exit, but which?"

"Can we just get started with somewhere?" Juan was feeling a bit agitated. "If the Aswangs are here, we shouldn't be!"

"How about purple?" Marikit suggested, shedding light on the tunnel. "Isn't it the governor's color?"

"Purple! Yes!"

Down they went on all fours, with Saturnina leading the pack. The soft glow of Marikit's lamp pierced through the dark, unveiling the small objects stuck in between the rocks: shoes that had lost their mates, a few headbands, lost earrings, cameo brooches, and bits of pearls.

"Does jewelry grow beneath the soil?" Marikit asked.

"They probably fell off when I was digging," Saturnina admitted.

"Rich people just find it easy to lose expensive things, huh?" Juan grumbled.

"Those things didn't matter to me. Not as much as my freedom," Saturnina reasoned.

Oh, Marikit realized. Everyone had different treasures. To some, it could be nice clothes or shiny jewelry, or all the yellow things. But to others, there were more precious things, like freedom, like friendship, like love. And as Marikit gazed down at her spinning needle, she felt her heart sway a little, as if it was not in the same place as it had been before. And that was not a bad thing.

After much crawling with nervous, bated breaths, they finally reached the end of the tunnel. "Here we are," Saturnina said, climbing a ladder and reaching a hole covered by another potted plant. The two girls peeked through the hole, which gave them a limited view of the cobblestone street at sundown, with horse hooves constantly clumping down in front of the four-wheeled carriages that transported the socialites across town. The orange light pressed down the almond-pink sky as a scattering of clouds shone with angry, vibrant colors before turning to dusk.

"Is that the exit?" Juan asked from below.

"No, just the main street," whispered the disappointed Saturnina, pushing the potted plant back to its place.

The three of them grumbled as they went back to the main tunnel, where Saturnina studied the many marked holes. "Oh, I think it's this one!" Saturnina pointed at a mint-colored marker that was dog-eared for a reason she forgot.

"I hope it is," moaned Juan.

Back to crawling they went. The wall was filled with small, wiggly worms wrapped in tulle cocoons dancing overhead. A few of them slowly emerged into brightly winged moths that stayed on Juan's pug nose before flying away. *Ah-choo!* Juan sneezed, turning away a few more of the flying creatures when another ladder appeared at the end of the tunnel.

Saturnina ascended, pulling another potted plant out of view. They were at the downtown proper, crowded by the elite in their best suits, many of them sitting by the alfresco restaurants, drinking hot chocolate. One lady, after making an exceptionally loud slurp in her cup, said, "Have you heard? Two kids trespassed in our town, and the Aswangs are after them. We better get home before dark, or else we'll be in danger."

"I think I know those kids," another woman answered. "One charismatic boy who asked me for directions, and a girl who wore a really strange dress and had greasy, frizzy hair."

Both women laughed so hard. "I wish you'd choke on chocolate," Saturnina whispered as she pushed the pot back to its place. "Not here, either," she reported.

"Well, could you try to find it—" Juan face-palmed, but then he paused, put his finger near his lips, and hushed the girls down.

"Quiet," he whispered, clearing every noise in his head until he heard it. A distant wail filled the stone walls—the sound of growling and slobbering, of claws scratching against the stones. "The Aswangs! They're here! Quick, to the next tunnel!"

The three scampered to the next tunnel without looking where it led. The route was so long that Marikit's hand grew tired from holding out the lamp, Juan's back ached from carrying the bag of silver spoons, and Saturnina could smell nothing but the scent of garlic after sticking her nose into her lei for too long. Finally, after much crouching and crawling, they saw the ladder.

Saturnina went up first. She groaned with dismay.

It was the cathedral.

Carefully, she pushed the flowerpot back to the hole, but just before she sealed it entirely, a pair of claws shone under the moonlight, walking past her.

"I can smell something. Children. Dirty, stupid children. But where?" A brown-furred Aswang growled. "Where could they be hiding?"

"They could be inside the restaurants, Mael. Hey, old man! Let us in! The governor gave us a warrant. We're searching for a young girl."

"Go!" hissed Saturnina. The three of them scrambled away from the tunnel, their heartbeats pounding loudly in their ears. *Quick!* They clambered on the stony floor, pushing their bodies against the sharp, cold rocks. With their bated breaths, they found their way back into the main tunnel, underneath the trapdoor that led to Saturnina's bedroom.

"What now?" asked Marikit.

Nobody answered. The only sound that they heard was a knocking on a nearby door.

"Nina?" Governor Panopio called out. "I have brought you cake. Can we talk about what happened earlier, Nina?"

The governor kept rapping at his daughter's door until he ran out of patience. "Open the door, Leticia!" they heard him say. There was the clunking of keys. The turning of the knob. The slight whimper of the door forced open.

"She's not here, sir!" came the maid's cry.

"What? No! Nina!" Governor Panopio cried. "The Aswangs! Oh, my Nina!"

There was the earsplitting sound of a plate crashing down, and maids tried to comfort Governor Panopio, who sobbed dearly, "My daughter! My daughter!"

Saturnina's face paled as she stood under the trapdoor. "They're looking for you," Juan whispered.

"I know that," she said, scowling.

Juan and Marikit stared at her, their eyes mellowed with unspoken regret. "You should say goodbye if you're leaving," Marikit advised.

It made Saturnina uneasy. "I c-can't," she stuttered, curling under the ladder. "I don't want to see him. What if I saw Papa's face and changed my mind? What if he tried so hard to convince me not to leave? I'd never get the chance to leave this room, not right now!"

"You'll never get the chance to say a proper goodbye, either!" Juan reproached her. "You'll regret it, I tell you. Don't give them the pain of waiting. The pain of longing, the pain of searching. I'd give the world to say goodbye to my parents, but the gods don't do retakes."

The lamp in Marikit's hand flickered. "You're lucky you still have your father," she murmured in her corner. "I lost mine at sea, and I'll never see him again."

Seeing the tears well in Marikit's eyes made Saturnina rise. She ambled up the ladder, her face too close to the wooden trapdoor as she cried, "Papa!"

Governor Panopio heard it. "Nina?" The panicky footsteps stopped. "Where are you?"

"Somewhere you can't see. Like a secret. Like what I've felt all these years."

Saturnina stood right under the trapdoor. "I've been kept inside for a long time, Papa. But I've made up my mind," she said, and, after glancing at Juan and Marikit, added wholeheartedly, "I'm going to leave my room. I'm going to leave Kapitolyo."

"Leave?" Governor Panopio was stunned. "But why would you do that, dear? You have everything you need here! I'm working so hard to give you everything you want!"

"Not everything, Papa." Saturnina smiled pathetically. "What I've always wanted is freedom."

"But, Nina. You'll burn!"

"I've been ready, Papa," Saturnina answered confidently. "I've been looking forward to burning. To swimming through waves and soaking in the rain. I want to live, Papa. Not as a Diwata's wife, but as a girl who can do things on her own. I'm going to have adventures. You should have some, too! Maybe you don't have to stay in the Kapitolyo! Maybe you don't have to keep working as the governor!"

"Oh, Nina. I—"

Bang! came an explosion. The trapdoor quivered as dust fell from the wooden plank. Marikit and Juan ducked, but Saturnina, recognizing the shrieks of her maid and the sound of her bedroom wall being torn down like paper, rushed up with alarm. "Papa?"

Clouds of dust welcomed her. Her once-beautiful room had fallen apart; her chandelier shattered, her closet spewing the remaining silver spoons she had hidden. The place reeked with the strange scent of metal and blood. From the gaps of the smoke, she saw her father's legs bound by claws. A pair of angry, red eyes stared back at her, its face covered with ashen fur and its sharp, rusty teeth glimmering with a menacing chuckle.

"Gotcha."

CHAPTER 22

TRAPPED IN
THE BLACK

Dilim. Filipino. n. *Darkness.* The loss of light, the sight of
shadows, the feeling of hopelessness and despair, especially
if you're inside a tunnel with no way out.

Governor Panopio lay flat on the carpet and looked
helpless under the Aswang's feet. "Run, Nina! Run!"
Saturnina scrambled down with a frenzy, her heart thud-
ding wildly in her chest.

"They're here!" she shrieked. "The Aswangs are here!"

But the warning came too late. An Aswang leaped
through the trapdoor, crushing the wood under its feet.
"Hah!" He licked his lips, showing off his rusty fangs as he
sang, "Three little children, running in the dark. Three little
children, I will tear your hearts!"

"Not if you die first." Saturnina took the lamp from
Marikit's hand and swished it at the Aswang's face. The

Aswang cried out as the brightness of the bulb burned his eyes, his wail echoing in the stone-wall mine. Intending to finish off her foe, Saturnina threw the lamp at him, setting his entire body aflame like a bonfire.

"I defeated an Aswang!" Saturnina could not believe it, even as fire began tearing through her sleeves. "I defeated an Aswang!"

"Good job!" said Juan. "Except that we have no light, we can't see through this tunnel, and for all I know, those monsters are on our tail."

As smoke rose, and the stench from the Aswang's burning body filled the air, a face appeared from the broken trapdoor, one with white hair and white whiskers and a purple collar. "Nina!" Governor Panopio asked. "Nina, dear, are you alive?"

"Yes, Papa!" Saturnina answered.

"Then I hope you stay alive. Go, Nina. If the gods are kind, we may see each other in the future. But tonight, run! Run to your freedom!"

"Come, this way." She pointed to the leftmost tunnel and crawled with Marikit and Juan into the spoon-dug hole, their hands brushing against the hard, stony pathway. It was rough and cold against their skin, but it didn't matter. They crawled and crawled, with bruised hands and bruised knees, seeing nothing but the borrowed shimmer of Saturnina's lost objects stuck inside the stones.

Suddenly, Juan stopped. "Shhh."

He narrowed his eyes and peered into the dark, tuning in to the echoes of the caves with his ears. There was a crouching. Rumbling. Snarling. The grazing of sharp claws against the hard rocks.

Marikit could feel her body tremble. Was it her heart? Or was it a tugging coming from her dress? From her pocket?

"The next tunnel!" Juan signaled to his crew. Marikit immediately followed as Saturnina crawled backward. There was the crouching sound again—this time, it was faster, like feet in pursuit. Stones tumbled, and the tunnels roared with thick, wagging tails grazing against them. "Hurry!" Juan hissed, stooping his already worn-out hands and legs on the jagged path when something breathed on his face.

A pair of red eyes opened in the dark.

"Found you," growled Mael, his blood-cavitied teeth smiling as he approached the kids on all fours. Lifting his paws, he showed his shiny claws, brighter than any small gem inside the mine.

"Three fresh children meat," another Aswang chimed in. Saturnina came face-to-face with a horrendous Nightmare in brown fur, smiling at her with a slobbering mouth.

He lunged his head, trying to snatch her with his teeth, but Saturnina turned her neck away, letting his nose sink deep into the scent of the garlic. *Hssss.* Smoke and fire burst on the Aswang's nose.

A smile broke on Saturnina's face. "Hey, lighten up!" She grabbed a bulb and pitched it straight into the Aswang's face—it burst like a bomb and spread all over his fur. Saturnina's skin spat out fire, too. It stung, yet Saturnina repressed her cry and swung her arm, using the garlic to scare the Aswangs away.

"Stop! Stop the fire!" the burning animal wailed. But none of the Aswangs wanted to help him. It was red fire. Aswangs hated red fire.

"Watch me set you all ablaze," Saturnina threatened, her heart bursting with so much bravado. She was burning, and it hurt, but she was not afraid.

"You've packed a few kiddie tricks with you, eh?" Mael wasn't impressed. "Let's see how you do with my claws!"

Juan's hand went straight to his sling bag and lifted a handful of silver spoons, entangling Mael's claws in them. Mael yelped and leaped back. He lunged toward Juan again, but every time Mael would flick a spoon away with his claws, Juan pulled another from his bag.

"Are you a cutlery shop?" hissed the Aswang leader. "Why do you have so many spoons?"

"To make soup out of you," laughed Juan, who threw a spoon right at Mael's face. The silver hit his eyes and fizzed, popping into tiny, angry embers and searing his furry lids.

"AAAHHHH!" came the furious Aswang howl, and it reverberated inside the rocky tunnel. The big, murderous king of Aswangs was crumbling in the hands of a child.

"Go!" Juan ordered, allowing Marikit and Saturnina to leave first. He crawled in reverse, careful just in case Mael made another attack. But the Aswang did not; he yelped and winced in pain, crying, "My eye! My eye!"

Saturnina climbed the stairs and pushed the flowerpot aside. "Come!" She pulled Marikit up. "We're going to get out of this. Alive."

The Aswangs had stopped pursuing them. *Good*, Juan thought, climbing out of the stairs himself. It was a relief to finally breathe fresh air, to finally be freed from the cramped, dark, spoon-dug tunnels.

And then he realized where the tunnel led them.

It was the glass end of the Kapitolyo.

"Great. Just great." Juan's heart sank, jabbing the cold glass wall as if he could break it. The sling bag that hung from his shoulder only showed him a few clinking spoons. Underneath him, the ground began to thud. There was a rumbling. The hole Saturnina dug gave way to a leaping Aswang.

One by one, the Nightmares jumped out. Angry. Burned. Humiliated.

"This isn't good," Saturnina said, trembling as the wind blew the fire on her skin. The garlic lei on her neck had loosened, the cloves dropping down at her feet like fallen fruit.

"The hunt is over," Mael ominously threatened, his one eye missing, but not his fury. "Now give us the girl. I'll make death swift and painless for you two."

"No." Juan stretched his arm over Marikit.

"What are you fighting me with, little boy?" Mael jeered. "Your tiny kutsara? You have no weapon!"

"Even with the last bit of silver, I would still fight!" Juan retorted.

I would still fight. Juan's words echoed inside Marikit's heart. What could she do? She was helpless. Weaponless. She was hardly even a Diwata. She was only a child.

Child.

Child of a Diwanlaon.

Manghahabi.

Something wiggled in Marikit's pocket. It had always been wiggling. She only paused to recognize it now. She slipped her shaking hands in her left pocket and felt the cold, thin strands of Mayari's hair.

We are here, they seemed to tell her. *Use us, Diwata.*

Child of a Diwanlaon.

Manghahabi.

"Manghahabi," Marikit repeated. It flashed in her head again—the image of the woman with a crown of beads and black hair, weaving threads of light in the air. *Manghahabi.* Her deep-red lips opened.

"Manghahabi!" Marikit shouted louder.

Raising her fists, stretching the moon threads, Marikit stepped forward. "Back off," she warned the king of Aswangs. "Or else."

"Or else what?"

"Or else be bound. For eternity."

"With what?" snickered the grand Aswang. "With a thread?"

"Yes," Marikit answered. "With *this* thread."

She remembered. She remembered it all. The way her nanay pulled light from the candlestick and made threads out of it. The way the tiny pink strings blossomed into dazzling loops of red. She wove the silver strands around her fingers, knotting them as she shaped the letters. *Nanay. Manghahabi.* In every touch of her warm palms, they grew. They stretched. They thickened in breadth, swirling with a mind of their own so that when Marikit flung them into the air, the ribbons went after the king of Aswangs, capturing him like a net made out of silver. They bound him from his neck to his toes, wrapping his snout, clamping his mouth so he could not terrorize anyone with his fangs.

With one pull, Marikit locked him in; the Aswang could not wriggle his way out.

Saturnina could only clap her hands. Juan could only stare with an open jaw.

"You can do that?" he gasped.

"I haven't told you? I'm a Manghahabi," Marikit said proudly. Turning to the Aswangs, she spoke: "Leave, or your leader will get hurt."

The ribbons tightened themselves around the king of Aswangs. His furry, sharp-clawed throng glared at Marikit with their red eyes.

"I said, leave!" Marikit shouted louder, pulling the strands tighter. Mael groaned. But the Aswangs did not step back. Nor did the smiles on their faces vanish.

"What's going on? Do you want him to die?" asked the confused Marikit.

Mael's stricken face stretched into a ridiculous grin as he loosened the ribbon around his mouth. "Foolish child," he began. "Do you know where Aswangs get their power?"

Before Marikit could answer, Mael opened his mouth and flicked his tongue, slurping Mayari's strands of hair as if they were pasta and gulping them straight down his throat. At once, his wounded eye opened with an enflamed glare, his fur brightened into a radiant tone of white silver, and his body gurgled into a mass double his former size, looming over Marikit as a bigger, more dreadful beast than before while hissing:

"From the moon."

CHAPTER 23

FIRE FALL DOWN

Apoy. Filipino. n. *Fire.* A hot, flickering element that makes up the skin of the sun and stars, constantly gurgling with razing energy that gobbles up everything along its path.

You just made me the most powerful Aswang on earth," Mael laughed. Marikit crumpled in despair, her legs trembling, her ribs shaking with cold, deathly terror. The Aswang made sure she saw his eyes when he spoke: "And now, to appease my wrath, I will avenge my child!"

The glass walls of the Impossible Bottle rang with the Aswangs' triumphant howls. "Marikit!" Juan and Saturnina ran to her, standing on either side of her, bereft of any weapon that could hold the Nightmarish throng away.

"Six spoons," groaned Juan, checking his remaining cutlery.

"Three bulbs," moaned Saturnina, letting the garlic cloves roll in her hands.

"No moon-hair," said Marikit, looking at her empty hands.

"We're under Bathala's grace now," Juan sighed.

Bathala, Marikit repeated to herself. The highest of all gods. Didn't she pray to him that September day, shouting with all of her throat? But he hadn't heard her. He hadn't brought back her tatay and kuya Emman. What made her think that he would hear her *now*?

But she had nothing left. Nothing but a small whisper, echoing in her heart as she folded her hands. *Please save us, Bathala. Please save us.* She watched as the Aswangs loomed closer and closer. "Please, Bathala." The prayer grew louder and louder, and so did her voice. "Bathala," she sobbed. "Please save us!"

Juan heard it. He looked up in the sky and remembered the many times he saw the great god peek through the white curtains of Kaluwalhatian. Maybe they only had to cry louder. "Save us, Bathala!" he begged. "Save us!"

"Save us!" added Saturnina, who grasped the remaining bulbs in her hands. There were no walls to protect her now. No room to hide away in. "Save us, Bathala!"

The three of them, trapped by the glassy wall, shouted with the same plea. "BATHALA, SAVE US!"

"We've got you now!" Mael led the throng as the Aswangs bellowed, speeding at the children with their clawed feet.

Clouds of dust covered the horizon. It was so thick that the Principalias gazing from their windows hardly saw anything. They did not see a comet sweep across the glassy horizon. They did not see it swing through the glassy entrance, the glass tunnel whistling as it came. They did not see it until it floated over their heads like a sun.

The ferocious Nightmares looked up and winced. It wasn't a sun. No. Suns didn't gurgle with fire. Suns didn't smash themselves into the ground. But this ball of light did. It swirled in the sky and swung down, piercing between the Aswangs and Marikit, unearthing a pathway into the stony street. It boiled and churned, like a massive bowl of energy about to throw a tantrum. Embers shot out of its body, hitting many of the Aswangs like bullets. It lodged inside their chests, beating. Burning.

"What is this?" they growled, watching their bodies fizz with smoke, their fur set alight. They found their answers when out of the embers came a sprout. A golden leaf.

It was a seed.

Some of the Aswangs tried to touch it, but it burned their hands like hot coals. It spread on their chests. Its roots grew so fast, slithering and swirling around their furry bodies, binding their hands, caging their feet, locking them inside a dark, hollow tree as its branches spread upward.

And then, out of the ball of light, a stomp. Like a strike on a drum.

All at once, the trees blossomed with fiery orange leaves. Like fire. All the Aswangs trapped inside were solidified into the wood, their menacing faces hardening into grainy bark as they screamed their last.

They turned into trees.

"Who are you?" cried Mael, terrified at the sight of his comrades. "Show yourself!"

The ball of light did not answer. Instead, it shot embers toward the biggest Aswang, planting on him a seed. Roots crawled, locking him in place. He attempted to claw his way out, but new embers flew at him, one after another, forcing him back.

Marikit watched in awe. She lay on the ground, fire gleaming in her eyes as each tree trunk burst with orange fire. Bathala had heard them! Bathala had listened to them! He had sent someone to save them, and there could only be one god with such fire. With such ferocity.

"Apolaki?" she asked.

"No, Marikit."

It was a familiar voice. She had heard it before, but it wasn't Apolaki's. No. It was merrier. Less mischievous. Less greedy. It was warm and joyful and comforting.

The voice of a friend.

The amber ball of light waned. It formed into the shape of a boy in a red vest, his pants trimmed with the same pattern by his knee. Inked geometric symbols swirled from his neck, arms, and legs, and his hair was wrapped in a dark-blue fabric. The boy gazed at Marikit with his bright eyes brown like honey, speaking clearly:

"It's me. Ali."

CHAPTER 24
THE FINAL DANCE

Sayaw. Filipino. v. *Dance.* The body graciously submitting itself to flow and rhythm, pirouetting with motions that evoke different feelings, such as joy, sorrow, or settling dues with enemies.

Marikit couldn't believe her ears. "Ali?" she asked again. "*My* friend Ali?"

The brown boy with long, disheveled hair smiled with a dimple on his right cheek. The bright light that shone from his brown skin was the same amber light Marikit first saw in Luntian Forest.

Could it be? She gazed at him.

He wore an open vest of gold. Intricate weaves of red and orange drizzled down his waist, his cropped trousers of the same embellishment. A sash of bright sunray draped his shoulder.

Could it really be?

"The First Life is a Life of Possibilities, I told you," Ali spoke, his voice unmistakable.

"Ali! It *is* you!" Marikit burst with gladness. "You've come back a Diwata, just as you have dreamed of!"

"Wait. Diwata?" Juan was confused. "Isn't he too young to break out of his shell?"

"My transformation was cut short," Ali bashfully explained. "I was going through my Banyuhay when somebody knocked on my bamboo vessel. I saw a light, and there was a voice: 'It's a tad too early, but you must wake up, my boy.' Then there was a crack, like the voice's owner opened my vessel with its bare hands. I went out, and then that's when I heard you, Marikit. I knew I had to save you."

"Hoy!" shouted the Aswang, who wasn't pleased at the arrival of the new visitor. "Who do you think you are? I have my revenge to settle!"

The king of Aswangs would not be ignored. Not with moon-hair inside of him. He crushed the hollow of the tree with his silver claws, grinning. "I will escape this prison, and I will eat you all. You will all go down in my throat, fuel for my body, and we will lay waste to the entire Kapitolyo this very night!"

"Not if I can help it!" Ali stomped his feet, and the earth vibrated, shaking with snakelike roots that thrust out of the surface. The roots attacked Mael, covering him from his toes to his hair. They twirled like a cord, their branches spreading, their tips blossoming with bright orange leaves.

Mael was trapped. Helpless. The king of Aswangs, subdued.

One by one, people soon filled the empty street. The Principalias gathered at a distance and watched in awe. They clapped their hands; the applause sounded like soft rain. "Bayani! Hero!" they told Ali. "You saved us from the Aswangs!"

"Saved *us*?" Juan growled. "You all were hiding in your big stone houses!"

But Ali, who had never been praised before, blushed and scratched his head shyly, murmuring, "So this is how it feels to be a hero!"

"Oh, you always have been!" Marikit spoke. "Even when you were a firefly, you always, always saved me! These are my friends." She made way to Juan and Saturnina. "Heroes, just the same."

"Thank you. I'm glad to be appreciated," Juan began, offering his hand to Ali. "Juan Tamad. Boy Scout. A Quart."

Saturnina, who kept her distance, only yelled, "Saturnina. Principalia. Please stay where you are, sir. I'm in a situation." Her skin began sparking fire whenever she moved one step closer, and she frantically tried to put it out.

There was a grunt, the sound of wood cracking, and

there was Mael, piercing through the trunk with his sharp claws. He chomped on the hole and made a way for himself. "I will not end here," he spoke in his deep, terrorizing voice. "I will not be shamed by defeat."

He crushed the roots with his paws and began to wriggle out of the bark. All the watching Principalias gasped.

"Oh no, you don't!"

Ali ran toward Mael. The god-ink scripts on his ankles and wrists began shining. He spun in a circle and hunched down, stretching his marked arms and sweeping the air with his fingers. He bent his knees, his inked feet sweeping as he twirled. Embers grew out of his palms, and he blew on them, straight to the squirming Mael, who had managed to break halfway through his hollow.

The seeds lodged themselves on Mael's fur.

Ali stomped his bare feet. The seeds began moving, shaking, sprouting, all at a magnificent speed. Up Ali twirled, swirling his fingers, brushing the wind with his arms. He landed on the earth and gave it another stomp.

Isa. The trunk stretched its branches.

Dalawa. Leaves began to sprout.

Tatlo. The roots wiggled from underneath.

Mael writhed with fury. "You will not defeat me, you *small* Diwata!"

Ali scowled. "I am *not* small!" He danced into the air,

whirling with his barefoot, ink-drawn legs before he made his final stomp. All of a sudden, golden leaves burst out of the tree. The trunk heaved itself from the ground like a spring—pushing and swinging until it propelled itself into the glass-sky, each fallen leaf exploding into a firework. The grand Aswang was stuck in the middle of the trunk, wiggling helplessly with a cry: "AAAHHHH! PUT ME DOWN! PUT! ME! DOWN!"

"Mabuhay!" The astonished Principalias celebrated, throwing their hats and abanikos into the air. At once, the trumpeters rushed out of their homes and began playing a merry tune. There was dancing and singing as the Aswangs trapped in trees slowly became one with the wood.

In the middle of the rejoicing crowd was a man, his hair white and his robe purple, dashing urgently out of the door of his broken house. His legs limped a bit, but no matter. He waved both of his hands as he approached the heroes. He was mouthing something.

Saturnina turned in the direction of the man. She knew who he was. "Papa!" She waved back. "We won, Papa! We won!"

But Governor Artemio Panopio wasn't glad. No. There was a troubled look on his face as his hands sprung up in the air, gesturing with an urgent motion. Saturnina squinted her eyes and tried to read her father's face.

He was mouthing, "No!"

He was pointing up.

And then she saw it.

The glassy horizon had begun to crack, and as Ali made his final stomp to make his fire tree burst, the walls of the Impossible Bottle shattered.

CHAPTER 25
AMAN SINAYA

Dagat. Filipino. n. *Sea.* A large basin of salty water set to keep islands afloat, usually rippling into bigger masses of liquid that wrap around the continents.

The last thing Marikit saw was sand. Shining, magical sand, all of it seeping out of the large crack that broke the Impossible Bottle. It spewed out in a flurry, creating a whirlwind of crystal glass shards and floating mansions and crying horses still latched to their carriages. Marikit remembered floating in midair, swimming against the rapid spinning of the wind to reach out for Ali's hand. But she missed his fingers by an inch, and he was lost, in a pool of velvet curtains and a treasure chest that vomited all its gems. Juan's silver spoons whooshed along the broken branches of fire trees. From the rustling depths, Saturnina squealed, "Papa! Papa!" Somewhere beyond the whizzing came a response: "Nina! Nina!"

Marikit wondered if someone would call her name, too.

Years ago, she had someone who would. His face clear and brown. Eyes that woke before the sun peeped from the clouds. A wise, large forehead and a tuft of hair, always shaken—not combed—by sea-scented hands. Thin cheeks. Broken teeth. A laugh that came right out of his chest. Warm and gurling and contagious.

She could remember his voice. The many times he called her name. The many times he saved her after she tumbled and fell and slipped and got hurt.

"Marikit! Do not lean too close by the water, you might fall down the boat!"

"Marikit, just stay where you are! I'm coming to get you!"

"Marikit, Tatay is here! Don't be afraid."

Tatay is here.

Tatay is here.

"Help! Please help!" she called out as she spun around in the air. There was screaming and yelling and things crashing down. Objects fell to the ground as the hurricane raged on. And then, a sloshing of the sand. Much, much sand.

From the hurricane gleamed something long and thin. Like a reel. It swung in the air, the same way Mang Fidel used to fling his fishing rod deep into the sea. *Tatay*, Marikit whispered, holding out her hand. The hooked end wrapped around her wrist.

Tatay is here.

Marikit closed her eyes.

She could remember it—that fateful September morning when she saw her tatay and kuya Emman last. She lay in her banig, reveling in the cold breath of a soft drizzle that sputtered by their window. Her mind was awake. Her eyes were closed.

"Marikit, we are leaving," said her father.

She stirred.

"Marikit Malikot!" Her kuya Emman leaned over her ear, shouting louder, "I said, we're leaving."

"Then just go," she mumbled as she rolled to the other side.

"Don't wake your sister, Emmanuel," ordered their tatay. "Come along. We'll be back by lunch, Anita."

There was the sound of a kiss. And the sound of the door whimpering open. "Bye, 'Nay!" came Emman's fare-well. "Bye, Marikit."

Bye, Marikit said in her mind, like it was a thing of no matter. They were going to return soon anyway. Like they always did. There was no news of the storm. There was no sound of the radio.

If she only knew what a difference that morning would have made.

I should have opened my eyes, Marikit told herself. *I should have said goodbye. I should have woken up. I should have seen them off.*

But she didn't.

And she never saw them again.

Hot tears dripped down her cheeks.

And then, Marikit opened her eyes.

The first thing she saw was the wooden ceiling. Old, grainy beams held the natural-colored plywood that bore nicks and cobwebs in its corners. The walls surrounding her were made of wood, too, decorated with fish-carved ornaments, wooden plates, and large wooden forks and spoons. An open capiz window had its panels slid halfway, allowing some of the sun to come in.

She rose from her makeshift bed and blindly felt her slippers underneath the bench. The wooden floor creaked from her weight. Almost everything was made of wood.

Like how it was back home.

Am I home?

A fishing line, Marikit remembered. She glanced at her wrists to find some of the traces still there. A fishing line had wrapped itself around her hand and pulled her away. Away from the hurricane. Away from death. There was only one person she knew who could throw a line like that. One who would, without hesitation, save her.

"Tatay?" Marikit began to call out. "Tatay?"

Impossible, said her heart. *He's gone. He's gone with Kuya Emman, and they will never return.*

After all, if they were truly alive, they would have come back. It had been three years.

Three years.

"Tatay." Marikit's mouth quivered as she stood by the doorway. There was the sound of a crackling fire and the scent of fish being fried.

Someone was here.

Maybe it's a dream. Maybe it's a miracle. Marikit rushed out with a jump, a name calling out inside her heart.

"Tatay?"

"You're up?"

Out of the cottage was sand. Heaps of white sand, powdery and refined, seeping through Marikit's rubber soles. She swung her head around the tall coconuts that rose above her. There was a grill. And there was a woman behind it.

A woman with a strange, strong charm.

She rose six feet high, with skin so brown and golden it glittered with the specks of sand. Her long, black hair turned to sea-blue, rippling down her ankles, spreading across the beach. Opalescent clams crowned her head as bright, white pearls hung from the braided strands of her hair. She wore a bodice made from overlapping seaweed that covered her bust and showed off her glittering navel. Her skirt was woven with a fish's silvery scales, gleaming under the morning light.

There was so much color in her skin, bursting whenever the light hit her, just like when daylight danced on seawater. Her colors were brave and bright and bold. There was a stunning sense of ferocity in her. Flowing, unflinching, eating up every onlooker.

Like the sea.

A blue, blue sea.

For a moment, Marikit only gazed at her with pure marvel. She glanced at her own skin, which was the same color as the woman before her—brown and sun-soaked and shining. Something blossomed in her chest. *Pride*, it said.

Morena, it said.

Marikit, it said.

Truly, unwaveringly exquisite.

"Don't just stand there, introduce yourself," the woman ordered, cutting Marikit's daydream short.

"I'm Marikit, ma'am," came the answer.

The woman gazed at her with glossy blue eyes and chomped on the freshly grilled bangus despite it being smoking hot. "Hmm, Marikit," she repeated, eating loudly and spewing the bones out into the floor. "What a name for a small, troublesome girl."

"W-w-who are you?" Marikit asked slowly.

The woman stopped eating. "Who am I?" Her already-furrowed brows furrowed deeper, her wavy, black hair started rippling like waves, and she rose from her chair, her fish scales popping out of her human skin. "You don't know who I am?"

Marikit cowered by the door. "I'm sorry, ma'am! I just got here, and I don't know a lot of people!"

"Am I too lowly of Bathala to not be revered as greatly as him? Am I less useful than Ikapati, or less magnificent than Apolaki? I am Aman Sinaya! I am the goddess of the waters!" And as she yelled, tides of water rushed through the house and exploded through the windows. "I hold the earth together! I breathe this planet to life!"

Water surged from all corners, washing Marikit back inside the wooden house as she cried, "I know now! I know now! Please don't be angry, Miss Aman Sinaya!"

Aman Sinaya took a deep breath and sat back on her chair. All of a sudden, the waves dispersed, the frothy tide disappeared, and everything in the house dried out as if it had not been flooded before.

"How did you do that?" Marikit wondered aloud.

"Do what?"

"The waters. You—" Marikit started gesturing with her hands. She didn't finish. Through one of the open windows, she heard a rumbling, like a downpour. Climbing up a chair, she looked out and discovered where she was.

She was in a hut in the middle of an ocean.

The next window didn't have the same view. Out that one, there was a placid lake, and boatmen glided through it on a sunrise. Through another window, Marikit saw lily-covered ponds.

Curious, she walked back. Ocean. Lake. Pond. As she peeked through the other windows, she found other forms of water—a cascading fall, a rippling river, a quiet beach, and a strange, pitch-black aquarium where light had failed to reach. Marikit kept running back and forth, making loud noises against the wooden floor until Aman Sinaya asked sternly, "What are you doing?"

Marikit paused. "I was just wondering, where exactly are we?" she asked shyly.

"What do you mean 'where exactly'?" Aman Sinaya raised her brows again. "You're in my home. My home has no 'where exactly.' I'm everywhere there's water. And everywhere, there's water."

"But how did I get here?" Marikit asked.

"Simple." The goddess spewed another set of fish bones down the floor. "I plucked you out of the sand."

Marikit remembered a line of string coming at her before she closed her eyes. "You asked for help, remember?" said Aman Sinaya. "That's why I saved you. You look disappointed, though."

Oh. Marikit's heart drooped. *It's not Tatay.*

"I thought you were someone I knew." Marikit blushed. "Someone I loved."

"Oh, but am I *not*?" Aman Sinaya scowled. "Is water a stranger? An element unloved? Far across the world, people seek it every day. No one lives without it. Nothing thrives in its absence."

Marikit turned her head around, hoping to see Juan sleeping on one of the benches or Saturnina playing by the beach outside the window. But neither was there. "W-where are my friends, ma'am?"

"What friends?"

"My friends." Marikit began making wild gestures with her hands. "They were in the hurricane with me! Ali, he's an Infinite who's now a Diwata. And Juan. He's a cursed Quart. Saturnina, too! She has never been out of the bottle."

"Hmmm." Aman Sinaya shrugged. "I didn't save them."

"What?"

"I didn't save them," Aman Sinaya repeated, throwing a fish bone out the window, where it became a live fish again. "I have a philosophy, see. No asking, no saving. You didn't even say my name back when you called for help, but I came for you anyway. Don't worry about them, kid." Aman Sinaya brushed off Marikit's concern. "Every lost thing goes to the Desert of Malikmata. Anagolay, the goddess of finding things, will definitely recover them." Then Aman Sinaya wrinkled her nose, looking as if she didn't believe her own words.

"That is, after the goddess finds herself. She's always lost, you know. Teen gods," she added.

Marikit slumped back to her chair. "But won't they die?"

"Not die. Just be, you know, unfound. Lost. Buried. Temporarily out of sight." Aman Sinaya tried to sound positive. "Look, aren't you happy? You're alive! You get to tell the tale! And, if you're lucky, if you live long whence-years, you'll probably see them again!"

"But I'm on a Diwata Journey. I have to go to X." Marikit pointed at the skirt of her dress.

"Much better. No distractions. No baggage," laughed Aman Sinaya. "Couple of lessons you need to learn—and take it from me, one of the gods of the beginning"—she patted Marikit's shoulder—"is that not everything you start with comes with you in the end. Second, and the most important thing . . ." Aman Sinaya lunged down, and Marikit smelled seawater on her. "Never argue with water. You won't win. Water will eat you up. Force you down the tides, turn you upside down. Just go with the flow, see." The goddess undulated her fingers like a drunk spider. "And you'll be all right.

Now, do you want some grilled bangus? Tilapia? Tawilis? I've got all the fish you want, if you'd just ask."

Marikit hung her head. "But my friends," she whimpered, her fists clenched as she bit her lower lip. "I have to save my friends. They came with me and fought with me and tried to save me from the Aswangs! I have to save them back!"

Aman Sinaya stared at Marikit with unblinking eyes. Marikit stared back unflinchingly.

"All right." The goddess shrugged. "I will lend you my vessel."

Marikit jumped with a joyful gasp. A goddess's vessel! She clapped her hands as a smile stretched over her once-troubled face. "Oh, Aman Sinaya! That is so kind of you!" Her eyes went so wide and her face so bright that the goddess, who was not used to emotions, covered Marikit's eyes with a clump of seaweed.

"I will let you use it"—Aman Sinaya spoke with emphasis— "for the sole purpose of saving your friends, whom, by the way, I won't help, because lending my boat is too much."

"That is enough! Thank you so much, Aman Sinaya!" Marikit shrieked giddily, pulling the seaweed off her face before throwing her hands around the goddess's neck. "I can save them! We can be together again! Oh, thank you! Thank you so much!"

Aman Sinaya didn't dislike hugs. In fact, she let Marikit

hang on to her for a few moments more, breathing in the child's skin and recognizing something familiar in it.

Sweat. Sun. Sea.

The smell she loved.

"All right. That's enough. Cut it out. Cut it out. Cut! It! Out!" Aman Sinaya finally pulled Marikit away with her strong, brown arms. "Before you go, I need you to remember a few things. One," she said sternly, "do not wander off from the sea. Because beyond the seawalls, the ones I have drawn, are other bodies of water—places I have enchanted, and places I have cursed. If you wander off, even a thread inside these waters, you will be trapped, and you will never escape again, do you understand?"

"Opo, Aman Sinaya," Marikit answered.

CHAPTER 26

THE OCEAN OF SUSPENSION

Tahi. Filipino. n. *Stitch.* The basic form of needlework, which requires a line of thread running in and out of the fabric or a boat's hull—whichever applies.

The goddess's balsa did not look at all magical. It was an ordinary raft, neatly trimmed to a square, with a mast and a flag that bore the emblem of the sea. "Take care of it," said Aman Sinaya, who didn't look like she wanted to part with her property. "No scratches, understood?"

Marikit nodded meekly. "Opo, Aman Sinaya."

The balsa started moving as soon as Marikit stepped on it. At first, she thought it was still Aman Sinaya controlling the balsa, but when she looked down, she saw a set of dugongs pulling the raft forward with their noses. "Bye, Aman Sinaya!" Marikit waved her hands as she went on her way. "And thank you!"

Aman Sinaya sheepishly waved back. The sea bubbled, and the goddess melted down into the water.

Marikit began treading the hundred-mile sea that was sandwiched in between two water walls. The central waters rippled with the luminous kiss of the sun. Schools of rainbow-colored fish shone beneath the surface. As Marikit turned to sit on the raft and gaze into the horizon, she could see the golden line spread from end to end of Aman Sinaya's sea.

The Desert of Malikmata.

Marikit gazed to her left. In that direction lay a tropical vista with thundering waterfalls cascading from the tops of the mountains, with plants teeming with crisp, green hues and birds of various sizes soaring in the open sky. Wild-flowers the size of a human head bloomed with bright colors. The mountain itself sparkled like crystal under the sunrays.

Marikit turned to her right, expecting another magical place, but her joy sank at the view. Blackened cliffs rose tall above the placid waters. Round lights in pale green hung in the air, as if their glow was suspended in a vacuum. Even the birds paused midflight. Nothing seemed to move.

It felt as if she was gazing at a still photograph.

She squinted her eyes and tried to recognize things from afar. In between the sharp rocks and the floating islets were damaged ships, torn bangkas, upside-down vintas, and all kinds of vessels that roamed the seas. Objects floated on the water. There were treasure chests left open, with coins of gold glimmering among the seaweed. Crowns hung on jagged rocks. Floating nearby were books with leather covers, and there were those with illustrated prints, like the ones in Marikit's elementary school.

The raft moved strangely, slowly trailing to the right. When she noticed it, Marikit turned her gaze around and pinned her vision in the other direction.

The raft moved along with her gaze.

"Whoa!" Marikit clapped her hands. When she swung her head to the left, the balsa followed. Then to the right. Then back. The balsa sailed on, the dugongs followed her direction without complaint. And as the balsa treaded circles across the permitted sea, the needle on Marikit's map started moving. She peered toward another direction, this time the frozen sea in black, and the needle pointed somewhere unexpected.

Slowly, unmistakably, it inched toward the east of south. The direction of X.

As if it was saying, *You're almost there!*

She looked on to her right, and the balsa followed her gaze, luring her into the water wall. She was close enough to see that many of the wrecked ships had sailors still in uniform, the little bangkas had men, and there were fishing lines thrown into the waters, held by humans who stood as still as statues. Not everyone wore the same clothes. Some had big, blue trench coats while others were half-naked. Some had big, feathery hats, while others sported floppy fabric caps or straw hats to keep the sun away from their faces.

Someone from the waters spoke. "Oh, I wouldn't go there, if I were you."

Amid the waves, a beautiful face appeared, her body soaked under the salt-sea, her curves shapely, her fins all purple that glistened with jewel colors.

"A sirena!" Marikit gasped.

"Yes, yes, you human-folks have heard a lot about us." The sirena rolled her long-lashed eyes. "But please, try not to stereotype. We *do* love enchanting people to death, except for the ones we fall in love with, but we *don't* love switching our fins for legs, that's rubbish. Oh, hey, you're getting past the line!" The sirena raised her hand as soon as the raft pierced through the watery wall.

It was just a small inch, the rightmost edge of the balsa entering the forbidden realm, and Marikit stopped in time. "Whew," cried the sirena in relief. "You scared me. This place is where Aman Sinaya gathers all the people lost at sea. Not even Anagolay, the goddess of finding things, is allowed here."

"Only at sea?" Marikit prodded.

"All of the waters, of course." The sirena rolled her eyes again. "It's just, you know, the word 'sea' is an umbrella of things. It might be the ocean, the river, the lake, some puddle beside your home. Everything comes down to one basin, a vast, blue place ripe for exploring and exploiting. That's where Aman Sinaya keeps watch and makes sure she punishes all delinquents. Pirates, ship captains, explorers. Oh, and her especial favorites"—the sirena smiled mischievously—"fishermen."

Something switched in Marikit's chest, clicking and waking all at once. Her heart started racing as she gazed at the shadows on the abandoned boats. The balsa inched to where her head turned.

Fishermen.

Never found.

The sea ate them, body and boat.

"Tatay," Marikit murmured. "Kuya Emman."

She held her gaze to her right. The raft followed it.

"Hold it, little girl," said the sirena, tapping the raft from underneath. "Are you volunteering to be trapped? If your body isn't anchored past the waters, you can never get back. Time will freeze you, and it will be worse than death. Some of these men are almost centuries old and their family never found them."

"Never. Found," Marikit repeated. There was that painful tug again, as if an invisible fishing line was pulling her to the forbidden precinct. *The sea ate them, body and boat.* That was all the fishermen could tell them.

Her tatay and kuya Emman were never found. They never returned.

What if they couldn't?

What if they were trapped?

What if they were *here*?

"Fishermen, you say." Marikit's voice quivered. "Do you happen to know where they're from?"

"Oh, they're from all walks of life," the sirena replied. "Fishermen with big boats, fishermen with small boats, fishermen who use dynamites, and fishermen who happened to enter holy waters and sacred reefs, which Aman Sinaya set aside as her sanctuaries. All end up the same, though. In these time-frozen waters where no one can get out."

Marikit lowered her gaze and tried to study the suspended sea by the corners of her eyes. She took note of everything—the shadows of the men, the scattering of treasures, the horrific images of sunken boats, the floating stars, and death. By the waters, she saw the pale reflection of the many strangers' faces. Above, she saw the jagged rocks and the flags waving from the ship sails.

And then, she recognized it.

She wasn't sure about the color, but she was sure about the letter. There was no missing it. There was a skull over a pair of two bones crossed together, forming an X.

The X. Marikit gasped.

The needle has settled close to the direction of the patch, but not completely. Maybe because past this watery gate was her destination. Maybe because she wasn't there *yet*.

Something rose from her chest. Didn't the Infinites mention something about a challenge? To overthrow kings, slay monsters, even compete with gods?

What if, perhaps, hers was to save her missing family?

"My father and brother *could* be there." Marikit pointed to the dreary, abandoned part of the sea. "They were fishermen, lost at sea. We've been looking for them for years, but maybe that's the reason why they were never found. Maybe Aman Sinaya has them!"

"What are you going to do, then?" The sirena played with her hair. "Get stuck with them here forever? Sheesh, humans and your emotions." She rolled her eyes and sank deep under the surface. "Whatever. I have better things to do than warn Halflings who roam in Aman Sinaya's sea. Better not break her trust, child; that goddess is hard to please, and much harder to appease. If you still want to go there, that's your choice. I'm out." The sirena swished her fins underneath the stale, gray water and swam away, leaving only trails of bubbles and Marikit peering into the unknown.

From where she stood, at the crossroads between a free sea and a suspended ocean, she saw the glimmering Desert of Malikmata. "I promise I'll save you." She clenched her fist. "But . . ."

Marikit glanced to her right. "What if they're there? What if saving Tatay and Kuya Emman is what I'm truly here for?"

Without another thought, Marikit made a decision.

The balsa followed Marikit's direction, until the dugongs stopped. The dugongs understood the peril. The dugongs put out their tongues and dived deep into the free sea. "Wait! Don't leave me!" Marikit begged. But the dugongs swam away, and Marikit could only watch from the edge of her balsa.

"How am I going to get there now?" She slumped down, gazing at the cascading water wall that enclosed the dangerous ocean. She was stuck. There was no moving forward. No going back.

"Should I ask for Aman Sinaya's help?" Marikit glanced in the direction of the hut. "But she'd be mad at me if she

knew. She won't help. I don't think anybody would, now."
She bit her lip.

Yet something throbbed angrily on her chest. It pricked, stung, and throbbed, as if it had a heartbeat. Marikit looked down.

It was the needle.

The small piece of metal, shining under the sun, danced and wobbled as if telling her, *Use me.*

I'm here. I've always been here. I never left you.

Marikit touched the needle and found it cold. She plucked it off. A strand of the stitch went with it, glowing under the light with a dazzling pink flame. *Nanay's light-thread.* Marikit pulled and pulled—it stretched longer, loosening the stitches of the first patch and unfastening it from its place.

The black-and-green-striped collar flapped in front of Marikit's face before slipping down onto the floor of Aman Sinaya's boat. The fabric blinked with its stitches, whispering with magic, *Use us.*

"How?"

Make us come alive.

Marikit bent down and placed her palm on the fabric. It was as if she could see it, the way her nanay wove each stitch with her Diwata magic. Strands upon strands upon strands. Sangdaan was right. Each patch was made of hope and light and love.

The collar glowed, quaking and convulsing until each of

the light threads hemmed in it burst out all at once. Ribbons of stalklike threads rose from it, stretching high like clumps of bamboo poles growing in an instant. They bent their bodies toward the vast sea, creating a bridge. It hovered past the boat, past the water wall. When the last thread had seeped out, all that remained of the fabric was a white canvas.

Marikit unwound the pink shimmering threads below her collar. *Everwhere*, she remembered. The thread was thin and strong, like Mayari's hair, like a wire. She slipped its end through the eye of her needle—her once compass—and tied it into a tight knot. "You will be my anchor now," she told it as she stuck the needle on the mast. The needle blinked with its silver light, as if it understood.

Marikit climbed the thread-bridge. It was warm and comforting underneath her, the threads blinking in rosy light as if telling her, *We are here.* As she reached past the bamboo-thread bridge, another patch fell from her dress. She bent down and lent it her magic. In return, it lent her its threads.

Bighari's Garden, the next fabric said, before its strands billowed into thick ribbons, exploding into a rainbow of many colors, flying across the waters. It ended midair, hanging as if it was anchored on invisible pillars. Marikit walked on it until all threads were spent. As the thread of Everywhere loosened on her dress, another patch fell.

Ikapati's Farm. The strands rippled forward, creating a pathway of golden wheat made by strings. Onward Marikit walked, using up all the strands as her makeshift path. Another piece of fabric fell. *The River of Dapithapon.* It swirled across the air like a glistening pool made of satin. *Barrio Bato.* A pathway with threaded knots—and a slab as big as Benny Bato—braided itself for Marikit. *Barrio ng Lagim. The Mountain of Ibalon. The Rainforest of Masigla. The Border. Meadows of Bino Bayabas. Barrio Ordinaryo.*

Marikit walked on a path where there once wasn't one, bringing to life threads of the map her mother wove for her. Patch after patch, Marikit traversed over the waters, across the craggy cliffs, and, finally, into the ship marked with the Big X, blanketed with ashen-colored gloom and the soft glow of the round lights that hung in the air.

She surveyed the ship. There was no sign of life, but there was no death, either—only stillness, only quiet. There was no compass to guide her now; the only direction she'd take was the one of her choosing.

She gazed at the frozen countenances, solemnly lit by the timid glow of the suspended lights. There were sailors and pirates, captains and slaves, small children embraced by mothers enveloped in their saris, travelers crossing seas to get to their refuge. "They're not here," she murmured.

Marikit climbed back onto her bridge and kept walking. She walked until most of her patches flew out of her dress and lent her their strands. She'd know they were spent when they returned to her in a blank white fabric, deprived of their threads and color.

Farther into the Ocean of Suspension she walked, until she knew she was running out of patches.

Deep in the dark navels of Aman Sinaya's sea, where the castaways were garbed in common clothes, was an assembly of fishing boats. As she drew closer, she spotted a

blue-and-white boat, too old and crusty-looking after the many nights it spent venturing at sea. It was marked with the name *The Anita*.

There were only two figures on the boat. One, older, had thinning hair on his head and a panicked look on his face, heaving a net that wouldn't pull out from the waters. The other, younger, was holding a bucket by the side, gazing at his father, holding out his hand as if some calamity has overtaken them. They were frozen. But they were *them*.

She was sure. She would never forget their faces.

"Tatay!" Marikit cried. "Kuya Emman!"

Marikit hung in midair. There was one remaining patch on her dress—the one woven by her knee, the one marked with X. It did not fall out, for when Marikit touched the X, she realized that it was not a patch. It was an embroidery, stitched with the light-threads as if it was the first thing her nanay wove in there.

"Let me down," Marikit insisted, tugging its thread, which was connected to the stitches of Everwhere. "Come on!"

But the X would not budge. The X stayed still.

Marikit pleaded with the threads. "I need to get to them! And I can't go forward without you. Please," she cried. "I need to save them."

Marikit closed her eyes. *Manghahabi*, she whispered, touching the thread with her fingers.

I am a Manghahabi.

She could feel the thread ripple, unleashing its breadth

into a warm, red ribbon, stretching, protruding, answering its master's call. *Manghahabi.* The word rang in Marikit's head, and the mysterious woman's face was slowly getting clearer.

Manghahabi. The bright-red strand blossomed into a cord, a cord she used to move down the bridge. Stitch by stitch, it unraveled, hoisting her down until her feet touched the floor of their boat. Like magic, *The Anita's* dust-blanketed surface started to have color. The color of the sea. The color of the sky.

"I found you." Marikit gazed into Mang Fidel's blank eyes. "I have finally found you both." She cried on his ash-smelling skin. She placed her ear in his heart, recognizing its soft beating. "Finally, I can take you home." Marikit wrapped their frozen bodies with the pulsating red cord from X and gave out a command: "Heave!"

Like a fishing line, the connecting strand reeled them up, light and fire and love blazing through its fibers. Stronger than metal. Stronger than death. She clung to them with her tightest hug, wishing that her warmth would breathe them back to life. But just as they reached the thread-bridge, the suspended ocean started moving.

Swaying.

Swelling.

Giant waves rose and rocked everything in it. The hanging stars began swooping down like falling comets. The boats began quaking, the rocks began cracking as the once-peaceful ocean churned into angry tides.

A shout pierced across the ocean.

"How dare you come in my forbidden waters!" Aman Sinaya screamed from underneath the waters. "You have abused my kindness. You have broken into my sacred precincts!"

"Please, Aman Sinaya!" Marikit cried, holding on to her father and brother as they dangled in midair. "I only wanted to find my family! I just wanted them back!"

But the goddess of the sea would not relent.

The ocean began tipping over like a hammock in the wind. The waves surged so high that the seawater poured on the vessels like rain, spinning smaller boats over as if they were tiny wooden tops. The tides pushed them against the rocks.

"And you dare to even ask anything from me?" Aman Sinaya rose from the waters, her black-blue hair cascading down to her waist. "You, whom I saved? You, whom I lent my balsa?"

"I'm sorry!" Marikit begged tearfully. "I'm sorry, Aman Sinaya! But please, let my family come home!"

"No one leaves without my permission, and I do not permit you," hissed Aman Sinaya, her scaly body collapsing into the water. The ocean turned into a giant whirlpool, a massive black hole that spun the powers of the wind, sucking everything in it. Ships rose from the waters, treasures flew in the air, the faint lights swooped in all directions, and frozen people bounced in midair as if they were light toys.

"Pull!" Marikit told her red thread. It obeyed, zipping up

speedily. Mang Fidel's frozen body landed at the center of the bridge. Emman only reached halfway. "Kuya!" screamed Marikit, running toward her brother, who was slowly slipping down. She caught his hand just in time, his frozen body dangling in the air.

She tied his wrist with a cord, but the bridge itself had begun to droop. The sea-salt storm weakened the strands enough that some of its parts slumped into the water. "Hold on, Kuya Emman!" cried Marikit as his body hung sleepily, his legs dangling close to the rushing waves. She tried to pull him up, but the strands had started to break.

"No!" Marikit groaned, braiding another strand and tying it around her brother's hand. Rain began to trickle, until it grew into a downpour so heavy, Marikit could feel each drop like a punch. Faint lights swung all around. Stars and tears, all raining from the sky.

She gazed out, far into the horizon where her bridge had slumped. It wouldn't take long until her entire bridge fell apart.

"I have no choice," Marikit whimpered tearfully. "This is all I could do!" With all her strength, she pulled her brother up, both of them falling back onto the bridge. She rolled the side of the now-drooping thread-bridge around her father's and brother's bodies, wrapping them like cocoons. "Take them, please!" Marikit sobbed. "Take them out before Aman Sinaya gets them!"

The light-strands—some of them now dead and wet from the water—glowed their remaining light. They heard Marikit. They heeded her call. They spun Mang Fidel and Emman around their bright ribbons, winding back each patch and pattern as they approached the water wall. The colorful ball rolled past Aman Sinaya. "No one defeats me in *my* territory!" she screamed, swinging her giant, watery hands, making sharp waves that cut the rocky cliffs. The boulders fell, aiming to crush the moving cocoon.

"No!" Marikit cried. Using her one last hope, she tugged the long stretch of thread that anchored her into the permitted waters and shouted, "Heave!"

At once, the needle, stuck safely in the balsa's cavity, unlatched itself and began rolling in the air, winding the thread into a giant spool, allowing Marikit to fly past the broken ships and push the ball of fabric out of harm's way. She zapped out of the Ocean of Suspension in a blink, falling straight into the sea.

Marikit opened her eyes to the broken pieces of wood that once were boats. There was no balsa. No Mang Fidel. No Kuya Emman. And before Marikit could gather her wits, a big, watery fist appeared before her, the placid waters boiling. "Get out!" screamed Aman Sinaya, before punching straight into the sea, spewing a tall geyser that shot Marikit straight into the clouds.

CHAPTER 27

X

Langit. Filipino. n. *Heaven.* Home to Bathala, often alluded to as Kaluwalhatian—glory. In many texts, it is depicted as a grand, sprawling palace full of fine things too opulent for the human heart to take in. The naked eye, however, only sees it as big blobs of clouds floating across a blue horizon.

Marikit hung in midair before the rapid fall. *Poof,* she went through the atmosphere, spiraling downward at a breakneck speed. *Poof,* she dropped straight from the heavens, slipping through the cloud-gusts passing by. *Poof,* the sight of the blue sky was replaced by a wide floor of white tiles, glimmering, sparkling, like a winter sea.

Marikit crashed into the cold floor, and pain washed over her in one giant wave. Her body was flung against the wall, her skin shivering. She couldn't move her arms, nor her legs, and in her heart stung a new kind of dread.

It dawned on her slowly, sharply stabbing her like a knife. She had failed her Diwata Journey.

And now, the gods would come for her memory and wipe it clean.

A small and sharp object glimmered on the floor. Marikit saw its metal body glint against the white slab. She reached for it, feeling its sharp tip against her thumb.

It was her needle.

With shaky hands, Marikit picked it up. It was cold against her palm. A while ago, she had felt her powers blossom like fireworks. Now, her hand felt helpless and empty. "You're the only one left," she mumbled, holding the needle close to her, attempting to latch it back on her dress. There were no patches on it now; the last strand of her nanay's rosy threads had evaporated into smoke. All she wore was a flimsy secondhand dress bereft of colors and magic. There was no map. Nothing to tell her where she was or where she would go. Nothing to help her save her tatay or kuya Emman. Nothing to help her return to Ali, Juan, and Saturnina.

She had failed them.

She had failed them all.

Thick clouds passed her by, their shadows blanketing her from the stark white sky. They slid across her face, like giant hands wiping the tears. "Child," came a voice, big and warm and distant. "Why are you crying?"

Marikit looked around. "Who's there?"

There came no answer, only the distant sound of pebbles dropping onto something hard.

"Who's there?" Marikit hoisted her tired body up. "Where are you?"

"I'm here," said the voice.

The layers of puffy, cotton clouds slowly pulled away, allowing Marikit a glimpse of a grand palace whose walls were made of cloud bricks and pearl strings, whose foundations were set by lofty pillars in gleaming, pure white, even brighter than the sun. In its very heart was an ornate door, carved in solid gold, beautifully sculpted with palm leaves and fruit, with the halves of sun and moon, with the stars hanging by its knob.

Marikit limped toward it. "Where?" she asked, motioning.

"Here."

"Where is 'here'?"

"Here, child. Just here."

Marikit groaned. "Here we go again, adults not telling me everything I need to know."

The sky tiles felt like ice cubes against her feet, but Marikit endured it all, dragging her legs as a golden door opened itself and let her in. There were many hallways, many rooms, all covered in spotless white tiles. Some were decked with crystal chandeliers and long, elaborate tables like those in the Harvest House. Some had beds decked with mother-of-pearl posts and gauzy curtains and clam-shaped headboards. Some had big rugs made of woven tapestries. Some had galleries of flowers painted in frames, and some, in quite an astonishing number, if Marikit had kept count, had many, many, many cabinets.

She followed the sound of objects falling. "Here?" she asked, craning her head inside the door.

"Here," he answered.

"I don't know if this is a trick, or you're just really just far." Marikit's voice echoed as she limped across the hallway. "Because *here* is very vague. And I don't like vague things. I don't like things that aren't spoken clearly. Or not at all."

But Marikit kept walking. "I have gotten this far without knowing a lot of things. Only learning. Only walking. Only growing and keeping promises and making friends along the way. I guess many things in life aren't clear. Maybe they don't have answers yet. Maybe the answers are just playing tag with me, like you."

Marikit began ambling along a flight of stairs. It led her up, then down, then spiraled leftways and swirled rightways. She slid, spun, split, then sprinted across the hall until she found, in a solitary room, a glowing, golden light.

The sounds of rolling and falling and clacking became louder. A deep *hmmmm*-ing thundered across the floor. Marikit gently peeped through the wide, arched entry, one embellished with tall palm trees and a tiny fountain rippling over the clear, white floor.

She finally saw who it was.

Snow-white hair hung from his beard. Snow-white hair hung from his mane, which was thick and wavy and covered his broad, bronze-colored shoulders. "Hmm," she heard him murmur. "Here, here."

He was talking to someone who looked just like him—a faux cloud-man with the same snow-white hair, snow-white beard, snow-white clothes, and a dreary face that gloomily gazed at the opposite tray of the sungka. Large cowrie shells rolled on the boat-shaped board as the golden-skinned man counted, "One, two, three, four," putting each cowrie shell in place. He was too busy counting to notice Marikit, who only looked on, taking in his bushy brows, his merry eyes, and lines that crinkled around them as he soberly accounted for his shells.

"Ahem," Marikit began.

"Oh!" The old man staggered, big cowrie shells dropping from his big fingers. Opposite him, the player made out of clouds vanished like powder. He turned around to see Marikit peeking from the entrance. "Why, it's you!" He beamed at her, stretching his arms as if for a big hug, his robe of pure white hanging down like a pair of wings. "You're here! You're finally here! Congratulations!"

Marikit walked inside, feeling a bit shy at the largeness of everything else. "Congratulations for what?"

"Why," the man said with a relish, "you've reached the X!"

"Excuse me?" Marikit stepped back.

"The X!" the man repeated, pointing to the floor.

Marikit looked down. The tile underneath her began forming a large X, in the same shade as the one that used to be embroidered on her dress. It gleamed and glistened, the rosy-red thread shining as if it was made out of real fire.

"This is X? This is where I'm supposed to go?" Marikit couldn't believe her eyes.

"Precisely."

"But, sir." Marikit paused to look at it again. "It's only a floor tile."

"Indeed," laughed the man. "All these tiles, across this room, across the hallways, are someone's X. And that is your X. Your one and only X. And you have done it, child! You have finished your Diwata Journey."

Rainbow-colored confetti fell from the ceiling, covering only her.

Marikit was confused. "I-I'm not really sure I'm in the right place," she began, wiping the confetti off her shoulders.

"Oh, you're in the right place all right. There's no righter place than here."

"What is *here*?" Marikit looked up at him.

The man face-palmed himself. "Ah! How dare I forget!" The man rose like a giant, his white hair shining, his robe dropping below his ankle. He stretched his hands and he glowed a bright light, booming, "This is Kaluwalhatian, home of Bathala, which is"—he winked—"me."

Marikit knew things about Bathala. They sang songs about him at mass. Her tatay would pray to him each morning, lisping hopes for a good catch. The elderly would fold their hands and ask for good health and provision. Everyone in Barrio Magiting would speak of his mercies.

Bathala, the creator. The god of all things.

"*You're* Bathala?" She shuddered.

"In the flesh. Or, should I say, in the spirit." Bathala chuckled. "People get confused, technically, but I'm generally Who I Am, and Who I Am is not just one thing or another, except for Who I Am."

Marikit furrowed her brows.

"Ah, forget it." Bathala waved his hand. "The study of Myself takes a lot of reading rotting scrolls sunk inside centuries-old ships, and none of them even captured my truest essence. Humans love writing books about me, but they'll never really know me unless they meet me. And you just did, so congratulations! Isn't this splendidly exciting?" The god clapped.

Marikit lurched down on her floor tile and stared at the rosy-red X. "But I failed you." She flinched. "I failed *all* of you."

Marikit quivered at the magnificence of Bathala, his snow-white hair looming over her like clouds. "I failed to save my friends. I failed to save my father and brother. I failed to defeat Aman Sinaya, and now they're all gone. They're gone now, Bathala! I won't see them ever again! I've failed!"

Marikit sobbed with all her heart, her cries ringing all throughout Kalwalhatian.

"Oh dear." Bathala brushed Marikit's hair gently with his thumb. "My little lightcloud, you must be mistaken. You didn't fail. You have saved your father and brother. You truly did."

Marikit looked up with disbelief. "I did?"

"Very much so."

The great god breathed into the air, and a cloud formed into a window. In a view of an open sea were Mang Fidel and Emman, riding Aman Sinaya's balsa, rowing with found scraps of wood as they navigated through the calm waters of the sea, bearing the ecstatic faces of two who were going home.

"You set them free, my dear girl!" Bathala's laugh was jolly and warm in Marikit's ears. "The minute Mang Fidel and Emman got out of the Ocean of Suspension, their frozen, suspended hearts began beating again, and they woke up! That blustery Aman Sinaya would never chase after them now. We have signed a treaty to never cause trouble to those who survive our best curse. And those two did, thanks to you!"

A small smile broke through Marikit's face. She could not believe it at first. It was far too much. "Is this a dream?" she mumbled, not taking her eyes off her tatay's brown face, her kuya's warm smile. "Am I dreaming?"

"No, my skychild. You have won the challenge. Just as I have intended you to do from the moment they were lost in Aman Sinaya's sea."

"You *intended* me to save them?" Marikit gaped at Bathala. "You knew I was coming here? Is that why you never heard my prayers?"

Bathala gazed at her affectionately. "I heard them loud and clear, little daisy-dove," he sighed. "I, too, made the sacrifice of holding out and bating my breath for these plans to take place. The waiting is toil in itself. Oh, how I wanted to reveal all these mysteries to take away your pain! But if I did, you wouldn't have grown. It takes patience, see, to wait all across eternity to see a flower bloom. A creator must not force open their creation. I only wait, for in waiting, beautiful things unfold. I could only guide you, direct you, blow the right wind to your sails. And entrust you to friends who would help you along the way."

The sudden, unexpected joy in Marikit's face vanished. She remembered Ali, Juan, and Saturnina. "It would be nice if they were here, to celebrate with me." Marikit hung her head. "I promised to come for them, to save them. But I didn't. Is it always like this, Bathala?" Her mouth fidgeted as she gazed up at the grand god. "Someone gets saved, and someone doesn't?"

"You can save them." Bathala's eyes glimmered. "There are many ways. You can go back and traverse Aman Sinaya's sea . . ."

"I can't do that!" Marikit trembled. "She just threw me up here, and I know she'll crush me if she sees me again!"

"Ah, you're right. That woman is a storm." Bathala frowned. "You can also get lost and let Anagolay find you so she can bring you to the Desert of Malikmata . . ."

"But I just got to my X! I can't get lost now!"

"Then there's one more thing." Bathala looked sideways, sitting on a chair and placing the tips of his fingers together. "A god's kiss."

"How do I get a god's kiss?" Marikit's eyes brightened.

The god of Kaluwalhatian peeped rightways and leftways before looming over Marikit and leaning in for a whisper: "By defeating a god."

CHAPTER 28
SACRED SUNGKA

Sungka. Filipino. n. A game of holes and cowrie shells, requiring two players to beat each other in acquiring most of the shells through tactics and, sometimes, luck. Except when you're a god.

How could one defeat Bathala? Marikit did not know. He towered over her like a three-story building wrapped in a glistening white robe, gold and fire radiant in his fingers. There was no way she could win against him. She could not wrestle with him, run faster than him, or defeat him with her powers. *This is hopeless*, she thought, as she stared below him. "I could never win!"

Maybe she had to go down and apologize to Aman Sinaya. Maybe the goddess would give her another chance.

Maybe she could try getting lost. Maybe Anagolay would find her, but that was if the goddess found herself first.

Or . . .

Marikit saw it from the corners of her eyes. It sat on the table, unmoved, with large shells waiting to be picked up and counted. She knew how to play it. She was itching to compete. The boat-shaped board waited with a half-finished game, tempting her to say the word.

Would she dare?

"I made a promise," Marikit said, exhaling. "And promises we break will break us."

She looked up to Bathala, who gazed down at her expectantly with his big, fiery eyes, and spoke with all her courage: "Bathala, I challenge you to a game of sungka!"

Bathala stared at her with complete surprise. He was not displeased; no, his face broke into a grin as he lurched down to gaze into Marikit's eyes. "In my infinite years of existence—which has no beginning, or end"—the smile on Bathala's face stretched so wide that Marikit could see the golden lines across Bathala's face—"nobody, not even the highest gods in this land, has ever asked to play with me."

His bushy white brows arched as his face brightened with luminous gladness. "Child." Bathala offered his big, bronze hand. "I accept."

Poof! Marikit opened her eyes and found herself sitting on the other side of Bathala's chair. Between them was the pearl-white sungka board. There were sixteen holes in the luminescent board; two rows of seven smaller holes, called houses, were the size of a large well. Each row faced the player, indicating the side of the board. Two larger holes at the ends—the heads—were lodged with almost-crystalline cowrie shells.

"Shall we?" Bathala began picking a batch of the shells with one hand and started filling up the seven houses on his side. The shells produced the familiar rolling drop Marikit had heard when she came in.

Marikit, on the other hand, found trouble in filling up her own houses. Since she was too small, she had to hold each shell with both of her arms as she wobbled to each hole. Bathala was finished in a flash, but Marikit took quite some time.

"Don't worry," Bathala told her. "I have all eternity."

Marikit grumbled. "I don't." She panted back to her base hole until it was emptied. When she was finished, Marikit sat on the edge of the board and surveyed her shells. "Sungka is all about foresight, Marikit," she remembered her kuya Emman teaching her. "You don't just take the shells from a house and start distributing them right away. You want to think about the ending. What do you want to happen? Where do you want to end up?"

"But that's *too much* thinking, Kuya!" Marikit would always complain.

"That's why I always win," Emman would reply with a smile.

Marikit gazed at the shells. Instead of Bathala, she imagined him—her kuya Emman—playing across her, sitting with his shoulders thrown back, his face bereft of any expression.

"Let's begin," Bathala said, picking up a group of shells from his house and dispersing them across the board. When he was done, Marikit stood up and did hers one by one, too.

The two of them took turns. Marikit required more time, more of her strength, more of her patience. Twice, she slipped down the sungka board and accidentally placed a shell in the wrong house. There was no repair to a mistake. Bathala ended up chortling, but Marikit scowled and stomped. "Ah! If only the sungka was the same size as me, I would win!"

"The secret to winning is this," she suddenly remembered her kuya say. "Never, ever think you're about to. Because as long as the game is still on, the other player could snatch an opportunity and end up turning the tables."

"How do I win, then?" Marikit asked.

"Keep on trying your best. Every single chance."

"I will, Kuya." Marikit hoisted herself up the pearl sungka board. It was easy when everything was smaller and she could survey her shells from above. But now, she had to crane her neck, count, walk across the sungka board and back again, all while carrying the giant shells in her arms.

"Ha-ha!" Bathala laughed as Marikit's shell fell on an empty pit, and she missed a turn. "I'm having fun. If you lose, I might assign you here in Kaluwalhatian to play sungka with me forever."

But Marikit did her best. She truly did. She took her turns with prudence. She surveyed each house, counted where the shells would fall, and hoped they would not end in an empty pit again. Alas! It happened again.

Oh, dear, persevering Marikit! The longer she played, the more fear overcame her. She kept making mistakes. She might not be able to keep her promise after all!

"Ali! Juan! Saturnina!" her heart cried.

She was in the middle of a choice, a shell lodged between her arms. Marikit surveyed the board with her doubting, throbbing heart. How could she win against Bathala alone? Her bravery was nothing but folly.

"You can do it, Marikit," she imagined Ali saying as he stood on one of the houses. "You're almost, almost there!"

"People with maps know the way," she imagined Juan saying while smiling at her.

"Sea treader. Shadow conqueror. Aswang vanquisher. What else can you not do?" she imagined Saturnina smiling at her approvingly.

"Just do your best, Marikit! Do your best!" She could hear them cheer for her. "We will be together again!"

"Hmm." Bathala glanced at her as he brushed his beard with his left hand. He picked a trio of cowrie shells and began distributing them. The shell landed on an empty hole in front of an empty row.

Marikit took heart.

There were four cowrie shells in one of her seven holes, opposite a handful of cowrie shells in Bathala's row. She had to count correctly. "One," she tearfully murmured, carrying the shell. "Two." *But what if I miscount again?* "Three." Her legs started shaking as she placed the shell on its hole. "Four," she whispered, carrying the shell near to her chest as if it was her entire world, and her heart almost made a jolt out of her chest when she saw the hole across her.

There were seven glimmering cowrie shells in that hole.

Tears started streaming down Marikit's cheeks as she took them one by one to her head base. When everything was over, she just sat there and cried, her knees still weak from all the running. "The game is not over, little one," Bathala reminded her, pointing at the few remaining shells. Marikit stood up, ready for everything to be over.

When the last of the shells were acquired, both players started counting their pieces. This was it. In a short while, they would know the winner.

Bathala picked up a shell, and so did she. It was an exhausting chore—Marikit's arms were tired and shaking as she picked up each of her cowrie shells. *One, two, three, four*—slowly, she removed the shells from her heap as Bathala did with his. *Five, six, seven, eight*—her heart was racing fast, holding out an image of her friends together again. *Nine, ten, eleven, twelve . . .* That hope started to droop. Bathala's mountain of shells seemed to be larger than hers.

Marikit looked at her remaining cowrie shells and sighed. *Twenty-one, twenty-two, twenty-three.* Bathala picked up a shell before tossing it into his heap. *Twenty-four, twenty-five, twenty-six, twenty-seven . . .*

She did the same, only slowly, dragging out the result of the game. *Thirty-one, thirty-two, thirty-three . . . thirty-four, thirty-five, thirty-six . . .*

"Kuya," Marikit started to whimper as she carried the next shells. *Forty-one, forty-two, forty-three . . .* Tears began dropping from her cheeks as she slowly went back and forth, her hands weary, her feet shaking. *Forty-five, forty-six, forty-seven . . .*

"Forty-eight," counted Bathala, showing her the glistening shell.

"Forty-eight," she repeated, picking up her piece. She then returned to her post and waited, watching Bathala's mouth, waiting for him to speak the next number . . .

He didn't.

When Marikit looked at the other large hole of the sungka, it was empty.

Hers wasn't.

"F-forty-nine," she nervously declared, her body shaking in disbelief as she gazed at one more glistening shell in her side's head. Then, everything sank in. "Fifty!" she declared, hugging the shell with tears in her eyes, repeating the number with a joyful exclaim. She did not let go of it, but she sat down, still quivering with immense gratitude, shouting, "Fifty!"

Bathala's face eased. He stretched out his hand, muttering, "Congratulations, Marikit! You have won this game, and I will grant your wish."

CHAPTER 29
THROUGH KALUWALHATIAN'S WINDOW

Bintana. Filipino. n. *Window.* An aperture in the wall covered by glass or without, where one can gaze into the world, or fly out.

Bathala folded the sleeves of his long, weighty white robe, the golden bracelets on his wrists twinkling as he stretched out his arm. It went longer and longer until it passed through the window, piercing through the clouds like a lengthy pole. A god's arm, it turned out, was quite stretchable. "Ali the Alitaptap," Bathala murmured, closing one of his eyes. "Juan Tamad. Ooh, here she is. Saturnina Panopio." He took his time before his arm slowly shrunk back in place, until the sleeves of his thick cloud-robes fell perfectly down his wrists. There was a trail of gold and sand swirling on the white floor, and when he opened his hand, Marikit could see three dust-covered children sleeping in his palm.

Marikit almost burst into tears when she saw them, but instead, she laughed. How comical! Juan lay flat with his arms stretched out, snoring loudly with an open mouth, sand and dust covering his face like a mask. Ali slept comfortably on his side, his body bundled with a blanket of fire-leaves that kept swaying as if he was a shrub. Saturnina rested like an angel, her head cushioned by her father's marble hand as if he had tried to make her comfortable even at the last minute.

They all looked like flour-covered espasol, except that the flour was bright, powdery yellow.

"Ali! Juan! Saturnina!" Marikit shrieked, clasping her hands. Her friends began to stir.

Juan roused first. He stretched his arms, the debris of the desert falling off him like fine powder. "Oh." He sat up promptly, blinking and scratching his eyes. "It's you, Marikit." He staggered before noticing the fluff of white hovering above him. He looked up. "Holy father of gods!"

Ali immediately sprang up and rolled his hands into fists. "What? Who? Where?" His god-ink shone in bright-yellow. Juan only pointed up. "Merciful Bathala!" Ali bent his knees.

"Bathala?" Saturnina finally opened her eyes. She brushed her silky black hair with the marble hand before her skin began breaking out with fire. "Oh my god." She gaped up.

"Rise, children. Rise," laughed Bathala gently, blowing

off the fire on Saturnina's skin. All three sprang to their feet. "Come. Your friend has been longing to see you."

The great god tilted his palm and gently put Ali, Juan, and Saturnina down on the white floor. Marikit didn't wait. She ran to them with her hands open and embraced them as tightly as she could. "I'm so happy! So, so happy! I thought I'd never see you!"

"Well, maybe not if we die from being strangled!" Juan coughed and began inhaling some of the sand right through his nose. He stepped back to survey Marikit, and then mumbled, cupping his chin, "Wait a minute. Something's . . . not there?"

All three gaped at Marikit. They turned her around, sniffed at her hair, then saw her dress. "Where are all the patches?" asked Saturnina.

"A lot of things happened after the hurricane," answered Marikit.

"How much?" muttered Ali.

"Enough for me to reach the X!" Marikit pointed to her tile.

Ali, Juan, and Saturnina slowly craned their necks down. "*That?*" they asked Marikit. "That's the X?"

"Yes."

"You're not joking? The X is a tile?"

"Most positively, and very strangely yes!"

Ali, Juan, and Saturnina gawked at each other. They

blinked, they shrugged, they erupted with screams like fireworks as they threw their hands at Marikit. The hall of Kaluwalhatian was filled with jumping and shrieking as they resounded in chorus. "Oh, you did it! You did it, Marikit!"

Joy gurgled in Marikit's chest. Not the sharp, proud, blistering kind. It was mellow, like the soft waves of the sea, rippling and lapping over and over with the tides of gratitude. "I couldn't have done it without all of you," Marikit confessed.

"Even though we were asleep on that last bit?" Saturnina asked.

"You were always on my mind," she said, a bit teary. "I wanted to go back to you. I wanted to keep my promise!"

Oh, there were so many words she wanted to say! Words upon words upon words. But this time, all she could do was beam with her widest, most wholehearted smile. Her Diwata Journey was over. Her family was saved. Her friends were here. How could she ask for anything else?

She was scanning their faces—faces she had thought she'd never see again—when Bathala drew his breath. The room blustered with a shimmer of clouds, and suddenly, Ali, Juan, and Saturnina floated in the air, their bodies soaring into the white-walled room.

"What's happening?" Juan cried as he flapped his arms.

"We can fly?" asked Ali.

"Oh, my dear children, I have a plan, see." Bathala twirled

his fingers, and the children gently rolled in the air. "Plans for each of you. Lives mapped out to intertwine in many different paths, in many different seasons. Trust me when I say that you will all meet again. As for now"—he drew the three children back to his palms—"I am afraid that you need go your ways."

"But we just got together!" Marikit cried.

"Separation, too, is a sacrifice. And one you must make," insisted Bathala, his golden eyes gleaming. "You, my heaven-hope, have found where you are supposed to go. But your friends, too, must discover their places in the world. I will, however, let you say your goodbyes properly, for so shall I."

The god of creation lifted Juan. "Juan Tamad." He poked the boy with his big finger. "You have survived the curse from your slovenly ways. And now your freedom is your reward. Set your mind to do great things, for there is a mountain of wisdom in it. In your journey, may you find the joy of working with your hands."

Bathala breathed in him, and Juan began swishing across the hall. "Whoa." He wiggled like a worm, making Marikit, Ali, and Saturnina laugh. "I'm flying, you guys! I'm flying!"

"Like an ugly caterpillar with wings," remarked Saturnina.

"Let's see you do this," grumbled Juan.

"How fun it seems!" Ali gasped, watching Juan approach the window.

It was then when Marikit knew that their separation was set. That in the length of the many whences, they may not see each other again. She sprinted after Juan, shouting, "You are the laziest, most honorable boy I've ever known. I hope that when we see each other again, you won't be sleeping under a tree!"

"Ha-ha," laughed Juan before flipping backward as he headed toward the white, arched window. "Goodbye! Goodbye, all! And thank you!" He tumbled as the wind turned him about, and the rest of the children laughed as he slipped through the window.

"Now you, Saturnina." Bathala picked her up, flicking away the marble hands that grappled her shoulder. "Doors are not the only prison, my dear girl. In many ways, you will carve your path, just as you caved those tunnels. Here is a chance to be healed from what kept you in. Make peace with the fire on your skin."

"Yes, Bathala." Saturnina gently nodded.

The god breathed and stretched his hand, allowing her to gently fly toward the sunlit arch. "I had only wished to leave my room, but now I am flying across Kaluwalhatian! Farewell, Marikit!" Saturnina blew a kiss. "And see you again!"

"Goodbye!" Marikit chased after her. "Take care! And please remember, traveling by Apolaki is hot and dreadful!"

"What do you mean?" Saturnina turned around.

Marikit smiled. "You'll learn things along the way!"

Saturnina drifted out of the window, her long, black hair trailing after her like the evening River of Dapithapon.

And then, there was one.

The fire Diwata floated on Bathala's palm like a young, noble knight, and the god beamed at him with pride. "You woke up too early from your ripening, my lad," spoke Bathala. "So early it deprived you of your full, adult Diwata body. But trust that nothing is too early or too late. Let your youth not be a hindrance to showing others how bright you can shine."

The god glanced sideways and cleared his throat. "You must know, the breaking of the Impossible Bottle is a breaking of law—one I will not take lightly—but you will learn. And you will grow."

Ali only bowed meekly. "I understand, Your Highness."

"Then go." Bathala exhaled a gentle breath, and Ali spread out his arms as he began to drift in the air. Orange-leaved shrubs sprung around Ali's soles and fingers, as if shielding him from the frosty clouds.

Slowly, he made his way toward Marikit. Slowly, Marikit made her way toward him.

She gazed at his face, trying to remember it all. How different he looked! "You were a tiny ball of light when we first met," she told him from below. "And now you have a body! Eat as many foods as you like. Just not too much, or you'll get constipated. And you can finally run—just be careful not to trip or tumble like me."

She strode as he drifted in the wind, faster and faster like a heartbeat. "I'm so, so grateful that you greeted me in that forest and went with me through that door. I'll miss you. All of you." She pursed her lips. "I will always think of you. And I will always be glad."

"So will I."

Ali reached out his hand, and Marikit hers. And as his inked fingers touched her hand, a tiny vine sprouted from the gaps between her fingers, coiling into a ring. It shone in golden amber—the color of Ali's light, the color of joy. Ali flew out the window, turning around to wave his hand. "Goodbye, Marikit! Goodbye! Infinity is a long, meandering thing. I will see you! I surely shall!"

"Goodbye, Ali!" Marikit waved back. "Until then! Until, hopefully, soon, then!"

She stood there, her fingers on her small flower ring,

her eyes following her friends. Surely, she would always remember him in every yellow, in every glow.

Surely, she would remember them all!

She watched her friends slowly disappear into the clouds, shrinking like dots in the blue sky, until they were gone. "How I'll miss them!" Marikit sighed and sighed, wiping the mild drips of tears that escaped from her eyes. She stayed there for as long as she could, until Bathala loomed behind her and gaped down with his big, fiery eyes.

"My canary-cot," he finally said. "It's time for you to be a Diwata."

CHAPTER 30

A CONTRACT FOR
A DIWATA

Pirma. Filipino. n. *Signature.* Handwriting indicating one's
name in letters or code, usually as proof of one's ownership,
or done in an act of being in accord to a certain rule.

The Diwata Journey"—Bathala went inside his room and
opened one of the drawers on his large marble desk—
"is not as complicated as it seems." He opened another,
scanned it with his eyes, and left it open. "All you have to do
is reach the X"—another drawer was opened—"sign an Oath
right on your birthday"—he opened another—"and *ta-daa!*"
A glittering white cloud puffed out of his fingers. "You are a
Diwata!"

All the drawers shut by themselves as Bathala moved
along.

"But, Bathala." Marikit followed as he flitted into the

next room. "I've been here for days. Many, many days. I've been walking for *so* long, I forgot the time!"

Bathala froze by the hallway and gawked at Marikit with surprise. "Has anyone never told you? Time works differently in the Land of the Engkantos," he began. "Why, hours in some lands will only take a few mortal minutes. That is, of course, unless you got into the cursed lands. Those take *centuries.*"

"It's still my birthday?"

"Absolutely right, darling child."

Bathala moved to another drawer and blushed sheepishly as Marikit trailed after him. "Of course, there are some setbacks when it comes to time. Like me. If you are several-infinities-old and have been busy keeping the world in order, you start misplacing things."

"What are you looking for?" Marikit stood on her tiptoes to get a view of the drawers, but Bathala was so big, and the drawers closed themselves in so quick of a blink that she hardly caught any glimpse.

"Well, child. To sign something, you need a pen."

Bathala kept searching, darting across the hall and pulling drawers open. There were many drawers in the room. And there were many rooms, each of them bright and sparkling and immaculate, the floors a spread of perfectly white tiles. But in some rooms, Marikit noticed as they went about, a few of the floor tiles were discolored—pale grays and rotting browns and rusty beiges, like her old, yellow dress.

A few of them had blackened completely, looking like lost teeth.

"Be careful of them, little one," warned Bathala as he trod across the white tiles. "They are void. There's no knowing where you'd land if you fall on them. I haven't replaced them yet, for I haven't had the heart to do so. A creator"—his voice slowly dwindled with unspeakable sadness—"cannot just erase a creation."

Marikit surveyed the many checkered tiles across the room, grays of different gradients, drumming with their darkness. One of the gray tiles began to dwindle, darkening and darkening before it thoroughly disappeared into a complete black.

"Why, it vanished!" she gasped, now seeing a whirling hole of the void. "Bathala, the tile has vanished!"

"And so it has." The god looked down. "How terrible."

"Why is it so?"

Bathala lurched down with a face of grief. "Do you remember how it feels when someone breaks their promise?"

Marikit nodded. *Ah, of course!* "It was saddening and disappointing and angering at the same time, like I was let down!"

"Let down, yes," agreed the god. "A stinging void, slowly replacing the colors of your heart into a new kind of emptiness. A wound that can never heal." Bathala's hand lingered on the vanishing tile as if he wanted to bring it back but couldn't.

"A wound?"

Oh. This was what Marikit had been seeing. A wound. In Kaluwalhatian. In heaven's most perfect palace.

Bathala let out a deep sigh before continuing his search, racking all the drawers and digging his great hands into them. Marikit was watching the next tiles blink when she heard a loud, thunderous shriek.

"I found it!" The shout filled the entire halls. "I found it! The Pen of Principles!"

"The pen of *what*?" Marikit staggered.

Bathala showed Marikit the crystal nib in his hand. "The Pen of Principles! The pen that signs all promises. It's made from Oaths-ink and rememberhymes, quite steady on the hand, too," Bathala made his pen shrink so that Marikit could hold it. "I liked my first pen better, but someone stole it and used it to rewrite laws. Now, the manufacturers have limited my supply and will not give me a new one." Bathala didn't look too happy about it. "Shall we begin? Back to your tile, please."

Bathala blew his cold breath on Marikit, and in a flash, she was back on her X.

She stood on it with the pen in her hand. Strangely, the tile began beating. Throbbing. Drumming, like a heartbeat. It seemed to call her with a name different from what she had. Yet strangely, she knew it was her.

And then, an image flashed in her head.

First, it was light, then it was dark, then it was threads. It was black hair dancing in the wind, and then, it was a loom, in the hands of a Diwata with brown outstretched arms, pulling the light of the sun with her nimble, inked fingers. The light became threads, and she wove them in her loom, bright and yellow and fiery. She wore a sash of gold, a woven tunic of many colors of red. Beads of many colors drizzled down her ears like rain. Around her forehead was a crown of gems. Her blouse glimmered with many woven patterns—threads of light, threads of life. Down her waist was a tapis that reflected the warm light of the sun. Her soles were bare. Her ankles were marked with ink.

The Diwata had curious black eyes and thick brows, lips that always furrowed and didn't know how to smile. She had the familiar listless expression of one who gave herself to her work, of one who stared beyond the threads and saw the possibilities it could become.

The Diwata looked just like her.

When the dream ended, when the flashing stopped, Marikit gazed into the white for a long, long time. "Bathala," she finally muttered. "I think I saw my future."

"Future?" Bathala lurched down and placed his warm

hand on Marikit's head. "Oh, child. Your future is not made yet. What you saw, my dear, was the past."

Past? Marikit narrowed her eyes. "How could I see the past?"

The god propped himself on the floor and let his white robes cascade on the tiles. "I shall tell you a story about a Diwata I knew." He touched her snub nose. "Now you must pay attention." He smiled at Marikit, lightly tapping her head. "What you will hear is a firsthand account."

He brushed his snow-white hair as he began with his big, deep voice. "Once upon a time, there was a beautiful Diwata from the Branch of the Manghahabi. She could sew sunsets and daydreams in light-breaths and sun-gold. She was an Infinite who broke out from a blue-green-colored bamboo shell with silvery-green leaves that grew in the Hills of Hiwaga. She was the brightest of them all, a Diwata whose loom gods sought in order to shield themselves from the fangs of the Bakunawa and the harsh kiss of Aman Sinaya's sea. She had no voice, but she spoke brilliantly with threads, so I told her to share her knowledge into the world. I opened a Door That Wasn't There, and she walked out, clothed in human skin and a little white dress, the first of her creation, bringing all her magical talents that oozed out of her fingers. But"—Bathala glanced away with sorrow—"mankind took all of her. And mankind has become her. When she was to return at an appointed day and time, the door was left open, and she did not appear. She had chosen to live with the mortals. And so, this Diwata broke the Bound Clause and allowed the kiss of our lands to fade from her skin. She broke her Oath and fled away from us, her world, her home. This broken Oath continues to bring me pain."

Bathala pointed to the tile on which Marikit stood. It had stopped throbbing, stopped flashing red. It had calmed down to its original color, and it was only then that Marikit noticed.

Her tile looked different. It was chipped to the edges and was slightly yellow. Yellow, like Marikit's old, discolored dress.

The god stooped down and touched the tile. It turned into a scroll. An old, brown parchment torn and crumbling.

"Broken Oaths rot and wither, see." Bathala's voice was morose. "Broken Oaths make the tiles disappear, make the foundations of Kaluwalhatian weak. They are a taint in the eyes, a pain in my soul."

The god sighed deeply. "I do not force hearts," he continued. "I do not bend wills. What Anita did was Direct Disobedience, but do I stop love? No. Love is Who I Am, and so I relented." He paused to smooth his tunic, which flowed over his crisscrossed knees. "But rules are rules. Disobedience means punishment. And that means becoming a Diwanlaon."

Diwanlaon, Marikit recalled in her head.

A Diwata-before.

"Diwatas who forgot their land never came back to it again. And so, I wrote a rule. A rule that would allow my Infinite breath to persist. To remake itself across time. A Banyuhay. That is the Diwanlaon." Bathala gently glanced at Marikit. "The taking of all the magic, of all the Infinite breath, and the perishing of a Diwata's former skin, so it could pass on to a clean slate. Another beginning, where their past sin is forgiven and forgotten."

There was a feeling in Marikit's chest, like a small, stinging throb. She didn't like it. Not at all. Most especially when she read a name on the scroll, and it was not hers.

It was written in script, in faded gray ink . . .

I, Anita Justo, a Diwata of the Manghahabi Branch, born June 21, day of the Thur, 2nd hour of the afternoon, 25th blink, sign this Oath to Bathala and the High Council of Kaluwalhatian, to which I abandon all other lives to live with the Engkantos in any Engkanto land of my choosing, to be mentored according to my Branch, and fulfill my duties as a citizen and subject of Kaluwalhatian.

Marikit only realized it when Bathala pointed at her.

"You, child, are that Diwata's Banyuhay. Her Infinite's new life."

Marikit remembered a story her tatay told about her nanay. That on the night she was born, her nanay almost lost her life. For many hours, Aling Anita lay still, cold and unbreathing, eyes closed—eyes that may have never opened again. Mang Fidel and Emman cried that night, both of them kneeling on the floor and asking, with loud voices, "Bathala, save her! Save her, Bathala!"

Marikit imagined the sound of it in her head, as if she was there, awake and listening. It was as if she remembered. It was as if the pain and sorrow were part of her memories.

Diwata.

Child of a Diwanlaon.

She remembered Sangdaan's face. She remembered how he said, "Condolences."

Is it because Nanay is not meant to survive?

"I was there, in that tiny midwife clinic where Anita struggled in pain," said Bathala. "You came out into the world on a June twenty-first, a Thursday, the second hour of the afternoon, the twenty-fifth blink, in the same way Anita was born. You were a small and bubbly child of seven pounds, of the brightest laughs. I bated my breath for a new beginning. It was expected. It was the rule. A rule among many rules. But, when you were born, something happened."

Bathala lifted Marikit's chin with his finger. "All Diwatas accept their fate, but when the life surging in Anita's veins was to be cut short, when her breath was about to be snipped off, a force more powerful than her Infiniteness bloomed. A force so strange and strong that she fought and wove back all that she could muster—the residue of her magic, the fragments of her memories—because of one thing. Do you know what it was?"

Marikit gaped at Bathala with now-teary eyes and shook her head.

"She heard you cry." Bathala smiled. "And when she did, she said, 'This child is her own life. *My* child, not my Infiniteness. A child who will face the world with her own wonder, with her own heart. So, I am going to live one more day. I have sewn for kings and heroes, and I will gift her nothing but the work of my hands. Clothes that won't tatter. Clothes that will keep her warm. Clothes that will make her safe from harm.'"

Bathala gazed at Marikit with affection. "That was her thought, day after day. To weave for you until you could walk and run and be out in the sun. And she lived, long enough to get you here, to have all the power and wonder and beauty she turned her back from. To help you on your way, so you could return home. Now, here you are, Marikit."

Across the air, the Pen of Principles drifted toward her. "This is the final step to the Banyuhay. An Oath. An Oath you make to me," spoke Bathala. "Write your name on the scroll, Marikit. Your name to replace the old. When it is done, there will be a new scroll. A new tile. And you will have the power of your Infinite in its entirety. You will be the Diwata I purposed you to be. All the power. All the wonder. All the beauty. *All this.*"

All the power. All the wonder. All the beauty, Marikit repeated in her head.

She would never have to wear old clothes again. She would never be poor. She could choose to not live in that wooden brown house and roam these magical lands without limitations. She wouldn't have to be afraid of any Nightmares or Shadows. She would ward them off.

She'd be Diwata.

A Diwata.

Child of a Diwanlaon.

Child.

My child.

Marikit flinched. "And then what will happen to Nanay, Bathala?"

Bathala had done this before. This was not the first Halfling to reach the X. He had watched his breaths come and go, leave and stay. And each time, he tenderly told them the truth. "Once you have fully written your name, once a new Oath has been established, the person that used to be there will disappear. In ink." Here he paused for a while, as if to calm the slight of pain that he himself felt. "And in life."

"No!" Marikit cried. "This can't be!"

"This is the rule, cloud-child. This is the sacrifice that must be made."

Marikit knew it. She had felt it in her heart of hearts.

The way Aling Anita said goodbye spoke so much of the sorrow about to come. *I was ready,* Marikit remembered her nanay saying. *Ready from the time I birthed you. Oh, all that I have given to be with you! Ten years was splendid. I wish there could be more. But there were ten years. I will always think of you.*

Always.

"But I want to go home." The weight of sorrow hit Marikit. "I want to see her again. I want to hug her and tell her I missed her, and that I'm sorry for all the things I said to her. I want to sit beside her and eat beside her and wrap my arms around her when we sleep in the cold banig. Oh, Bathala! I don't want my nanay to die! I don't think I'll ever want to be a Diwata if she would be gone!"

The god slouched down and met Marikit's mournful gaze. "It is the only way, child." He placed his hand on the rotting tile. "A broken Oath will continue to rot. It will wither until there is nothing but a dark, empty hole. A hole that will impair Kaluwalhatian. I cannot fathom the pain of removing my own breath from existence. Yet if you will not mend this, there is only death for you, too. A black void. Forgotten, unforgiven."

Marikit clutched the pen tightly, as if her little hand could break it.

She hung her head and gazed at the rotten, yellow tile blinking underneath her. There was an emptiness to that tile. Sorrow upon sorrow piling up into the void. "I don't want you to disappear, like all the other tiles. I don't want to break a promise. I don't. But . . ."

But Nanay.

I have to mend this, Marikit told herself. *I'm the only one who can. But how? How can I mend this?*

Mend.

Rat-tat-tat-tat-tat, resounded the sewing machine in her head. *Rat-tat-tat-tat-tat.* She could hear it. Aling Anita pressing the big metal pedal with her two feet. Callused hands pulling the balance wheel, sewing and seaming and stitching things together. All the broken and torn parts, made whole with patches and scrap fabrics. All connected with neat trims and stitches. All bound together.

All made whole.

Marikit could feel something spinning. Tickling. Turning and whirring. She felt it with her hands. The pointed edge pricked her finger.

She opened her eyes.

It was the needle. Her needle.

Diwata.

Child of a Diwanlaon.

A Manghahabi.

"Mend," Marikit muttered, pulling the needle off her dress. Gone were the patches. The patches that were woven with all of her nanay's powers. There was nothing but an off-white tattered canvas and small drops of red that came from her wound, slowly trickling down in long, thin drops.

Like a thread.

She recalled Sangdaan's words. *Magic has to be manifested through something. A medium. A channel. If not, it'll just dissipate in the air and vanish like dust.*

Diwata.

Child of a Diwanlaon.

A Manghahabi.

Marikit looked at Bathala and said behind her teeth, "I will mend it. I will mend it for me and my nanay. I will write you an Oath."

Her thumb on her bleeding finger, she began pulling. The end of her finger started sparking like fire. It hurt, like skin being pulled. *Sacrifice.* Marikit closed her eyes. *As Nanay has made so many sacrifices for me.*

And now, it's my turn.

Marikit screamed and pulled. From her finger, a thread as red as scarlet stretched. She stretched and stretched, with tears in her eyes and a shout behind her teeth. "I am a Diwata!" she hissed. "Child of a Diwanlaon. A Manghahabi!"

Pull she did, her finger shaking, the rest of her hand sparkling like tiny firecrackers. With her trembling left, she finally put the ends into the eye of the needle, and she began sewing.

Right into the scroll.

With her scarlet thread.

All the broken things. All the crumbling things. She sewed them all with clean stitches like her nanay taught her. And when all parts were mended, from the peeling tip to the brittle edges, Marikit tied the final knot and cut the thread with her teeth.

And with the pen, she wrote, *Anita.*

And Marikit, she scribbled second.

She opened her eyes, and she heard a laugh.

CHAPTER 31

THE WAY BACK HOME

Tahanan. Filipino. n. *Home.* The place where one is surrounded by the people they love, not minding if it is within the security of concrete walls or flimsy wooden dividers.

The laugh echoed across Kaluwalhatian, across its cold, white hallways; across its splendorous rooms and lofty ceilings, across the many tiles that bore Infinite breaths. "Ha-ha-ha!" came the laugh from the depths of Bathala's throat—merry, hearty, twinkling with such bursts of brightness that Marikit was quite sure an Infinite must be born in Luntian Forest. "Look at what you've done!" the god exclaimed with pure astonishment. "You wonderful, wonderful child!"

Marikit stood on a tile that sparkled in pure, spotless white—one without yellow stains or chipped edges or impurities. The X throbbed with a dazzling red light as the scroll in her hand began to illuminate with a golden glow. And when all the shining and gleaming had stopped, she saw her scroll mended in all corners, each crack, each tear beautifully connected with bright red stitches, and on the middle of the parchment was her name.

Marikit.

And her nanay's.

Anita.

Diwata.

Child of a Diwanlaon.

It was finally over.

Her needle dropped to the ground. Marikit wobbled back, the smart pain in her finger stinging all across her arm. "It's love, isn't it?" Bathala's face eased. "Love mends all things. Love never fails." He stretched out his hand, muttering, "Congratulations. Oh, my cloud-child, you will never become your full Infiniteness now that you share a life with your mother. But I think you have found something greater than any power, any wonder, any beauty could ever give."

The great god took the Pen of Principles and drew a door in the air. It opened onto a mesmerizing view of chocolate-brown hills under an eternal sunset. "Up there, in the Mountains of Marilag, are the rest of the Manghahabi, waiting for you," Bathala said. "They will show you how to harness your power, teach you how to weave the strings of the sun, help you create the dreamy blue dress you so desire."

A blue dress formed from Bathala's clouds, with a billowing skirt made of layers of chiffon, creating gradients of blue and silver, shining against the silk band. The bodice glimmered with faint rainbow colors like Aman Sinaya's scales, and the sleeves fluttered like butterfly wings, waiting for her to put it on.

"My dress," Marikit mumbled. "My birthday dress!"

"That, and many more dresses, should you choose to stay." Bathala pressed on, "You will have more adventures. Discover new places. And meet friends, old and new."

"My friends!" Small, warm tears flooded Marikit's eyes. Even now, she could still feel the fascinating sensation of walking through the enchanted lands—the glow of firefly wings fluttering around her, the spread of long fields over the blue sky, a Tikbalang inhaling the smoke of tobacco, a long evening river teeming with life, gurgling lava spouting over the caldera, birds chirping inside a dense rainforest, a single tree in the spread of grass, the crashing waves of the angry sea.

But she glanced at her flimsy, tattered camisole, its patches empty, but not her heart. Oh, there was something more filling than the magic the Engkantos could give. "I have finished my journey, Bathala," she answered, her eyes full of conviction. "I am ready to go home."

Bathala lovingly gazed at Marikit, his cheeks round

and merry as he smiled. "I knew for sure what you wanted, but I could only try to persuade you, little daisy-dove. The choice is yours. You shall return here when you find a Door That Wasn't There. For now"—the god kissed Marikit's forehead—"home, you shall go."

Bathala blew his cloudy breath, and at once, all the white from Kaluwalhatian transformed into the dusty vista of Barrio Magiting. Gone were the giant pillars; what she saw now was just the vision of the tall mango trees all ripe with yellow fruit, lining the yard of their neighbor. Gone were the grand halls, the flamboyant mansions, leaving only the rundown bungalows with weathered walls and broken windows and wooden fences. There were no shiny gems, just rocks and pebbles children used as markers for hopscotch. No enchanted people, no Tikbalangs or Principalias, only the barrio-folk in their sandos, shorts, and dusters, fanning themselves as they walked under the sun.

Marikit stood in the middle of the road, surrounded by the noise of Sampaguita Street in all its familiar glory—the mothers gossiping, the stray dogs barking, the stray cats whining, the children sprinting away from the bamboo groves, and an elderly man shouting after them, "You've been warned! Engkantos lurk there!"

Marikit giggled. *Oh, yes, they do!*

When she looked down, she saw her patchwork dress, as if Kaluwalhatian's clouds had magically pulled each piece and stitched them back together. Her dirty feet were cradled by her old rubber slippers, shabby and almost out of shape. But they beamed at her from below, telling her that they had brought her from the journey far and now, they were home.

"Marikit!" the sun-drenched children called to her, pausing from their game. "Isn't today your birthday?"

"Oh, it *is*." Marikit looked back.

"So, where is it? Your dress? The dress that looks like a Diwata's?"

Marikit surveyed the many eyes that now gawked at her. Then, she glanced at her dress. She could still see it—the wild prints, the uneven cuts, the bright pink stitches that connected every patch. It was not anywhere close to the blue dress she told them about.

But she was not the girl from the day before. There was a shift in her ribs, like a new heart had been placed there. Marikit clutched her dress and surveyed it with loving eyes, understanding that each stitch, each patch, was made for a purpose.

"It's *this* dress." Marikit pointed.

The children took a moment before breaking into laughter. "That dress? That dress that looks like a rag?"

"Where's your blue birthday dress? The dress that would

make you look like a Diwata?" a girl whose mouth was occupied with a lollipop asked.

"Yeah, the dress like Jana Solomon's!"

"My birthday dress is this dress," Marikit insisted. "And I like it. It's strange, but it's practical, has nice pockets, and most importantly"—she twirled around and showed them every patch, every stitch—"my nanay made this for me. Now, if you'll excuse me, I need to get home."

She sprinted away, her slippers skidding against the unpaved ground, her untamed hair flying in the wind.

Marikit's home, the quietest house in Sampaguita Street, was still. There was no winding and spinning of the sewing machine from their wide-open window. No pair of eyes peeking from below the sill. Aling Anita, instead, sat by the doorway, the last of the day's sun shining on her head, her face buried inside her hands now wet with tears. "Isn't it your birthday?" her neighbors said. "Why won't you celebrate?"

Ah, but there was nothing to celebrate, Aling Anita wanted to answer. They did not know of her pain. They did not know of her sacrifice.

What she did not know, however, was that her gift was to come soon: a girl stepped into their flower-gilded entry, shouting with all her heart, "Nanay!"

Aling Anita looked up. *I must be dreaming*, she thought.

This must be a dream. But when Marikit ran to her and clung to her neck with her warm, magic-wounded hand, *ah*, Aling Anita's heart was awash with the brightest joy. *This is not a dream.*

Marikit clung to her nanay and gestured with her hands, words upon words upon words. *Salamat, Nanay, for everything you've done.* And love wrapped them, like the soothing touch of the sun after a rain or the first kiss of water in the heat of summer. It did not end there, for two familiar faces appeared by the street, two familiar voices called out their names. Mang Fidel and Emman arrived home with their sea-drenched clothes, taking both mother and daughter inside their sun-soaked arms in yearned-for joy.

That afternoon, the small house of the Lakandulas was filled with so much sound. Not the usual spinning of Aling Anita's sewing machine, but the gracious melody of being found, of being home, and the gathering of their neighbors who rejoiced at this miracle. Yes, there were still Shadows, swelling with their dim bodies as daylight waned, but what could Shadows do? The setting sun covered Marikit with its sticky, bright-orange embrace—light and joy and love. When she turned her gaze at the distance, where the tall bamboo poles rose like needles to the sky, she could see the Alitaptap sparkle like stars, and the tiny bud around her finger unfurled to a bloom.